Enduring Havoc

Enduring Havoc

Montana Mayhem
Book 6

Millie Copper

Written by Millie Copper

Edited by Ameryn Tucker

Proofread by MDC Proofreading and WMH Cheryl

Cover design by Dauntless Cover Design

Also by Millie Copper

Montana Mayhem Series

Unending Havoc: Montana Mayhem Book 1

Ruthless Havoc: Montana Mayhem Book 2

Merciless Havoc: Montana Mayhem Book 3

Cruel Havoc: Montana Mayhem Book 4

Relentless Havoc: Montana Mayhem Book 5

Havoc in Wyoming Series

Wyoming Refuge: A Havoc in Wyoming Prequel

Havoc in Wyoming: Part 1, Caldwell's Homestead

Havoc in Wyoming: Part 2, Katie's Journey

Havoc in Wyoming: Part 3, Mollie's Quest

Havoc Begins: A Havoc in Wyoming Story

Havoc in Wyoming: Part 4, Shields and Ramparts

Havoc in Wyoming: Part 5, Fowler's Snare

Havoc Rises: A Havoc in Wyoming Story

Havoc in Wyoming: Part 6, Pestilence in the Darkness

Christmas on the Mountain: A Havoc in Wyoming Novella

Havoc Peaks: A Havoc in Wyoming Story

Havoc in Wyoming: Part 7, My Refuge and Fortress

Nonfiction Books

Sourdough for Your Food Storage: Add Nutrition and Variety to Your Baked Goods

Sprouts for Your Food Storage: Add Nutrition and Variety to Your Diet

Stretchy Beans: Nutritious, Economical Meals the Easy Way

Stock the Real Food Pantry: A Handbook for Making the Most of Your Pantry

Design a Dish: Save Your Food Dollars

Real Food Hits the Road: Budget Friendly Tips, Ideas, and Recipes for Enjoying Real Food Away from Home

Join My Reader's Club!

Receive a complimentary copy of *Wicked Havoc: A Montana Mayhem Prequel*. As part of my reader's club, you'll be the first to know about new releases and specials. I also share info on books I'm reading, preparedness tips, and more. Please sign up at:

MillieCopper.com/Wicked

Chapter 1

Beverly
Friday, September 4
MSU Campus, Bozeman, MT

Ringing out the cloth, I then dab at my daughter's dripping face. The hallucinations take a toll on her body. Her heart is pounding; her skin is blotchy and drenched in sweat, like she just ran a six-minute mile.

Doc Sanderson said she could even have an arrythmia, where her heart beats irregularly. With this episode, I don't think that happened, but it's hard to really know. All I do know is my little girl is in a fight for her life.

As Emma settles into a restless sleep, I lean back in the chair and close my eyes. The doctor said to sleep while she does. He wrinkled his forehead and crooked his finger at me. "Don't try to be a hero, Beverly Pitney. This is a marathon, not a sprint. If those girls are sleeping, you'd best be sleeping too. Just like when they were babies."

Of course, then there was always so much to do—dishes, vacuuming, and a never-ending pile of laundry. Baby clothes, diapers, my own shirts that always smelled of spit up . . . along with the full load generated by Chad when he'd return from wherever his assignments had taken him.

Even though he took a full two months off after Emma was born, it didn't feel long enough. And just like now, I was alone during nights of colic and illness. Even with all the terrible events of the past fifteen months, the best part is Chad being here. With our world upside down, my husband has no choice but to be here.

My eyes shoot open. But he wasn't always here, was he? No, just like now—off on a much-needed hunting trip to bring in meat for the town—he was gone last spring when I needed him. Had he been here . . .

I shake my head to will away the memories. I let out a long breath, then inhale nice and slow. One more in and out. That's all. That's all

I'll allow myself. Too much and my mind may let go, my thoughts could drift to places I can't allow.

Sleep. Sleep now while my youngest daughter Kylie is snug in the other room, not afflicted by this terrible illness. Sleep while my poor Emma is between fits, while the fever seems to be waning and the mania—the delusions—aren't plaguing her. Sleep a deep, dreamless sleep where I don't have my own nightmares.

My girl is one of dozens who are sick. When Emma first let out a scream of terror and started scratching at her arms and face, I wasn't sure what was happening. Was she drugged? Her little sister Kylie was so scared. I was scared. I sent Kylie running down the hall to find help. Sal Reese, a recently orphaned neighbor boy, went after Doc Sanderson.

She was upset over her sister's illness, but at least eight-year-old Kylie isn't sick too. I'm doing everything I can think of to keep her well. I've moved her out of the room she shares with Emma and into my bedroom—mine and Chad's. She's staying in there continually, using it as a safe room to keep this weird and terrible virus from spreading. I'm sleeping on the futon of this small apartment on the Montana State University campus, our home for the past year.

Although living here isn't ideal, we do have consistency, as far as knowing that each day will be another day of hard work and a struggle to survive. And at least here, in the safety of the campus, we have food. With the summer growing season coming to an end, we're harvesting an abundance of fruit, vegetables, and grains.

Right now, we feel practically rich with our winter preparations. But is it enough to feed the thirty thousand or so people still living in Bozeman until next summer? Last winter was so hard. A winter of death. Fitting, considering we'd had a summer of death too. A summer when everything fell apart.

Running a hand through my hair, I glance around the sparse room. What a difference from the life we used to have. Chad's work required him to jet off to various places around the globe at a moment's notice, but it also provided a very comfortable life.

My time was devoted to our girls. A couple of years before everything fell apart, I started a business I hoped would give us a new future. A future where Chad could be choosier about the jobs he took—the jobs that took him away from us.

Claudia, our daily housekeeper, kept our home clean and running smoothly. Although she didn't live with us, she was there eight to five every weekday. That's all changed.

Chad had arrived home just a day before the first attacks grounded air travel when five planes were purposely crashed while landing. Claudia came to work the next day, though I'd called her and told her she could take the day off to mourn. She insisted she didn't want to be alone and would rather work than think about all the poor lost souls.

It was shortly after lunch when the second attack happened. Bridges across the country were destroyed, killing hundreds. The news reports suggested suicide bombers were responsible for the devastation, but Chad shook his head and said he'd be surprised if they were.

It wasn't thirty minutes later when his cell rang. Our good friends and Chad's business partners, Rey and Kimba Hoffmann, were heading our way. The bridge near their home was among those destroyed, severely damaging their multilevel condominium in the blast.

With the destruction, and the craziness they feared could happen, they thought a few days in the quiet of Bozeman, Montana, was a good idea. That was the last time we heard from them.

The following day there was another attack, a cyberattack that took out all the electricity and phones. When the attacks continued, with oil refineries targeted, railways devastated, and hundreds of elected officials murdered, it became less likely our friends would reach us.

With the power out and the oil refineries gone, fuel became an issue. What was still available in town was restricted to official use only for the police, fire department, and others considered worthy. Claudia was no longer coming to the house.

On the last Saturday in June, nine days after the planes were shot out of the sky and a week after the cyberattacks, the phones started working again. Not reliably, but enough to give us hope.

We tried to call Rey and Kimba but couldn't get through. The call to Claudia did go through; she said she was doing well and might even ride her bike to work on Monday. I assured her it wasn't necessary. Without electricity, not much could be done, but she was welcome to come and stay with us if she'd like.

The next morning, our hope of a return to normalcy was destroyed when our newly working phones let out a shrill whistle. Chad grabbed

3

his phone first, going pale as he read the screen. I glanced at my screen and caught only one word. Missile.

The next minutes were chaos as we hustled the girls to the basement. With them in the windowless bathroom of the apartment space, Chad ran back upstairs after food and water. He ordered me to stay downstairs and empty the extra pantry of anything that didn't need cooking.

We knew we were better off than most, having made extra provisions in the years before, including buying this house in a new subdivision of large two- to five-acre lots with rural features.

The buried propane tank gave us the ability to cook. The water well, with a special pump by Apocalypse Well Pumps out of nearby Belgrade, gave us water. Not water coming out of the faucets, but fresh clean water we could easily get out of the ground.

The missiles never landed. At least not in Montana. We later learned both coasts were devastated by multiple nuclear ground detonations. For us, and the rest of the flyover states, we were spared the fireballs but not the ruin.

When our phone screens went blank and wouldn't power up, it took Chad mere seconds to realize what happened. A high-altitude nuclear device did enough damage to change our lives forever. The electromagnetic pulse, or EMP, took out the electricity and phones for the foreseeable future.

Even though we didn't think we needed to worry about radiation, we stayed in the basement for several days and continued to sleep down there for the rest of the time we were in our home. It just wasn't worth the risk.

A few days after the EMP, Chad took his mountain bike to check on Claudia and bring her to our home. He was too late. Someone had broken into her house and shot her before taking what little she had. I still feel awful for not insisting she move in with us before the EMP. We didn't know. We didn't know it was going to get so bad.

"Go! Go away!" Emma swats the air as she screams at the top of her lungs. "No!"

4

Chapter 2

Kimba
Saturday, September 5
Great Falls, Montana

Our pace has been slow, almost leisurely. In some ways, it's more like a cross-country backpacking adventure than an end-of-the-world journey. If I try hard, I can almost forget the lights are out and people are dying. *Almost.*

We arrived at the transport company headquarters late yesterday afternoon. Unlike when we traveled to the Dosen ranch, hiking a trail along the Sun River, this time we stuck with the paved roads. Once we reached Simms, we used the state highway until it connected with Interstate 15, a major highway that used to connect the Canadian and Mexican borders. Now only sections are safe for travel, and rarely by car.

The interstate was busy—mainly full of walkers, but we also saw bicyclists, people on horseback, military vehicles, and even the rare personal car or pickup truck. As we walked, we were continually on edge—heads on a swivel, searching for danger.

I've healed enough from the gunshot wound to my side that I'm able to take watch. But I have no doubt Rey's sleeping with one eye open and is at the ready. He doesn't even take his boots off.

Atticus and Axel Dosen gave us a brand-new four-man tent. The size of it makes it too big to carry in one of the backpacks, so we divide up the pieces. It isn't ideal, especially if we're separated, but it's nice to have a little more space.

When we reached the interstate a few miles north of Great Falls, we started seeing signs for *His Way Public Transport Company.* The signage made it easy to know where to exit the freeway and how to find our way to the church hosting the bus company. We arrived at the perfect time. The buses only run two days per week, and tomorrow is one of those days.

We bartered for our seats, using jewelry we'd collected during our journey, along with things the Dosens and Conner Brower gave us. Not only were they generous with barter goods, but they also sent us with a generous amount of food—cans of tuna and sardines, pasta, and more, all of it from the cabinets in the small house.

The bug-infested cabinets.

While I know the weevils can't get in the cans, the rest of the stuff grosses me out. My oldest daughter, Nicole, made a point of double—maybe even triple—inspecting all the food before we left, but I still see her turn up her nose at the contents sometimes, sure there's an errant bug walking around on her food.

When they were getting the food ready for us, I was still taking it easy. I did help some, but from the comfort of a chair. It really took all my energy to recover from the shooting. I've been shot before, in my former line of work I'd been a target on more than one occasion, but this was different. The combination of a year of food rations and walking partway across the state of Montana, along with the grief of losing my only son, my body just didn't heal as I thought it should. I give an involuntary shudder.

"You cold?" Rey furrows his brow.

I wave my hand. "I'm fine, just thinking about something."

His eyes linger on me before he dips his chin. "No fever?"

"Truly, I'm fine." The smile I give him is genuine. While we're still working out some of our issues, we're better now. Losing our son, Nate, took us to an ugly place. The sadness is still there—will it ever go away?—but we're now facing it together. Tears sting my eyes, causing me to blink rapidly.

Rey puts a hand on my cheek. I turn toward it and kiss his palm. His eyes cloud as he pulls me close. "You're ready for this? We could— "

"No, I'm ready. This is the right path for us."

I feel him nod against my head. "It'll be good to see Chad and Bev, make sure . . ." Rey clears his throat. "I'm sure they're fine. Them and the girls."

"Chad had a good setup." I step out of Rey's embrace and look up at him. "We may have laughed at his provisions, but he was right all along."

Our youngest daughter, Naomi, jumps up and down. "I hear something! Is it the bus?"

Rey's fingers lace with mine as the four of us gawk up the road. Within seconds, the front of a semitruck comes into view.

With a confused look, I glance to my husband.

"Weird." Nicole shakes her head.

"Well, I'll be," Rey mutters. The cab comes into full view, towing a long fifth-wheel trailer.

When we got our tickets last night, we were told they had a small fleet running on biodiesel. The woman was pretty excited as she shared the fuel-making process. Something about wood ash turned into lye, a still to make some kind of alcohol not suitable for drinking, and oil. They're using any old cooking oil they can find and producing more from oily seeds.

I'll admit to only halfway paying attention, but it sounded like quite the setup. I'm glad they're doing it, though, since we can now ride instead of walk. But I sure didn't expect a travel trailer.

As the truck pulls to a stop, Rey grabs his pack. "Let's get our gear. Looks like a line's forming."

This bus will take us only as far as the junction of I-15 and I-90. The lady at the ticket counter said they have a sister business running on Interstate 90 and we'll be able to obtain tickets to Bozeman.

We're going just over a hundred and fifty miles on this part of the trip, but we won't reach the stop at the I-90 junction until after seven tonight. Considering it isn't even nine yet, it's going to be a long day.

A woman wearing a dark blue ball cap and a bright yellow T-shirt takes our tickets, inspects our weapons to ensure they're unloaded, and hands us four cards. "Be sure to put this card above the seats you choose, that way others will know they're occupied if you get off at the stops. Likewise, don't choose seats with cards above them."

Wooden steps have been put by the door of the long fifth wheel. I enter first, with Nicole on my heels. I was under the impression this was the first stop on the bus route and am surprised to see many more people than just those who boarded before us.

The interior of the camp trailer has been reconfigured to a wide-open space with bench seats, like a city bus. A full row of seats is across the front, facing the rest of the group, and there's also a full row at the back.

I choose two sets of seats, one in front of the other, and step aside while motioning for Nicole to take the inside seat.

"Here you go, squirt." Rey ushers Naomi into the row in front of us. The seats are spaced well, giving us enough room to put our backpacks at our feet. I dig a sock out of my pocket and hand it to Nicole to use for protecting and cushioning the muzzle of her shotgun as we travel. I have a second sock for my heavy rifle.

For the .22 I carry in a sling on the backpack, I've reworked it slightly so the lighter rifle's muzzle goes down instead of up while we're on the buses. I've had muzzle safety drilled into me for so long, this is all second nature but still important to remember.

When we bought the tickets, we were told our guns would be inspected to ensure they were empty. The ammo must be stashed in our packs. Neither Rey nor I were happy with this rule, but we've complied—with the visible weapons anyway. Had we been asked if we were carrying concealed, we would've fessed up and emptied those guns too. I'm glad it didn't come to that.

Another rule: no eating on the bus. We'll have about thirty minutes to an hour at each stop, so we can get off and eat. We've been saving our tins of tuna and sardines for quick meals and still have a good supply of deer jerky. Connor Brower also gave us each a bag of beef jerky and several bags of dried vegetables: tomatoes, zucchini, powdered greens, and more.

We had breakfast while camped outside the church—instant oatmeal, which appeared to be bug free—but there's already a rumble in the pit of my stomach. I take a swig of water and wonder how long it'll be until the first stop.

I let out a content breath. This may not be the most comfortable seat I've ever sat in, but I am sitting. It feels like a bit of normalcy in our new world.

We wait and watch as more people board the makeshift bus. We knew there'd be quite a load, based on the people camping and the ones we talked to. The ticket lady said many will disembark in Helena, the state capital, and others will get on there. She said it was good we arrived when we did; they'd sell out and people would have to wait until the Wednesday bus.

My eyes are on the door when an elderly woman steps on. Her face is haggard and her hair's stringy. Behind her is an equally worn-down man.

They're followed by a rough-looking guy in his twenties. Apparently, they aren't moving fast enough for him, because he gives the old man a push and says something vulgar. An equally rough-looking guy behind him laughs. *Great.* That's all we need. A couple of jerks on a long bus ride.

"Enough!" A man wearing the same bright yellow T-shirt as the ticket taker points at the pusher dude. "You get one warning. Anything else happens, and you're off. No matter where we are. We'll pull over and boot you."

Pusher Dude gives a sloppy salute. "No problem, man."

He walks toward the back of the bus. As he nears our seat, his eyes travel my body before drifting to my daughter. He raises his eyebrows with a leer.

Behind him, his buddy makes a clicking noise with his mouth. "Mm-mmm. Some fine scenery on this bus."

I keep my head high, my eyes straight ahead as I tap Nicole lightly on the leg. I feel her shift, straightening and avoiding eye contact.

"Seems they think they're a little too good for the likes of us." Pusher Dude eyeballs us as he walks by.

"Might have to change their minds."

"Five minutes. That's all I'd need . . ." Pusher Dude's voice drifts away.

As they move toward the back, I feel the air rush out of Nicole.

I lean into her. "We're fine."

"Everything okay?" Rey asks.

I answer with a nod, ignoring the tightness in my empty stomach. Then I force a smile and reach out to caress Rey's shoulder. "We're fine." He puts a hand on top of mine. The knot in my stomach melts away.

Within a few minutes, the bus is nearly full and the woman in the yellow shirt steps on. She smiles at the man dressed like her before turning to the passengers.

"Alrighty, folks. We're minutes away from leaving. If you need to use the facilities, this is your last chance. Our next stop is in the small town of Ulm, about twelve miles from here. We'll be traveling at a modest speed, not to exceed fifty miles per hour, but often much slower."

A spattering of groans sound throughout the bus. Fifty miles per hour isn't fast at all, but it sure beats walking.

9

She lifts a hand. "I know, I know. We're not the only ones on this road, so we're mindful of those who have other, slower modes of transportation."

We soon discover not only do we need to mind our speed for the others sharing the road but because the interstate is already falling into disrepair.

The stop in Ulm is also at a church. Rey stays on the bus to watch our things, while the girls and I get off and have a snack.

"Won't Dad be hungry?" Naomi asks, gnawing on a dried tomato.

"He'll get off at the next stop."

My daughter's eyes go wide. "Can I eat then too?"

My laugh is light and airy. "I think you'll be okay waiting a bit. We'll stop often enough you won't go hungry today."

Chapter 3

Beverly

Clad in a long gown covering his clothes, wearing a hat, gloves, and a tight-fitting face mask, Doc Sanderson looks more like he's ready for surgery than to examine my sick daughter.

"Eight more people came down with it last night. I'm not sure exactly what it is yet, but it's fast moving. A virus, I'd suspect, but I've never seen anything like it. We're going under quarantine."

My brows crinkle together. "The college?"

"The town. Did you hear the gunfire this morning?"

"I heard something, but I thought it was . . . I don't know what I thought. It didn't sound like we were being attacked."

"No, not by an outside force." He lets out a sigh. "Hugh Vardy was working in the large livestock shelter with— " he clears his throat "—his wife and son-in-law, plus a few others. No one knew he was afflicted with the sickness, the hallucinations. He freaked out and started shooting. Three are dead, including his family, and two more are wounded."

I close my eyes as my hands go to my mouth. Hugh Vardy was a friend. His wife too. They were always so willing to help me in the goat barn when I was learning how to care for the different breeds. "What will we do?"

"Like I said, we're locking down." Doc Sanderson motions to the lockbox on top of my dresser. "Plus, there are orders to confiscate firearms."

"Even those of us who keep them locked up inside the house?" My voice comes out as a squeak. The idea of giving up my gun doesn't sit well with me. I've taken to wearing it every time I leave the dorm. I can't help but think . . .

"Everyone. They'll be cataloged and secured in the armory."

"And how do we know whoever has the key to the armory won't get sick and freak out? I'm not okay with not having a way to protect my daughters."

He raises his hands. "I hear you. I don't disagree, but there's nothing else we can do. The sickness is here, in your house. Who's to say you won't get it and . . ." His eyebrows shoot to the top of his head.

"I'd never."

"I'm sure Hugh would've said the same thing. Listen, Beverly, this is a bad thing. I've never seen anything like it. I don't know what it is or how to treat it. You know what it's doing to Emma. Is Kylie still okay?"

"She's fine. We're being careful. I don't let her out of the bedroom except to go to the bathroom. And I'm cleaning everything I touch."

"And you're not going into her bedroom?"

"You said not to." My eyes sting. "She's alone in there. All alone. What else can I do?"

"Not a thing. That's my point. What can any of us do? We're doing what we can in hopes of stopping the spread of this . . . whatever *this* is. And maybe we'll be able to contain it, stop it from traveling beyond the people living at the college, beyond the town. But for us . . . I just don't know."

Swallowing the lump in my throat, I tell him I'll do whatever is necessary to keep my girls safe. He gives me a weary smile.

"What about my husband? Is he okay? The rest of the hunting crew?"

"Hopefully no one was sick when they left."

"Chad was fine, not sick at all. Everyone that left was well, remember?"

"I do. We had a handful of people sick when they left. Correct me if I'm wrong, but Emma was symptom free then, too, right?"

I let out a sigh. "True. You're saying Chad could be sick? Anyone on the hunting crew could be?"

"And they could infect anyone—*everyone*—they meet."

"What could be done to stop it if . . . if that happens?"

Doc Sanderson reaches a gloved hand toward his face, catching his motion midway and yanking the hand away. "Right now, we worry about here, about keeping people healthy. Since your family has been afflicted, it's important for you to remain in your living quarters. Meals will continue to be delivered. I'll continue to make house calls."

"What about you? How can you keep from getting sick?"

"PPEs—N95 respirator, gloves, gowns—plus, I'm only making rounds. I won't socialize with anyone else. When I'm not tending to the sick, I'll be in my dorm. My physician assistant is following the same protocols. We've divided up those affected by location."

"How many?"

He lifts a hand. "Too many. Dozens. The mayor is in contact with the Army out of Billings. They're sending help."

My brows furrow. "Soldiers?"

"Some. Doctors and nurses too. We need to try and get ahead of this."

I close my eyes and let out a long breath. "How do you get ahead of a virus?"

He shakes his head. "We're hoping quarantining the sick will help. If it's airborne, that should make a difference. Plus, we're counseling everyone on handwashing and not touching their faces."

I quickly move my finger, which was pushing up my glasses.

"Yep. It's hard not to, especially for those of us wearing glasses." He moves his eyebrows, causing his frames to bounce and the face mask to shift. "If people develop symptoms, they need to return to their dormitory. We're working on a way to come up with a signal so we'll know of new illnesses."

"What kind of signal?"

"Probably something simple, like hanging a shirt out the window. The mayor is sorting out the details and finding spotters."

"But if everyone's in their apartments— "

"No, no. Our town is locked down, so no one can enter or leave. They're stopping the buses when they arrive tomorrow, unless they can contact them by radio before then. But anyway, those who aren't sick can still go about their business. Ordering healthy people to stay in their apartments wouldn't make much sense."

"Really? It seems it might. If everyone is in their homes, then we shouldn't be able to spread it as easily."

"Someone needs to do the cooking and other stuff. How do we decide who stays locked in their dorms and who doesn't?"

I lift a shoulder. "What about Chad? What happens when he and the rest of the hunters return?"

"They can't."

"What? What do you mean they can't?"

"That's part of what the Army is doing. They'll set up a waiting area. Chad and the rest of the hunting party will be screened for the illness. If they are sick, they'll be taken to the hotel at the edge of town . . . you know the one I mean?"

I give a slight nod.

"Okay, good. If they're well, there's a camp being set up. Anyone who was gone waits there. If they can't stop the Missoula or Billings buses from arriving, they'll wait there too."

"Wait for how long?"

"Unknown." Doc Sanderson shakes his head. "At least until we know what we're dealing with. This isn't like anything I've ever seen. Of course, I'm just a small-town doctor. What do I know?"

Doc Sanderson was one of a couple dozen health care providers at the college. He and his colleagues provided medical services for the sixteen thousand plus MSU students. When the attacks started, summer session was happening, meaning there was a fraction of the usual students.

Several of Doc Sanderson's coworkers only had contracts during the school year or were taking advantage of the downtime for vacation. Before the attacks, Doc Sanderson lived off campus—just like most of us who now call MSU home.

His wife and two kids were back east visiting her parents. They'd left a few weeks earlier, driving and seeing the sights along the way. He was supposed to fly out the following week for a short visit before driving home with them. When the first attacks grounded air travel, his plans changed. He considered renting a car and going after them, but the cyberattack and the mass amounts of people on the gridlocked roads forced him to stay in Bozeman.

He hasn't heard from them since the morning of the EMP. He now doubts he'll ever hear from them again. They were outside of Baltimore, Maryland, one of the areas confirmed to have received a direct nuclear strike.

Knowing the doctor's family is likely dead, I hate to make a big deal about Chad not being able to come back to the dorm. I lift my chin and force a calm look on my face. "Well, I'm sure it'll all be fine. Emma seems to be doing better, don't you think? She's sleeping more and isn't having the dreams as much."

"Keep doing what you're doing. You'll receive a jar of broth each day. It'll arrive warm and in a cooler. Make sure she drinks the entire quart. We're going to provide other soft, nourishing foods too. She's young and strong. She'll bounce back in no time."

"And Kylie?"

"If she shows any symptoms, or you start having symptoms, we'll make sure you get the treatment you need too."

"I can't get sick! Who will . . ." I shake my head. "No, I'll be fine. I'll take care of my children."

"If you do get sick, we'll have someone move in and care for you. We'll work it out, you'll see. I'll be back this evening. Maybe we'll have more things figured out then too. The signal and . . ." He shakes his head. "There're a lot of moving parts, but it'll come together and we'll start healing."

After Doc Sanderson leaves, I sink onto the futon in the living room. I bury my face in my hands, then remember I'm not supposed to touch my face. What does it matter? I've been caring for my daughter for a couple of days. If I'm going to get it, I'll get it.

"Mommy?" Kylie sticks her head out the door of the bedroom. "Did he say Emma will be okay?"

"Yes, sweetie. Emma just needs to rest. And you and I are going to stay in the house while she gets better. Other people are sick, too, so we want to stay here where it's safe."

She crinkles her forehead. "I thought you always said fresh air keeps us healthy? If we could go outside— "

"Not this time. Nice people will bring us our food, and we'll stay here while they treat us like princesses."

"You won't have to work? Who'll take care of the animals? Milk the goats?"

I swallow the lump in my throat as I think about Hugh. He and his crew tended the larger livestock while I, along with my team, took care of the smaller animals. Hugh and his wife taught me how to milk the goats. Now his wife is dead. I didn't even think to ask about Hugh. Does he know what he did, or are the hallucinations so severe he has no idea he killed his wife and son-in-law?

"Someone else will take care of them, sweetie. Just for a few days until Emma is better and we're sure you and I won't get sick."

"What food will they bring us? Do they know I can't eat the bread because . . ." She makes a face.

"Even if they bring it, you don't have to eat it. We'll be fine. Do you have enough toys and art supplies?"

15

She gives an exaggerated shrug. "I guess."

"Doc Sanderson said we have to wash our hands. I'll bring you a basin of water, but I'm going to wash my hands first so they're nice and clean."

As I add tepid water from a jug into a plastic bin, I think about Kylie and her stomach troubles. In some ways, the end of the world has been helpful to her digestion. She isn't tempted to eat cakes and cookies, along with other gluten-containing foods. We didn't even have bread until recently when the wheat and rye harvests happened. Now we have an abundance of cereal grains, and for most people, it's their main source of calories.

But for Kylie and Chad, both with the same gluten sensitivities, they're still existing mainly on meat and vegetables. Even so, Chad is certainly in the best shape of his life. While he'd always taken care to work out regularly, he'd started getting a bit of a waistline.

He quit eating bread and sweets years ago, before Kylie was even born, but there was still the occasional slip when on the road or when we'd go out with friends. It was after a meal out with friends for pasta that he put two and two together and realized his body could no longer handle gluten.

When Kylie started showing the same symptoms, we tried an elimination diet for her—for all of us, since it was easier—determining she, too, had issues with gluten. Emma and I didn't have these problems, but we chose to make our house completely gluten-free.

It's only been since the wheat harvest that Emma and I have started eating bread again. I have to admit, it's pretty amazing. The kitchen crew bakes outside over campfires, making the most amazing biscuits, loaves, and flatbreads out of sourdough. Sometimes, I feel bad Kylie and Chad are missing out on it. But with the way our bathroom facilities are, risking an upset stomach and the accompanying diarrhea isn't worth it.

While we do have a bathroom in the dorm, the sewer system doesn't work, so the toilet is lined with a garbage bag. We add sawdust to the bottom and then sprinkle more shavings over the top when we've done our business to help keep the odors down. Like everything else, garbage bags are rationed and reused after dumping the contents in a large compost pile. There's talk of using the compost on crops in the future . . . I hope it never comes to that.

"Mommy? Did you forget?"
"No, sweetie. I'm bringing you water now."

Chapter 4

Kimba

The bus from Great Falls makes plenty of stops on the way to Butte. The next break is at an old rest stop on I-15. Dozens of people are camping there, but only a few get on.

Rey steps off, taking Naomi with him. When they return, she has a piece of jerky stuck on her shirt. I motion to the chunk of dried meat, and she picks it off and then plops it in her mouth.

I should reprimand her, point out her manners, but we have so little these days. While manners still matter, being squeamish about food doesn't. A little stuck on your shirt, picked up off the ground, bugs crawling through it . . . whatever. Looking at some of the other passengers on the bus, with their hollowed cheeks and vacant expressions, we've had it good.

The stops continue, with Rey and I taking turns getting off. Naomi gets off each time; Nicole often stays on the bus, her eyes closed. Pusher Dude and his weird friend are still with us and continue to make comments and gestures whenever Nicole or I move from our seats. Nicole was shooting them dirty looks, but I whispered for her not to antagonize them, to pretend they didn't exist. I received an eye roll for my effort.

I get it. While I may tell her to ignore them, it's not easy. I'd like to punch them each smack in the nose. Or at least give them a piece of my mind and tell them how to treat women. I know Rey agrees, but we can't risk getting kicked off the bus for causing trouble.

At one of the stops, I meet another lady who says she got on the bus in Great Falls, at an aid station in the park.

"Oh, I see. I thought the church was the first stop."

"Used to be, but since they had to drive near there anyway, they added the aid station stop to help people out. Plus, it's safer."

"Safer?"

"On account of the bears. They've been a real problem, and people were taking shortcuts to get to the church. There have been several encounters. Why, I even heard about a poor lady hiking along the Sun River who was ripped from her tent."

My breathing turns shallow, and I feel myself pale. I swallow hard. "That's terribly sad." I choose not to tell her the lady was my dear friend Jennifer.

"Anyway, I'm not sure what people are going to do. We took the land from the bears, and now they're taking it back. Did you know, historically, the grizzlies' range was from the West Coast all the way into the middle of the country? And from Alaska down to central Mexico? It might be like that again someday. Of course, with the western states now being nuclear wasteland . . . maybe not."

My forehead crinkles. "Isn't it just a few coastal cities with severe radiation?"

She lifts a shoulder. "Don't know. I heard from one of the Air Force guys they've declared the western parts of Washington state and Oregon, all of California, and parts of Nevada as wasteland. That's what they're calling it, the Wasteland. Same thing on the East Coast, but I didn't pay much attention . . . geography isn't my thing. Those still alive in the Wasteland are being evacuated and relocated to new areas. But . . ." She shakes her head.

"I don't think there're many survivors. Nukes killed a lot, then the radiation sickness followed by winter . . . either they starved or killed each other for food." She leans closer to me. "I even heard there're cannibals. Not just in the Wasteland either. All over the place."

My eyes dart to my daughters. They're far enough away and engrossed in their own conversation, with Naomi animatedly talking about going fishing when we were at the ranch, so they don't hear the woman.

The bus conductor calls out a five-minute warning, and the woman and I say our goodbyes. She's getting off at the next stop, on the edge of Helena.

I was hoping we'd see some of the state capital, but we stay on the interstate and stop before we reach the city and again after we've passed. We've heard rumors the governor of Montana is still here, trying to do what he can to help, but staying out of sight.

In the early days of the terrorist attacks, many members of Congress were killed. I guess he thinks his life may still be in danger. Same with the president of the United States. While we've heard a few of his addresses, no one really knows where he is. Some people think Texas, others think Cleveland, Ohio. I've even heard rumors he might be in Colorado or Kansas, maybe even one of the Dakotas.

After we leave the stop on the other side of Helena, our speed often lags as we climb the hills. My ears fill up somewhere along the way and drive me crazy until they finally pop. After so many months of traveling through flat prairies and ranch lands, we're in the mountains.

Nicole leans into me. "Will they do this in winter?"

"The bus?" I look out the window and shake my head. "I bet they get some serious snow here. The elevation must be— " I give a half shrug "—six thousand feet at least. No snowplows, so I can't imagine they would."

"Are the snowplows diesel? They could run ahead of the bus."

"True. Seems like a lot of effort, though."

When the lady in the yellow shirt tells us we're at the final stop before the end of this line, I let out a sigh of relief. Beats walking, but it's been a terribly long day.

It's less than an hour until sundown when we pull into our stop. Yellow shirt lady announces the time as 7:23 p.m. and welcomes us to Butte, Montana. We're not really in Butte, more on the edge at a former elementary school.

She tells us the ticket office is open until nine if we're planning to continue south on Interstate 15, but the bus won't run until Monday as they take Sunday off. While someday they hope to have bus service all the way to Las Vegas, for now they only go as far as Pocatello, Idaho. Las Vegas was said to have received fallout from the nukes. I wonder if it's part of the Wasteland the woman was telling me about earlier?

If we want to travel I-90, which we do, we need to use a different kiosk, which is now closed but will open in the morning. This bus does run on Sunday since the company offering it keeps a Saturday Sabbath. We'll be able to get our tickets early, but the buses—one traveling west and the other east—won't arrive until midday.

Bozeman, where Chad and Bev Pitney live, along with their two girls, is only about eighty-five miles east of Butte. Eighty-five miles until the end of the journey we began so long ago, when we fled our home in Denver for the safety of the Pitneys' quiet home.

"Well, I guess we'll settle in for the night." I keep my voice light and cheery, trying to hide the tiredness I'm feeling.

We find a spot at the edge of the dry grass, and Rey points to the taller mountains in the west. "Looks like rain."

Butte isn't quite the elevation as some of the passes we went over on the bus, but it's still fairly high and mountainous. It does smell like rain. If Atticus Dosen were with us, he'd be able to not only tell us if we were going to get rain but how much and for how long. He's like a walking weather station.

I miss them—Atticus, Axel, Victoria and her sons, Patti and her babies.

When we were in Great Falls buying our bus tickets, Nicole asked about mail service. To our surprise, they said to leave it with them. Someone comes by every week or so and picks up whatever is collected. They did caution us there's no guarantee it will be received and people are just doing their best.

Nicole has written several letters to our friends. Tamra Nicholson—who traveled with us the first few weeks of our trip, when we were using cross-country skis because there was still heavy snow—is in Joliet, Montana, a small town not too far from the Wyoming state line. Tamra's letter wasn't terribly long but had the necessary information.

The letter to the Monroes—Leanne, Sadie, and Sebastian, along with Donnie McCullough—was a little longer. They all settled at Leanne's aunt's place in Lewistown, Montana.

Two letters went back to Bakerville, Wyoming, our home for the months after the world fell apart and until we started this journey. The first was to our traveling companion Rochelle Bennet, who'd left the safety of the mountain to find her son who was at summer camp when everything happened. The second was to Doris Snyder, who Nicole considers an adopted grandma.

Nicole plans to write everyone again after we're settled in Billings—or Bozeman, if we decide to stay there—so they have a way to write us back. She says she'll write to the Double D ranch then, too, so we can stay in contact.

We've barely finished dinner when Naomi starts rubbing her eyes. I walk her to the bathroom, a pair of outhouses set up with a washing station between them, then take her inside the tent. Her head has barely hit her pillow—a folded sweatshirt—and she's asleep.

21

Nicole, Rey, and I sit on stumps as we watch the last bits of light fade from the sky. The waning full moon is already casting a decent amount of light.

"Ready for bed?" I ask Nicole. Rey told her she has the night off from watch. He'll take a long first watch, and I'll take over at two o'clock to finish it off and watch the sunrise. My favorite time of day.

My daughter gives a big stretch followed by a noisy yawn. "I suppose. If I thought it wouldn't rain, I'd move my bedding out here. It's a nice night."

"End of summer." Rey motions with his arm. "Won't be long until the snow is flying. We need to be settled before then."

"I think . . ." Nicole pulls her lower lip between her teeth.

Rey and I share a glance while waiting for her to continue.

She gives me a smile that doesn't meet her eyes. "Want to walk to the toilet with me?"

With the sun nearly set, and just barely enough light to see, I pull my small flashlight from my utility belt. Another gift from Connor Brower was new batteries for all our lights. We left our walkie-talkies at the ranch as a thank you for the things they provided. Rey and I went back and forth on whether or not it was smart to leave them. Our final decision: nope, not smart, but it was the right thing to do. They'll need them for their security measures.

Nicole has her own light, a small penlight version with the name of a car insurance company on it. She takes it into the bathroom with her. While her light is nothing fancy and completely disposable, it was still very generous of Conner to make sure we were so well set for our continued travels. Especially considering everything that happened.

Of course, in some ways, our leaving there was better for Conner. I'm sure every time the boy looks at me, he sees the person responsible for the death of his entire family.

When I step out of my outhouse, Nicole's near the washing station holding her pen light between her teeth while she digs in a bag.

"Here, let me help you." I shine my light in her direction, allowing her to get rid of the one in her mouth.

"Thanks. Want me to get yours out?" She motions to my bag.

"Just shine your light in my direction."

Once we have our toiletries organized on the shelf above the repurposed utility sink, I tell her I'll take care of the lighting while she cleans up. Without running water, they've set up a large barrel with a hose. There's a sign above it saying it's potable but not to fill water jugs; it's for personal washing and teeth brushing only.

We already knew this from when we met the camp host earlier and were given the rules of the campground. That was also when we passed off a tennis bracelet with small diamonds as payment for our night of lodging. The man made it clear he'd rather have food, but he didn't balk too much at the shiny trinket.

When Nicole's finished, she takes over light-shining duty. I'm wetting my toothbrush when there's a noise in the brush. I spin toward the sound.

"Hey, *girls.*" Pusher Dude from the bus is holding a pistol in a side grip, directed at me.

"Mom?" Nicole's voice sounds young and strained.

I raise a hand. "We don't want any trouble."

The pain is instant and searing as my ponytail is yanked and I'm pulled to the ground. I open my mouth to scream when the punch comes in hard and fast. My vision blurs with a kaleidoscope of colors and stars. Nicole lets out a muffled scream. A sweaty hand covers my mouth.

"Get them to the woods." The voice sounds far away.

I take a deep breath though my nose, inhaling the disgusting odors of the man's palm, working to regain my senses as I rapidly blink my eyes. The one manhandling me is the weird friend from the bus. Pusher Dude is still holding the gun on me, still turned at the ninety-degree angle made popular by gangbanger movies.

Where's Nicole? I dart my eyes to the side, trying to find her. My heart sinks when I find my daughter being marched with a hand covering her mouth by a third man I don't recognize. The gun that's usually in a holster on her hip is missing. Did they find her backup piece? The .22 revolver is carried on her left side—her weak side—tucked low and concealed below the belt of her loose cargo pants.

I'm on the ground, being drug under the arms. The man's in an awkward, off-balance stance. Since Nicole's hip gun is gone, I assume mine is also. But the Baby Glock at my ankle, which has saved my life before, has probably gone undetected.

Nicole's eyes are trained on me. When our gazes meet, she raises her eyebrows. She's been trained and knows if they get us to the woods, take us away from where we were abducted, things are likely to go badly for us. So bad, neither of us will ever see Naomi or Rey again.

But I'll be with Nate.

A feeling of comfort washes over me. My little boy. To be with him again . . .

With an almost silent whimper, I push the thought away. I don't want to die. And I don't want my daughter to die. With Pusher Dude's gun trained on us, things still may end badly, but I'm not going down without a fight.

Hoping Nicole can remember the very brief Morse code lessons we've had—and hoping my own rusty skills are correct—I blink out two long and one short followed by three long. After I repeat the signal, she gives me a brief nod. A fraction of a second later, I see the change in her body as she shifts her center of gravity.

It's go time.

Opening my mouth, I search for the meaty flesh of the man's disgusting hand. I don't get as much as I want, but my bite elicits a scream as he yanks his hand away. Hot liquid runs out as I turn my head and spit out the chunk of flesh. At the same time, I throw all my weight toward his knees.

"Hey!" Pusher Dude yells.

The man holding Nicole cries out in obvious pain. I don't see what's happening but know she's doing what she must, what she thinks will help her survive. As the weird friend loses his balance, a gunshot rings out. There's another cry of pain as I reach for the gun at my ankle. I move and turn, trying to get myself stabilized into a shooting position so I can be sure of my target.

Catching a glimpse of movement, I see Nicole darting toward a skinny tree. She's drawing her revolver. Another shot sounds as the handgun clears the holster, throwing bark from a tree in all directions. My senses tunnel as I turn toward the percussion.

Pusher Dude's gun is trained on my daughter. He closes one eye and lifts the muzzle. The air is electric as I pull the trigger of my semi-auto at the same time Nicole does with her nine-shot revolver. My bullet hits him in the bicep, Nicole's the center of his chest. We both fire again, our bullets following his movement. He crumbles to the ground and folds in on himself.

I order Nicole to get behind the trees as I scurry for my own cover of brush. The guy who was holding me is on the ground. The one who had Nicole is out of sight.

"Hold it!" a voice calls out.

I spin toward the voice.

"Toss your weapons! You're surrounded," a man orders.

My heart's pumping in my ears. *What is happening? Another attacker?*

"Kimba? Nicole?" Rey yells.

After a few more seconds of confusion, I'm in Rey's arms with my daughter beside me as the three of us hold each other tight.

Chapter 5

Kimba
Sunday, September 6
Butte, Montana

Rey hands me a steaming mug. I inhale the rich aroma. Black tea. A caffeinated name brand, part of the care package put together by the Dosens.

After Nicole and I were attacked, I couldn't really settle in to sleep. The caffeine will be welcome and will hopefully help me get through the day. Of course, we have so little of the stimulant these days, it'll probably hit my bloodstream and I'll be bouncing all over the place—good thing, since all I can think of right now is a soft bed with a fluffy pillow.

Well, not all. My mind is still churning from the events of last night. I reach a hand to my swollen cheek. It's bruised and my eye is black. Nothing's broken, I don't think. But man does it hurt.

Nicole ended up with only a few scrapes and bruises, minor physical injuries. But emotionally . . . I hate what she had to do. She tried to be so brave last night. Stoic. She kept it together fairly well until we made it back to the tent.

The pain and memories aren't the only thing on my mind. Today is Nate's thirteenth birthday. Or it would be, had he not died when a freak tornado ripped through our camp a few months ago.

Rey rests a hand on my knee. "You want to go lie down for a bit?"

I cover a yawn. "I've become spoiled after our time at the ranch. The hard ground isn't nearly as inviting as the beds were. Did you get any sleep?"

He tilts his head. "A little, leaning up against the log with the tarp draped over me. At least the rain did little more than drizzle, so I stayed dry. You know how it is, not really sleep but rest."

"I could— "

"No, I'm good. I don't think I could sleep anyway. Today . . ." He bites back a sigh. "I wish we could do something. I was thinking how we should've waited until after . . . after today to leave. We could've done something with everyone."

I close my eyes and let out a long, four-count breath. "Like what?"

Rey bites his lip and shakes his head. "I don't know. A special Bible study?"

"We can do that. We'll be with Chad and Bev tonight. We'll do something with them."

He chuffs. "A Bible study with Chad and Bev?"

"Okay, maybe not. But something. We'll do something special."

"I've always heard the firsts are the hardest. First birthday after a death. First Thanksgiving. Christmas. I can't— "

"Right. I can't imagine it'll ever be easier."

Rey's hand moves to mine, and he moves his body closer. I rest my head on his shoulder as my tears fall.

"I'm so glad you and Nicole are okay." His voice is thick. "I don't know what— "

"Shh. We're fine. Nicole was amazing. She . . ." I let out a noisy breath. "It was all so fast. I'm still trying to sort out in my head exactly what happened."

"From the evidence, I'd say you two kicked some butt."

I snort out a laugh. "Not sure my body would agree with you."

"Good thing the shooter wasn't any good. How he managed to shoot and kill his buddy and miss you and Nicole entirely, it's a . . ."

"A miracle?" I offer.

"Indeed. And the third guy, bleeding out with Nicole's knife in his leg."

The variety of emotions coursing through me is nearly overwhelming. Pride in my daughter for doing what was needed to save herself—to save us. Plus, a profound sadness because she was forced to do so, forced to kill.

We've practiced with knives, concentrating on how to defend against them. A few months ago, our traveling companion Sadie Monroe was kidnapped along with her brother. She stuck a knife in her captor during their escape.

At the time, Nicole had commented she didn't know if she'd be able to do what Sadie did, that it was too up close and personal. Her lack of confidence resulted in several one-on-one classes where she and I reenacted Sadie's escape. The repetition was a lifesaver.

27

Rey and I sit together for many minutes, our bodies pressed close, each lost in our own thoughts. I lift my head when the people camping nearest us unzip their tent and step out. The entire camp is beginning to stir.

"Not too far between Butte and Bozeman." I motion with my hand.

"Not too many miles, but if it goes like yesterday, I'd estimate the trip to take four or five hours."

"It's been so long since we've seen Chad and Beverly. I hope— "

"They're resourceful."

Rey has never doubted the Pitneys were fine. Their home, on the edge of Bozeman, was in a good location to ride out the apocalypse. And we know Chad had several provisions in place. Years ago, when Rey and I first started our consulting business and contract work, we met Chad through a friend of a friend. Straight out of high school, he'd spent a dozen years in the military before moving on to the private sector.

We'd heard rumors about him and his skills in hand-to-hand combat, with weapons, and also with computers. I'm not sure exactly what I expected, but Chad was not it. Meek and mild mannered, but with a quirky, sometimes over-the-top sense of humor. He's an average, everyday looking guy. A few inches shorter than Rey, but stocky. At first, I thought we must have the wrong guy. No way could this ordinary man be an elite fighting machine.

After our initial meeting, I told Rey Chad wouldn't be a good fit for us. We needed someone more dynamic. Rey disagreed, saying we needed a gray man—someone who'd fit in, someone people wouldn't look at twice. Someone who would blend in.

Then there are those like Rey and me, often put into jobs where our good looks and charm were essential. I lost track of how many times I was the honeypot. Rey, too, was often enlisted to go after wealthy socialites suspected of devious antics.

With his crooked nose and thick unibrow, we likely wouldn't use Chad for romantic capers. But the skills test proved he did have some serious abilities. All the rumors were true. Not only was Chad amazing with computers, but his fighting and marksmanship skills well surpassed ours.

After several small jobs, the three of us had a large operation infiltrating what was believed to be a terrorist network. *Homegrown terrorists*. Nicole was about a year old then, and it was the first field work I'd done since I'd left the government. I went undercover, once again as the honeypot, while Rey and Chad stayed on the outside to back me up.

We thought it'd be an in and out thing—a week, two tops. Six weeks later and we still weren't sure what the situation was. While it certainly seemed they could be terrorists, or at the very least antigovernment, judging by the multitude of guns and ammo, there wasn't any talk of attacks.

Other than the stockpile of weapons and rooms filled with bulk foods, they were normal, everyday folks. They'd formed what they called a Mutual Aid Group. They even had a name: The End of the Line. They trained with their weapons, but it was more defensive maneuvers than offensive. Still, little things were said by a few people that led me to wonder what was really happening.

In the end, our employer had enough proof from what we gave him to call in the official guys. Often, we were hired by rich executives getting dirt on their competition. Not in this case. This job was off-the-book work for official channels.

Even though the off-book work paid the bills over the years, those jobs were the ones I hated the most. When we were working for private companies, it was usually research. It rarely got gritty. Unofficial government jobs were a different story. Anything could happen and often did.

I can't tell you how many times I'd read a newspaper article or watch the news and *know* whatever catastrophe just happened wasn't the act of some random madman but was a staged event.

A false-flag operation.

Only a month or so before the attacks changed our world, I was certain a school shooting in Wyoming was one such event. The attack was stopped by a husband and wife who killed the shooters. In the days following, a school secretary and the gym teacher both died under suspicious circumstances. The husband and wife who stopped the shooting disappeared and many, including Rey and I, thought they were dead.

Imagine our surprise when we discovered they were alive and well, living in Bakerville, Wyoming. Learning what actually happened at the school, and in the days following, confirmed our original beliefs about the school shooting. The incident was well orchestrated and well funded.

It was no different than the series of attacks against the US—the plane crashes, bridge explosions, cyberattacks, assassinations, and more. All were planned with precision. Deep in my gut, I can't help but feel the school shooting is somehow connected to the attacks.

Rey and I have often discussed who could be behind these things. It could be a foreign country or terrorist group or, as our friend Donnie McCullough believed, it could be an inside job. While I love my country, I'm well aware of what could happen behind the scenes. Not everyone has our best interests at heart.

The conspiracy theories of the Deep State and other shadow governments could very well be real. I have no firsthand knowledge of these clandestine forces, but nothing would surprise me. After all, we worked for the government in secret positions, hired to help with deniability.

Over the years, I've met plenty of people who could most certainly be part of a hidden agenda. I give a shudder as I remember a particularly vile group of operatives. Like us, they were off book. Unlike us, they had few qualms taking on the worst of the jobs.

Their team, led by a former special forces guy by the name of Jankins, was ruthless. We ran into them during the last job I did in the field with Rey. While we'd known of Jankins for several years and had crossed paths before, we'd never been on the same job. They were brought in for mop up, to finish what Rey, Chad, and I started. To do the dirty work.

I was surprised to find Jankins had a new member of his crew: Eric Bohm. I knew Bohm, who everyone called Doc, from my time as an operative. When I first met him, I found him charming. So much so we started dating. The better I got to know him, the more I realized he wasn't charming, he was manipulative. And psychotic. He took way too much pleasure in his job.

Eric Bohm had special skills to convince people to share secrets. Those skills are what earned him the nickname Doc. No one wanted a visit from Doc Bohm; it wouldn't be a pleasant experience. Why Jankins added someone like Bohm to his team, I don't know. Maybe he felt he needed someone well trained in ruthless interrogation techniques.

When I saw Eric, he gave me a full body scan and a leer. "Man, Kimba, you haven't aged a day. Just as hot as ever." My stomach churns just remembering the way he was.

"You seem deep in thought." Rey gives me a weary smile. "Still thinking of Nate?"

I lift a shoulder. "Always. He's always in my head . . . and my heart. Also, Chad and Beverly, and other things."

"Worried about what we'll find?"

"I'm trying not to worry. If anyone can ride out the apocalypse, it's them. Chad had some good things set up. The MAG we infiltrated really got him thinking. Why didn't we do the same thing?"

"Why didn't we become survivalists?"

"Chad didn't call himself that. He said he was a— "

"Doomsday prepper, just like the television show." Rey lets out a laugh. "Remember when we went to visit them? They'd just moved to Bozeman."

"Beverly was pregnant with Emma, and I had just found out I was expecting Nate." A tightness fills my chest.

Rey reaches for my hand.

"I'm okay. It still hurts, of course, but now when I think of him, it's different." I give Rey a weak smile as my eyes cloud. "I want to remember the good things. Like how Bev and I loved sharing our pregnancies. When Emma was born, she was over the moon. When Nate arrived four months later, it was perfect. I loved how we got together so often in those early years. Then, when they had Kylie . . ." I tilt my head and give him a small smile.

"And with Naomi so young, the distance between Bozeman and Denver seemed to double. We've only seen them, what? Twice since Naomi was born?"

"Three times. At least we had FaceTime and Zoom."

"Are you getting nervous?"

My mouth goes in a tight line. "Like you, I think they were well set for this. But then I remember the place we stayed outside of Roundup, Montana. They seemed well set, too, but . . ." I shake my head as memories of finding the murdered family rush over me. When we found them, it hadn't been long since they were killed—a week, maybe two. Marauders took what was easy and left the rest.

"Chad's smart. He would've organized with the neighbors and done things like we did in Bakerville."

31

I raise my eyebrows. "Did you forget— "

"I meant those of us who moved up to the ski lodge. I certainly didn't forget about the massacre. I wish we could've convinced them to . . ." He shakes his head. "People have free will. It's easy to want to force them to do what we think is best, but it doesn't work that way."

I puff out a breath. "Are you sure Chad was still prepping? I hadn't heard much about it lately. Maybe he was on to his newest obsession?"

"Well . . . there were the banana labels."

I snort out a laugh. "I forgot about those. Who would've ever thought collecting the stickers on bananas would be a real thing?"

"Leave it to Chad. With his worldwide travels, he found some good ones. To answer your question, as far as I know, he was still gung-ho on the preparedness stuff. Bev put the kibosh on a few of his loftier plans and brought him down to earth. Of course, now . . ."

"Yeah, now it seems maybe he was the one who knew what was going on and we were the ones with our heads in the sand."

An old VW Bus pulls into the driveway of the school. I lift my chin. "You think they're the ones selling the tickets to Bozeman?"

"I suspect so. It looks like a line's starting to form by the kiosk. Guess I'd better get to it." Rey lightly lifts himself off the stump and offers me a hand. "You want to start waking the girls?"

"I will. I hope Nicole's okay today."

"She was great last night, kept herself together when it counted. The adrenaline crash, though, that's something we need to train her on, how to not fall apart after the immediate danger passes."

I give a solemn nod. "Learning how to control emotions isn't easy, but it's one of the keys to preventing an adrenaline dump. Plus, realizing it'll happen. She hasn't been in these situations enough to know. There was the trouble at Brower's where she had to shoot the guy, but then she moved right on to the next event. And with everything . . ." I let out a sigh.

"I hate she has to learn this. It's not . . ." I slam my mouth shut, realizing I'm rambling and working toward a rant. "Anyway, I'll talk with her. You should too. Give her your perspective on this."

"I will. But now I'd better go get in line if we want a seat on today's bus."

We do get seats. Today's bus is more what I expected us to have yesterday: an old school bus that belches out smoke. They've removed every other seat, giving us space to stow our packs at our feet and still be able to stretch our legs.

Nicole's much more pulled together than I expected. We discuss how her body's reactions to the stress of the attack and fighting back were normal. How anything she is feeling today is okay and expected. She only gave me a single eye roll during the conversation.

Before the bridges exploded and we fled our condo in Denver, Nicole and I had the typical mother and teenage daughter angst. Plenty of eye rolls then and lots of snotty comments and heated arguments, from both of us. While I always thought I'd be more understanding than my mother was when I was Nicole's age, it didn't end up that way.

When things fell apart around us, we developed an unspoken truce. Our truce remained until shortly after Nate died. With me snapping at everyone around me, and the troubles between Rey and me, a divide occurred with my eldest daughter.

I think she felt she needed to take sides in the marital issues. She saw I was treating Rey unfairly and sided with him. She was still respectful and understood our situation—continual danger—but a wall went up between us. The eye rolls increased, and more than once I got a sideways glance.

Now, with Rey and me working on our relationship, Nicole sees us trying. She's opening up to me more. The occasional teenage attitude is to be expected, though. We chat off and on during the drive, and Nicole spends some time writing.

When I ask her if it's more letters, she shrugs. "It's . . . yeah. It's a letter, but it's kind of dumb."

"Okay? Who are you writing to?"

She leans her head close to mine. "It's for Nate, for his birthday. I thought . . ." She shakes her head. "I told you, it's dumb."

A lump forms in my throat. I swallow hard. "Not dumb. Not at all."

It's after five o'clock when the bus takes exit 309 into the town of Bozeman. The roadblock waves us through. My stomach's slightly knotted, excited and nervous to see our friends, but also wondering about the town itself. It's easy to see it hasn't fared well, with several burned-out buildings and other destruction.

"Look, Mommy!" Naomi exclaims from her spot next to Rey. "A *Welcome to Bozeman* sign."

"It is! And good job reading it."

She furrows her brow and turns serious. "I can read."

"I know, honey, sometimes I just . . ." I wave a hand. "I'm so excited we're here."

Just beyond the welcome sign, we pull into an old car repair shop. This place is still standing and looks unharmed. The bus conductor, a man only a few years older than Nicole, bounces off. As we gather our things, he steps back on the bus.

"Uh, folks, those of you getting off here, we need you to meet on the edge of the parking lot. There's been a . . . a development."

"What's happening?" Nicole whispers.

I answer with a shake of my head.

Rey turns to meet my gaze, his mouth a grim line. "We'll know soon enough."

Chapter 6

Kimba
Bozeman, Montana

In a brief look shared with Rey, I can read his every thought and concern about what's happening in Bozeman. Neither of us know exactly what the trouble is, but it's something serious. The look on the bus conductor's face was fear. Pure and utter fear.

I straighten my spine and force my concerns into a box before pasting on a fake smile. "Let's hustle off the bus, girls, and find out what's happening so we can get on with . . ." I tilt my head. "Get on with things."

As we step off the bus, the conductor gives me his own fake smile, his panicked eyes resting on my red swollen cheek and discolored eye. As his gaze leaves my face and lights on Nicole, the smile changes. He doesn't leer, not exactly, but I feel my mama bear instincts rise. After what happened last night, I don't want anyone looking at my daughters.

"Nicole?" I touch her arm.

She takes a step closer to me, avoiding the boy's scrutiny. I give her a slight smile, letting her know I'm here and we're fine.

If last night's attack had happened six weeks ago, I don't know if we would've made it. I was such a wreck, so lost in my grief, I'm not even sure I had the presence of mind to fight back like we did. Of course, Nicole's a big reason we survived. She kept her head during the attack. She did what was needed. She was a warrior.

I drape an arm around my daughter's shoulder. "All will be well."

She wants to say something, to argue with me. Her lips purse as she shakes her head.

I give a nod. "We'll be fine. We will."

A tall lady in a military uniform, with salt and pepper hair pulled into a tight bun, stands next to the bus conductor. She whispers something to him. He shrugs and then points toward the bus where the elderly couple from yesterday, the ones Pusher Dude was bothering, is slowly making their way toward our group.

Once they arrive, the woman with the bun gives them a tight smile and then looks around, meeting our questioning eyes. "The town of Bozeman is under quarantine." Her voice is emotionless, matter of fact.

After a beat of silence, there's a cacophony of questions, all sounding off at the same time and all expressing essentially the same question: what's happening here?

The military woman raises her hand, motioning for silence. "There's an illness going through the community. The hardest hit area is the college, where most people live, but we've put the entire town under lockdown."

My arm tightens around Nicole, and Rey pulls Naomi closer to him as she asks what a quarantine is.

Another murmur runs through the small gathering.

The lady waves her hand. "We have an aid station set up at Lindley Park. There's camping and conveniences to keep you comfortable until we have more information as to the extent of the illness."

"Is it a virus?" someone asks.

The officer glances around the crowd, meeting several people's eyes before giving a curt nod. "We're operating under that assumption."

Rey lifts a hand. "When did it start?"

"The illness started several days ago. The lockdown was initiated about forty-eight hours ago. We tried contacting the bus line via radio to stop them from coming here. We've decided the aid station is an acceptable solution . . . for now."

"Did it get out?"

Her mouth goes into a hard line as she meets my husband's gaze. "We don't believe so. There was a group of Bozeman residents who'd left on a hunting expedition around the time the symptoms started. They returned yesterday morning. All were examined and none have symptoms."

The bus conductor furrows his brow. "What does this mean for us? For the bus line?"

She gives a grim nod. "It means this is the last bus in or out until we get this illness under control. Those with Bozeman as their final destination will need to get off at Belgrade or go on to Livingston until further notice." She nods in our direction. "We can accommodate those already here, but we won't have the ability to house any additional persons."

"You think we should stay here?" a voice calls out. "Won't we get sick?"

"It's possible. No one would fault you for getting back on the bus and heading on to Livingston, or wherever you wish, until this is resolved."

I raise my hand. "Just to clarify, the entire town is under lockdown? Are there any neighborhoods excluded?"

"Until we know what we are dealing with, it's the entire town."

"Is it possible to get messages to people? Or find out their status?"

"You may be able to learn more at the aid station. They have limited information available. Those of you staying in Bozeman, please make your way to one of the trucks. We'll transport you to the park."

Rey and I have a silent conversation. He gives a slight nod, which I mimic.

"Let's go, girls." My husband's voice is dull and monotone.

We climb into the back of an old, green, rusted-out pickup truck with Illinois license plates. It strikes me as funny a truck like this would be so far from home. It looks like such a wreck, I can't even imagine it could make the drive.

The elderly man and woman from the bus slowly totter to the same truck. Rey gets out to help them, when the soldier standing nearby says they can ride up front with him if we'll keep their bags. There's another couple from the bus in the bed of the pickup with us. The woman has a very young baby in a cloth carrier, similar to the style Patti wore on her chest.

"How old?" I ask.

The young mother scrunches her nose. "Three months, maybe? It's hard to keep track these days."

The man's smile is proud. "Three months sounds about right. The lady who helped with the birth said it was the end of May. It's . . . what? September now, right?"

"The sixth." I nod. "A girl?"

"Yes." The new mother beams. "Do you think this is something serious? My parents live here. I wish I would've asked just how sick people are getting."

"I'm sure we can ask more questions when we get to the park."

The man scoffs. "Whether they'll answer or not is another subject. Hard to find out the truth about anything anymore. Did you hear about the president's latest address?"

I glance to Rey, who lifts a shoulder. I answer with a shake of my head.

"Yup. Last night. At least, that's when we heard the replay. They had it on at the campground in Missoula. Another guy there said he heard it for the first time earlier in the day. Makes me think it was fairly recent."

"And?" Rey tilts his head.

"Mostly the same old same old. They're working to get things back to normal, obey the orders from your local officials and the military, blah, blah, blah. Like we have a choice? It's getting to be shoot first, ask questions later. Anyway, he said something rather cryptic about remembering we're Americans and what that means to us in the coming days. He said we've been an independent nation since 1776, and that isn't going to stop now. What do you think he meant? 'Cause I know what I think. I think he's hinting someone's trying to take us over."

Stifling a scoff, I give the man an indulgent smile. "Oh, I'm sure it's nothing so dramatic." I clear my throat after realizing just how close I sound to my fake Kim persona. I'm done with her. Done pretending and manipulating to get what I want.

The man snorts. "Look at how things are! You think this was an accident? We were attacked, probably by another country. Russia, China, maybe even North Korea. You know, it could've been— "

"Honey." The woman gives him a look and shakes her head.

He lifts a hand. "Anyway, *someone* orchestrated all of this. Softened us up just so they could attack and take us over."

Rey taps a finger to his chin. "Maybe so. But it does seem a little odd that another country would destroy so much of America in order to conquer us. I mean, the early attacks make sense, when they were localized sabotage . . . to a degree. But the EMP and coastal nuclear detonations gives them a country in ruins. Living here would be just as difficult for them as it is for us."

The man furrows his brow. "What if it was an accident? What if they didn't plan on the EMP and nukes, but someone working with them . . ." He scrunches up his mouth. "Like a double cross. Shoot, the president could've even been involved. I mean, look what he's done, siccing our own military on us. That's even against that Posse law."

The wife gives a patient smile and pats his arm. "I'm sure these fine folks don't need to hear about this."

"But it is! Our own military isn't supposed to be used against us. We're told we aren't under martial law, but look." He motions to the driver of the pickup truck. "Aren't they acting like police, telling us what we can and can't do? What gives them this authority?"

"We've talked about this." The woman's voice is low and understanding. "There was probably some law or rule passed to allow it. It's not like we get all the information with the way things are."

The pickup truck turns into a driveway and pulls to a stop. The greenspace of the park is littered with a couple dozen tents and makeshift shelters.

Rey helps the elderly couple with their suitcases as we all move to the check-in area. We're given the rules, essentially don't cause trouble and don't leave the park until the quarantine is lifted.

The couple with the baby registers first, giving her parents' names and address. After checking the records, they're told the neighborhood was evacuated several months ago. All survivors moved to the college. The woman tries to ask questions about her parents but is told the college will have more information when the quarantine's over.

The elderly couple, here for their son, are given a similar answer about his block being evacuated and moved to the college.

Rey leans into me. "I won't be surprised if the Pitneys also live at the college."

"No doubt," I mutter.

We were right. We aren't told anything exact, but when we give the Pitneys' address, he says it's listed as evacuated and relocated to the college. As for the Pitneys themselves, they have no information about how they're faring. Once the quarantine is over, we may be able to find out more.

After we're told where to set up our camp, which is in the same area as the others from the bus, Rey thanks the man and motions us to start moving.

"Interesting how so many were moved to the college," I say, keeping my voice low.

"Isn't it?" Rey agrees. "Entire neighborhoods. Definitely interesting."

39

After our camp is set up, I ask the girls if they want to go for a walk. Nicole sucks in a deep breath, her eyes wide. "I'll be right with you." I give her a reassuring smile. "After two days on a bus, I need the exercise. And maybe we can find a spot to do a little sparring practice."

"Me too?" Naomi asks.

"Of course."

Nicole gives a reluctant nod, while Naomi bounces up and down with excitement. We take our time walking along the grass. While there are quite a few tents set up, they're well spaced, giving decent privacy.

We make our way to the far edge of the park, where several large white tents have been set up. There's a cluster of horses fastened together near the tree line. Several fires are burning as the smell of cooked meat permeates the air.

"Hello." I wave to a woman nearby. "Were you hunting?"

"That's right." Her voice is low and gruff; she sounds like her nose is stuffed up.

I take a step back, urging the girls to move with me. Does she have the virus responsible for the quarantine? The Army woman said they were examined and cleared.

"Looks like you were successful." I motion to a deer carcass hanging in the trees. "You live in Bozeman?"

She gives a weary nod. "At the college, along with most everyone else still alive. Our families are still there. They aren't telling us much. I guess you know about the quarantine?"

"We just arrived on the bus. They told us. My friends live in Bozeman. We were told they moved to the college. Do you happen to know Beverly Pitney?"

One side of the woman's face lifts in a slight smile. "Hey, Chad!" she bellows. "Someone's here asking about your wife."

Chapter 7

Kimba

A look of confusion covers my old friend's face as he steps around the large outfitters tent. With his hand on his sidearm, he scans the area, his gaze quickly resting on me.

Chad Pitney portrays a myriad of emotions within a fraction of a second, ending with a broad smile. "No way!" He rushes forward and smothers me in a hug. "Kimba Hoffmann. I can't believe it."

He releases me and takes a step back. His eyes grow wary. "Rey?"

"Here." I nod. "We're on the other side of the park. Beverly? The girls?"

Chad purses his lips. "At the college."

"She said you were hunting." I motion to the lady, her eyes not moving from the spectacle of our greeting.

Chad nods and then turns to my girls. "Look at you two! You've grown so much. Why, Naomi, you were just barely walking the last time I saw you. My Kylie, too, she's all grown up now. And Emma, she's as tall as Beverly."

"You look different than on the computer," Naomi blurts out.

He throws back his head, hooting in laughter. "I guess I do. You know they say the screen adds ten pounds."

She turns to me with wide eyes. "Does it, Mommy?"

"It's just a saying, honey." I pat her shoulder. "You look good, Chad. Things here have been okay?" Even though he's lost a considerable amount of weight, he's toned and muscular—not sickly looking like so many these days. He's aged since I last saw him. The sprinkling of gray he had before is now a silver helmet, and even his bushy eyebrows have a frosted look.

A cloud crosses his face. "We've been okay, managing to get through a day at a time. Is Nate back with Rey?"

My smile freezes as tears flood my eyes.

He closes his eyes briefly as his shoulders sag. There's a catch in his voice. "You lost Nate."

Blinking away my tears, I lift my chin. "On the twenty-second of June. It was a freak windstorm, a tornado maybe. We . . ." I shake my head. "It's been difficult."

He moves close and rests a hand on my shoulder. "I don't know what to say."

I swallow hard. "Can you come to our campsite? See Rey?"

"Absolutely. Let's just tell 'em where I'm going."

He nods to the woman still watching us. She lifts a hand in acknowledgment as we step around the canvas tent. Chad hollers he'll be back shortly, his voice carrying to several small fires where strips of meat are being dried.

As we walk across the park, he talks about the quarantine and being separated from his family. His eyes dart to Naomi, who's hanging on to his words, as he downplays what he thinks may be happening. The bottom line, though, while there were a few people who seemed ill when he left, it wasn't something overly concerning. Living in close quarters, sharing illnesses is expected.

"What kind of symptoms?" I ask, thinking of the nasally woman at his camp.

"Nausea, vomiting, just a general malaise. A few of the sicker people had bad dreams. One girl around Emma's age may have been hallucinating."

"Really?" Nicole asks. "What'd she see?"

"Birds, lots and lots of birds. Oh, and itching. One woman was so itchy she scratched herself raw. A few others, too, but not as bad. There's also been some bad infections. Ugly. Rotting the skin. We thought it was people being careless with cuts or wounds. But now I'm wondering . . ." He shakes his head.

"How long has it been going on?" I ask.

He lifts a shoulder and puts a finger to his bearded chin. "Several weeks? A month? Maybe longer. You know how time is these days. I was thinking about a lady living in our building who died a few weeks back. She had a seizure. Doc said he thought it stopped her heart. Now I'm wondering if her death was related to this. Another guy had a seizure a few days later, but he didn't die from it."

I give Rey a wave. He pauses only a second before pumping a fist into the air. He and Chad begin to move at the same time, closing the distance between them. Their embrace is decidedly manly but still with plenty of affection.

After Chad gives his condolences to Rey, we all find seats and he repeats what he told us about the illnesses. I watch him as he talks, assessing how our friend is truly doing.

There's a change in him.

Before, even with his history in the military and the less than savory things we were sometimes required to do, he was still talkative and funny. Chad had a great sense of humor and found the good in just about everything. Particularly disturbing jobs affected him as they should, but he was the best at compartmentalizing and putting the troubles aside.

But now I'm not seeing that. There's something different about our old friend.

"I'm surprised they didn't quarantine your group." Rey motions to the large tents.

"None of us had symptoms before we left, and we don't have any now. They examined us and decided we aren't a threat."

I raise my eyebrows. "The one lady, the first one we met— "

"Gina. She always sounds all clogged up. Besides, this isn't a head cold making a person hoarse and stuffed up. They were sick-sick. Like a stomach bug and the other stuff. I'll admit, I wouldn't think it'd be something to issue a quarantine over. Something more must've happened."

"Beverly and the girls?" Rey asks.

"Nope. No symptoms. I'd like to think they're not only quarantined from outsiders but also those who are showing symptoms." He gives a somber bob of his head. "I'm sure Beverly and the girls are fine." His voice belays his confidence.

I give him an understanding smile. "What happened to your house? When we registered, they said your neighborhood was evacuated?"

"They did, huh? That's not quite what happened."

Rey narrows his eyes. "What did happen?"

Chad rubs a hand through his stubbly hair. "They scammed us."

My eyebrows draw together. "Meaning?"

"You remember what our place was like? Our community?"

"Sure." Rey lifts a hand. "Edge of town, big houses, affluent."

"Yup. We were pretty well set. Not just Beverly and me with our . . . um . . . *enhancements*, but really everyone. Each house had their own well and septic. Plus, it's a green community, set up to

43

reduce the carbon footprint." He raises his eyebrows. "Everyone had solar power. A few, including us, added wind."

"Right." Rey nods. "But for you— "

"Mm-hmm. We had the guts of the solar system swapped out. Where most people were selling back to the power company, we set up an independent system, allowing us to store power and use the batteries. It was perfect, really."

"I'll never forget the grief Bev gave you over changing out the system." Rey lets out a low laugh.

"I know, right?" Chad plunges his chin in agreement. "Turns out, she was right. The EMP fried the guts of the main system. Spent an insane amount of money, and we still lost the solar and the wind."

"I thought you got the hardened version?"

"So did I. Guess not. Anyway, we were just as in the dark as everyone else."

Rey and I make murmuring noises. When we set out from Denver, our goal was to reach Chad and Beverly. Chad had given us an open invitation to show up on their doorstep if things ever warranted. We left our Denver home before the EMP. When it hit, and we discovered just how widespread the damage was, we wondered if their plans worked.

A wrinkle cuts across Chad's forehead. "We weren't sure if Bozeman was getting fallout, so we moved to the basement. Hey, do you think the sickness could be radiation poisoning?"

I shake my head. "Radiation poisoning would've shown before now, right? We met a man and woman who'd been exposed. It was obvious early on, not long after the missile alerts. That's how we first found out about the ground detonations. We didn't even know for sure what was happening, other than nothing was working."

"Yeah, did you know it was an EMP?"

I can't help but smile. "We suspected. But we, uh . . . we were with some people who— "

"Don't tell me!" Chad laughs. "You didn't."

"She did." Nicole tosses me a side eye. "It was so embarrassing."

Chad's mouth goes into an *O*.

"We told the children. They know about the work we did together." I raise my eyebrows. "The basics, anyway."

Rey reaches for my hand. "Kimba put on quite the show. We heard the alerts on the phone of the ladies we were traveling with, a pair of sisters. We stayed in a railroad tunnel for several days."

"That sucked." Nicole gives an exaggerated shudder, while Naomi disagrees and insists it was fun.

Nicole opens her mouth to say something else to her sister, but I lift my chin and shake my head. "Girls."

"Well, it did suck." Nicole can't help but get in the last word.

She's not wrong. It truly was awful. Adding to its awfulness was me being in full Kim mode, annoying and negative about everything. My cheeks flame as I recall some of my words and attitude.

While Rey knew it was an act, and we'd told the children if they thought I was acting funny to not worry about it, Sylvia and Sabrina Eriksen had no idea. More than once, they held their tongue instead of telling me off.

I motion to Chad. "Please, continue your story."

"We figured it'd be better to be safe than sorry, so we stayed in the basement near the back and away from the patio door, especially the girls. We kept them restricted to the bathroom and bedroom. I taped plastic over the bedroom window as an extra precaution. We had plenty of food and water, games and books. It wasn't terrible. Kept thinking you all might be showing up soon too."

"We were trying." Rey shakes his head. "That's why we were in the train tunnel. We were on our way here when the car ran out of gas. We started walking when everything went pear-shaped. Then we got a little . . . sidetracked."

"Oh!" I exclaim so loudly everyone jumps. "You won't believe who we ran into."

Chad leans forward. "Same here. You won't believe who *I* ran into."

"Who?" I ask.

"Jankins."

"Jankins!" Rey and I blurt at the same time.

The hair stands up on the back of my neck. I glance around. "Is he— "

"No longer a threat."

A sigh escapes me. "What happened?"

He raises a hand. "In a minute. But tell me, who'd you run into?"

I assume a smug look. "Meagan Wright."

His eyes go wide. "No! She said— "

"Yep. Next time she saw me, she'd kill me." Even though Chad met us after my government service and the incident with Meagan, he knew full well of the drama: the witch hunt she'd led and the threats she leveled against me. "For a few seconds, I believed she would. Then . . ." I tilt my head to the side and lift my hands.

"She's my grandma Doris." Naomi has a tender smile and dreamy look.

"Come again?" Chad says.

I let out a small laugh. "When she didn't kill me on sight, things changed. It was tense at first, but now . . ." I lift my hands. "We're friends."

Rey takes my hand. "More than friends, even. They welcomed us into their community. Meagan calls herself Doris now. It might even be her real name." He looks at me for confirmation.

I give a combination nod and shrug. Maybe it is. Maybe it isn't.

"Anyway." Rey lifts his free hand. "We're like family. It made leaving there hard. But we'd made a commitment, plus we wanted to see you."

"What commitment?"

We quickly detail our journey of seeing the Dosen family home and the others we dropped off along the way. We spend many more minutes talking about Nate and how losing him was so hard, plus the deaths of Asher and Jennifer Dosen. Once Chad has the overall info on our trip, I give him a nod. "Back to your story. What happened at your house?"

Chad looks to the sky. "Where was I? Oh yeah, the EMP. About a week later, we moved out of the basement. Things were going okay. We were working together with the neighbors, figuring out water and things. Several days later, an old truck came rumbling through the neighborhood. A guy in the back, from our city police, was using a bullhorn. He said there was a gas leak and we had to evacuate."

"Really?" I shake my head. "Caused by the EMP? Or maybe the cyberattack?"

"That's what we thought. A neighbor down the street was going door to door after the police went by. He said they'd be back in two hours and we had to be out so they could do whatever work was needed. Another neighborhood had the same problem, and it sparked a fire. We'd been smelling smoke since the night before, so we left."

"Did you go to the college then?"

"We did. Our neighborhood and several others were all affected by the *gas leak*." The way he says gas leak tells me there's definitely more to this story.

"The next day, even more people were relocated to the college. Good thing it was summer and the place was nearly empty, because about half the town was there. About midafternoon, we saw a column of smoke in the direction of our place. We started organizing people to go fight it, but . . ." Chad shakes his head.

"By the time we got there, we couldn't even get close. The whole area was burning down. It was a week before things cooled enough to make our way in. Our house, along with everyone else's, was gone."

"That's rough, man." Rey shakes his head.

"It was. And it got worse. They were passing out supplies at the college, and I recognized some of the things as belonging to me."

"What?" My eyes go wide.

"I wasn't the only one. Practically everyone found something of theirs. We thought it had all been lost in the fire."

"I don't understand." Nicole shakes her head. "They stole your stuff before the fire started?"

"They stole our stuff before *starting* the fire."

Chad continues on with an almost unbelievable tale of a group masquerading as the police and evacuating neighborhoods like his to go in and loot before destroying the houses to hide the evidence. A few from the actual police department were involved, but most had been murdered.

"How'd your stuff end up at the college shelter?" Nicole asks.

"One of the police officers who was helping the looters grew a conscience, too little and too late, but he thought he'd give back what they rejected."

"Not very smart."

"Nope. Even less smart was them not moving on right away. Instead, they'd holed up on the edge of town. That's when I found Jankins."

"He was part of them?"

"Yup. Not the brains behind the operation, of course."

"Of course not!"

"But he was one of the ringleaders."

"What was he doing here?" Rey asks. "I mean, last I knew, he was living in Washington state, in the Puget Sound area. Figured, since we heard Seattle was hit with a nuke or two . . ." Rey lifts his hands.

Chad looks around at the neighboring camps. His eyes travel to Naomi, who's moved over by the tent and is playing with a bug or something in the grass. He leans in closer and lowers his voice. "He tried to cut me a deal. Said he knew this was happening and was on his way to a rendezvous in Billings."

"What?" Nicole's eyes go wide.

I lean back, shaking my head like it's on a swivel. Donnie McCullough had been vocal about his opinion of the attacks. Rey and I had been quieter, discussing it only in detail between the two of us. But it sounds like Donnie was right. We were right. It was an inside job.

Chapter 8

Beverly
Wednesday, September 9

With the Army now in Bozeman, things are different. We're still quarantined to our apartment, that hasn't changed, but they brought medicine and more doctors.

Doc Sanderson is still making his rounds, along with his physician assistant. He says most of the Army is outside the lockdown zone, but a few doctors and nurses are helping with the sick in a makeshift medical ward set up at the Strand Union Building. SUB's central location and nearness to Swingle Health Center make it a logical choice for a hospital.

The day before yesterday, Doc Sanderson started sedating Emma with meds provided by the Army. So far, the sedation seems to be helping. She's no longer thrashing around and screaming about the awful things she sees. The point when she starts to come around makes me worry. But she needs to come out of it enough to eat and take fluids. The food delivery continues.

Sal Reese, a young man who lives on the floor below us and recently lost his mom to a heart attack, delivers our food. Like Doc Sanderson, he takes precautions to not get whatever Emma—what the three of us—may have. Most of the time, he knocks and lets me know the food is there.

Through the peephole, I've seen him wearing a bandanna over his mouth along with leather driving gloves. Doc Sanderson wears a tight-fitting mask and disposable gloves. I did notice in the days before the Army set up shop, his mask wasn't looking its best. My guess is, he only had one or two, and they were being overused. I guess they don't have an extra for Sal, and he's doing the best he can.

This morning, when Sal drops off our food, he speaks through the door and says they think they've figured out what's wrong with everyone. He overheard a few of the Army people talking with one of the history professors living on campus. He didn't completely understand, but did catch enough to believe it's not a virus and not contagious by person-to-person contact.

"Really?" I call out. "Then how— "

"I don't know. They were excited and walking away from me while talking. I couldn't follow without it being obvious I was . . . you know."

"Eavesdropping?"

"Mm-hmm. But maybe Doc Sanderson will come by soon and tell you. Then you won't need to stay locked up in the apartment. How's Emma doing?"

"She's better. Resting. The food helps. And thank you for making sure there's plenty for Kylie to eat. I appreciate you ensuring there are gluten-free things."

"It's no problem. I'd hope someone would do that for me, too, if I couldn't eat bread. But today it didn't matter. No one got bread."

"Really? Is everything all right in the kitchen?"

"Seems so. I could smell the bread baking earlier. Maybe it just didn't get finished. The drizzly rain might have affected the fire— couldn't get it hot enough to cook the bread? I don't know, I'm just guessing. Weird though, huh?"

I glance out the peephole. Sal's still wearing his leather gloves, but the bandanna is pulled down around his neck instead of covering his nose and mouth. "Do you really think they know what's wrong? That they can treat Emma?"

He jostles his shoulders. "Sounded like they might. They were sure excited. I did hear—well, the professor said something like, 'There's no cure.' But one of the doctors said, 'But now we know how to better treat the symptoms and prevent anyone else from getting it.' That's one of the last things I heard before they ran off."

His entire face scrunches up like he's suddenly deep in thought.

"What is it?"

"Um, you know. They, uh, they didn't go to the Swingle. I mean, it would seem they would, right? There or to the SUB? You know where they went?"

I let out a slow breath. "No, Sal. I have no idea where they may have gone."

"Right. They were going to one of the food storage areas."

"The food storage areas?" My forehead crinkles. "Why?"

50

"Don't know. But weird, huh? Anyway, I'd better get going. I still have a few people to deliver to. I hope, maybe soon, they'll let me bring your food in for you."

"Maybe soon they won't make you bring me food." I smile at the door. "I'm very grateful you've taken such good care of us. Thank you, Sal."

"Oh, yeah, sure. I'm glad they're letting me help deliver the food and make rounds to look for the window signals. It's fine. There's lots to be done with so many people quarantined to their apartments, so I pick up other jobs too. I've also been helping in the goat barn. That's your crew, right?"

"Yes. How is . . . are they all okay?"

"The goats are great. I really like the ones that don't have ears. They're unique looking."

I relax into a smile. "They are. I meant the workers, my crew. I know with what happened to Hugh . . . we all were friends."

"Oh, that." His sigh is loud. "You heard Hugh died too?"

I lean against the door as tears fill my eyes. "I hadn't heard."

"Yeah, it's sad. Lots of people are dead. A couple dozen at least, and hundreds are sick. Some just a little sick with the squirts—I mean, diarrhea or throwing up. But others are like Emma and hallucinating. And you heard about the gangrene?"

"Gangrene? You mean the cuts?"

"That's what they thought. Doc didn't tell you?"

I furrow my brow. "He didn't say anything. Well, he did ask if I'd noticed any sores on Emma. He's been checking her feet and legs."

"Mm-hmm. Probably looking for the gangrene. They've had to amputate on a few people. You know Skelly? He was the first one who was complaining about a sore on his foot. Works in the woodshop."

"We just assumed he'd dropped something heavy on his toe and tore the skin."

"Right. Well, he lost his leg all the way to the knee. Not sure he's going to make it. But now he's not the only one. There were a few others with cuts that are now infected. Yesterday, someone said they thought it was part of the virus. The history professor today said, 'It even explains the gangrene.' So, I guess we'll know more soon. I'd better go, Mrs. Pitney. I'll see you tomorrow, huh? Maybe you can even open the door then. Bye."

I lean against the door as I wait for Sal to make his way down the hall. Wouldn't be good to get careless now, not this close to maybe having answers and being released from our small apartment.

Kylie has been a trooper. She spends her time in the bedroom, playing quietly on the floor or reading in the queen-size bed. Although we do leave the bedroom door open, in some ways our interactions are much the same as between Sal and me. I haven't touched her since Doc Sanderson told me I could spread Emma's sickness to Kylie by contact.

When I get our daily food delivery, I bring it in and then wash my hands. I even wipe down the food containers before dishing up Kylie's portions. While I'm doing that, Kylie goes to the bathroom and washes with the water I leave in there.

I do my best to keep the bathroom, kitchen, and all areas that I touch as clean and disinfected as possible—not easy when we have no way to heat water and limited cleaning supplies. Thankfully, we were given a spray bottle of disinfectant to use. It's more than halfway gone already.

If the sickness isn't viral, I'll be able to hug my baby again without fear of spreading it.

According to Sal, the professor said there's no cure for whatever Emma has—whatever is affecting our town. But if they know what it is and can better treat the symptoms, maybe they'll ease up on the sedation and she can start coming around. The hallucinations were so bad, I was truly beginning to fear for her sanity. I was afraid she'd try to hurt herself.

Seeing just how badly she was affected helps me understand how Hugh did what he did. And why the guns were all confiscated. Not only the guns but even all our knives were seized—defensive, hunting, and kitchen knives. Doc said the knives weren't taken from anyone not currently showing symptoms, only from the homes of the actively ill.

In some ways, it makes sense. In others, it doesn't.

Rumor is, Hugh Vardy had zero symptoms before his shooting spree. But what can we do? Lock up anything that can be used as a weapon? Cain killed Abel with a stone. While I don't put much stock in those Bible ramblings any longer, I do understand that true evil can't be stopped. Not only do I understand, but I've also seen it firsthand— experienced it.

And seeing my sweet, innocent girl thrashing and out of her mind, I can see how a good man like Hugh Vardy may not have been in his right mind. If this illness can cause the appearance of evil where there is none, locking up the guns and knives isn't going to help.

"Mommy?" Kylie calls from the doorway of her bedroom. "Did Sal bring our food?"

I send her a smile. "He did. Give me just a minute and I'll have it ready for you."

Chapter 9

Kimba
Thursday, September 10

I drop a kiss on Naomi's head as she cuddles next to me while we read. The blanket across our laps helps keep away the chill of the late summer day. While it feels like rain is on its way again, we're taking advantage of the break for a little fresh air. Especially since the last few days have been drizzly, forcing us to spend most of our time in the tent.

The quarantine of Bozeman is still in effect. With each day that passes, Chad becomes more and more agitated. He's tried to get info about his family, but no one seems to have any details of who is sick and who isn't.

Being here hasn't been too terrible. They've not only provided us books but also a generous lunch each day. We've even had bread and butter. Lovely dark, chewy loaves slathered in rich, creamy butter, along with meat, salad greens, and fresh tomatoes.

"There're several gardens and greenhouses," Chad said. "That's one good thing. After we regained control of the town and took care of the, um, riffraff, we really banded together. The college had some good things in place and lots of land. We started planting crops last summer and haven't stopped."

I took an appreciative bite of bread, letting it melt in my mouth. "I know Montana was well known for growing wheat, but I didn't think it was a big crop around Bozeman."

"Not so much. Most of it's grown in the north, the Golden Triangle they call it. They grow a lot of winter and spring wheat there. Around here, it was more hobby growers. But they've expanded. Not just wheat but barley, oats, rye, and a few other cereal crops. The bread you're eating is mostly rye from the looks of it."

"Well, it's delicious. You still don't eat bread? Even now when food is so scarce?"

"It still makes me sick. Runs right through me like . . . never mind. Besides, we have plenty of vegetables and meat. Our hunting parties go out regularly, plus we have paddocks of cattle, pigs, sheep, goats, even rabbits and chickens. We make a point of foraging too. Wait until you see the setup we have. I'm proud of the things we've done.

"Beverly's a big reason for it all. Growing up in a small town like she did, she really took to helping with the animals and gardens. Even though her family didn't do any of those things, she had friends who did. And she's just a natural. She's in charge of the dairy goat operation. 'Course, our good works may have made the military happy to stick around. I suspect things will change soon."

The talks turned to what we think the reconstruction efforts will look like. While Chad and Beverly have been happy in Bozeman, his eyes lit up over the prospect of joining us in Billings and maybe even moving on with us to Denver. Like us, he wants to help our country. But we all know something more is happening.

There's been many whispered conversations between the three of us, after the girls have gone to sleep. The more we compare notes about what we've seen and learned in our travels and what has happened in and around Bozeman, the more we're convinced this isn't over.

I mentioned the guy from the truck who said the Army shouldn't even be operating on US soil. Chad said he heard there was an Executive Order allowing it, as long as the governor of the state allowed the military assistance. And according to Chad, most states have, but a few haven't. Texas said they were fine on their own. South Dakota said thanks, but no thanks.

I asked Chad how he knew about this. He shrugged before answering he didn't really know. It's all rumor. With people traveling more, they're hearing more.

While most of our conversations are a variation on the current events, I've noticed Rey weaving in Christianity, but Chad isn't interested. He's nice enough about it but usually says something like, "You and I both know the world is what we make it."

I try to be gracious about it. Before Nate died, I know I tended to be a little heavy handed with my beliefs—to the point I'm slightly embarrassed about my behavior at times. While I am certainly not embarrassed about God or sharing about Him, my methods may not have been the best. And then I turned so far the other direction, blaming God and everyone else for Nate's death.

Now things are different. I no longer blame God, but I've also come to a new place of understanding. I want to share God's love with Chad but know I can't force him to accept it. Like all of us, Chad has free will. I pray he'll come to a place where he wants to know more, but all I can do is plant the seeds.

The day we arrived in Bozeman, Nate's birthday, ended up being a good day. Hard because of discovering the quarantine but good with finding Chad here. Our celebration for, and of, Nate was low-key, with Rey reading Psalm 23 and all of us talking about him and sharing stories. It was good. Difficult, but good.

"Is it almost time for lunch?" Naomi asks, unwinding her finger from her hair as I close our book.

"I believe it is, sweetheart. Let's find your dad, then it should be time to make our way to the kitchen area."

The elderly couple from the bus, Mr. and Mrs. Kingsworth, give us a smile as they hold hands and totter their way to the eating area. The couple with the baby is at their side and talking animatedly. The man's excited about something. We meet up with Rey and Chad on the way. They've been at Chad's camp this morning.

"Hey." Rey gives me a look I can't quite interpret.

I raise my eyebrows. "What's up?"

"There's going to be an announcement. We think maybe— "

"They're lifting the quarantine." Chad claps his hands together. "That has to be it, right? It has to be."

When we reach the food station, a line has formed, but the serving hasn't started. We take our place at the back when one of the Army guys stands up in the bed of a truck parked nearby. He hollers out for our attention. "You'll be pleased to know the quarantine is being lifted."

A shout of approval goes up. I glance to Chad, whose smile is nearly breaking his face. There're several questions yelled out to the man about what happened and if they're sure the sickness is no longer contagious.

"We're certain the issue is under control. It wasn't a virus, but rather a bacterium." Another Army person, standing next to the truck, says something to him. He nods, then yells out, "Make that a fungus."

"A fungus?" I mutter.

Rey shakes his head.

"Well, I'll be," Chad whispers.

"What's a fungus?" Naomi asks.

The same responses and questions are traveling through the camp.

"If you can wait a moment before we begin serving, Captain Mercer can give you additional details."

The person on the ground steps onto the truck. I can now see it's the woman who first told us about the quarantine when we got off the bus. She sends a kind smile to the gathered crowd. "I'm Dr. Abigail Mercer. As the major said, we are dealing with a fungal disease known as ergot."

"Ergot." My hands cover my mouth.

A wave of conversation runs through the crowd.

Mercer raises her voice. "It is a known pathogen, somewhat common in North America, which affects wild and cultivated grasses. It's most common in rye but also wheat, oats, and barley."

"Are you saying it's food poisoning?" someone calls out.

"Essentially, yes. We found the fungus in some of the grain crops, what was being used to make bread and cereal. Eliminating the affected grains will stop the spread. Those who are sick are being treated. You won't get sick from the ill people, only from ingesting the contaminated grains."

Gina, from Chad's camp, yells, "What about our families?"

Another person I recognize from Chad's camp adds, "You destroyed our food?"

"You can see your family. We're lifting the quarantine, and you can go back to your homes. And, yes, all affected crops are being destroyed. That's the only way to prevent the illness." She takes a deep breath and straightens her shoulders. "I regret to inform you, there has been loss of life."

The crowd loses control.

Captain Mercer allows it for a few moments before she raises a hand. "I heard the question of how many deaths. I don't have the exact number at the moment. Those of you who live at the college will be able to find out about your loved ones there. If you don't live at the college and your loved one was ill, they were taken to the field hospital set up in the Strand Union Building.

"At 1430 hours, we'll begin transports. Please have your lunch and then take down your camp. We'll set up a staging area here once food

57

service is finished. I can take a few questions, except for answering to the conditions of specific individuals."

A lady near the captain asks a question too quiet for me to hear.

"Yes. Correct." Captain Mercer nods. "That is a theory."

"What'd she say?" a man calls out.

The captain straightens and lifts her chin slightly. "She asked if this ergot is the same as the kind from the Middle Ages and believed to be a component of the Salem Witch Trials."

Another murmur travels through the crowd.

There're a few more questions and clarification from the captain. When the questions die down, she motions to the servers and reminds everyone the transports will begin after lunch.

Chad's mouth is a tight line. "I don't think I can eat. I'm going to tear my camp down. I'll meet you at your tent to help with yours."

I touch his arm. "I'm sure Beverly and the girls are fine. You said they didn't have any symptoms?"

He nods. "Kylie can't abide by bread either. She has my intolerance for it. But Emma . . . she loves it. She's been so excited to have something new in our diet. Beverly eats it, too, though not as much."

I give Chad what I hope is a confident smile, while Rey says, "I'm still praying."

Chad responds with a vacant nod before stepping away. He's not the only one. A good portion of those in line leave. After getting our food, we sit at a picnic table with the Kingsworths and the couple with the baby. The Kingsworths' son is a pastor at a local church and has a campus ministry at the college. At least they, like Chad, will soon have answers.

"This food won't make us sick?" Naomi asks, peering suspiciously at the bowl of soup.

"No, dear." I pat her arm. "They know what's causing the sickness, and they've made it stop. Your soup is fine."

After lunch, the girls help me tear town our camp, while Rey helps the Kingsworths. We're just about finished when Chad shows up. He gives me a wan smile before asking if we need any help. I assure him we're fine and motion to the food area where a line is already forming. "Don't feel like you have to wait for us. Go on and find out about your family. We'll be there when we can."

58

Just then, Rey and the Kingsworths start in our direction. "Ready to go?" Rey calls out.

Chad claps his hands together. "You know it, bro."

Chapter 10

Kimba

A couple of school buses and several pickup trucks are lined up and waiting to haul people to the college. I step onto one of the buses behind the elderly Kingsworths as they wobble up the stairs. Chad and his hunting group are behind us.

Unlike the long-distance transport we rode from Butte to Bozeman, this bus has all its seats in the proper place, making it a tight squeeze with our gear.

There's little talk. The news of the ergot poisoning has people turned in to their own thoughts.

Chad looks physically ill. His face is ashen, and even his lips have lost their hue. I catch his eye and send him a hopeful smile. He lifts his chin in response before quickly looking away.

The tension in the bus increases with each second of the ten-minute ride.

When we pull in, a uniformed man in the front seat stands. "We've set up a registration table. You'll check in there and then be told where to find your loved ones. Your patience is appreciated—and expected—as we work to reunite you. If you aren't inquiring about loved ones and have lodging on this campus, you'll still need to check in. Some of the quarters have been converted to house the infected."

There's a minor mutter among those on the bus as he dismisses us to stand in the already swollen line.

Rey whispers in my ear, "I wonder if we ought to find a place to relax. Let Chad see them on his own, then he can find us."

I answer with a slight nod and glance around. There's plenty of grassy space to set up camp.

"Nah, man." Chad loudly cracks his knuckles after Rey tells him what we're thinking. "I'd like you to stay with me. I understand if you don't want to, but I'd appreciate it."

"Kimba?" Rey raises his eyebrows at me.

"Of course we will."

The line moves quicker than I expect. We soon discover the main reason is because no one's given any information, just sent to secondary locations. Most are sent to the apartment or dormitory they were living in before the lockdown. It's easy to tell the relief the assignment gives.

A few people are sent to large meeting halls. This caused one man to completely lose it, yelling and screaming about how he wanted to know immediately where his wife and child was. He was quickly ushered away in a none-too-gentle manner.

Chad stands completely still. His head is held high, his back straight. His posture makes his previous training clear. It's easy to tell a military man or woman at times like this. He's shed some of his pallor, though he doesn't look as healthy as he did before the announcement of the ergot poisoning.

When he's motioned forward, his voice is crisp and clear. "Chad Pitney. My wife, Beverly, and I live in Shiloh Court with our two daughters."

The soldier gives him a single nod before running her finger down the sheet in front of her. "Mr. Pitney, please proceed to your apartment."

Chad lets out an audible sigh. "Thank you, Corporal."

She responds with a curt nod. "Please remain in your apartment or the greenspace nearby. Certain areas are off limits for now."

Rey claps Chad on the back as we move out of the line. "Lead the way, my friend."

"It's only about a ten-minute walk." Chad weaves around a group of people to an open space.

We've cleared the bulk of the crowd when Nicole whispers, "Mom?"

"Hmm?"

"How do we know they're okay?"

I raise my eyebrows, then open my mouth when the meaning of her question suddenly makes sense. Giving him bad news in his own apartment, as opposed to a public area, would be the right thing to do. "I . . . I'm sure they're fine. Let's keep praying."

As we walk, I send up my petitions to God. While I'm no longer angry at God and lashing out, I also don't have the warm fuzzies I experienced in the early days of my accepting the gospel. I know He's there and the Holy Spirit is with me to provide guidance. But I miss the way it used to be, the feelings I had before Nate's death and my turning away from God. Will I get those back?

Chad sets a fast pace, his strides eating up the ground as the girls and I scurry to keep up with him. We're in what is obviously the housing section of the college when we hear a mournful wail from one of the apartments. Chad stops in his tracks.

He looks back at Rey, once again ashen and gray. "What if— "

"Let's go on, friend. We're with you."

Chad's neck veins pulse as he works his jaw. "Let's do this."

At a much more sedate pace, we finish the walk across a green field and begin to climb the stairs to his top-floor, two-bedroom apartment. He hesitates at the door before slowly turning the knob and poking his head inside.

"Chad!" Beverly's voice carries out of the apartment and down the common hallway.

My hand goes to my mouth as tears fill my eyes at the sound of my friend's voice.

Nicole lets out an audible sigh.

We step next to Rey, who's standing near the open door. Chad and Bev are locked in an embrace. Kylie is at their side, one of Chad's hands on her shoulder.

He releases his wife to bend and lift his daughter in the air. "Hello, mite."

"Emma's sick." Kylie bursts into tears.

Chad looks to Beverly, and she nods.

"What'd she say?" Naomi whispers.

Bev jumps and turns toward us, her hand going to her hip. From the reaction, I expect to see a gun nestled there, but it's bare.

Rey lifts his hands. "Beverly."

"Rey?" Her eyes travel from my husband to me. "Kimba. Oh!"

A microsecond later, I'm hugging my friend and we're both in tears.

"Where's Emma?" Chad's voice is thick.

"She's in the bedroom." Kylie points.

"Doc Sanderson left a little bit ago." Bev runs a hand through her dark brown hair. There're new strands of silver weaved through and, like my own mane, it's in serious need of a washing.

"Can I— "

"You can see her." Beverly dips her chin. "She's resting. They've . . . did they tell you why people got sick?"

Chad repeats what we learned at the park.

Bev wraps her arms around herself. "She started hallucinating. I didn't even know she was affected until then. Did you hear . . ." She clears her throat. "Did they tell you why they did the quarantine?"

"Just that people were sick. We didn't know about the ergot until today."

"The hallucinations, that's why they did the quarantine. There were too many affected, and some were . . . dangerous."

"Your sidearm?" Chad motions to her hip.

"Taken. They confiscated them in case someone freaked out—it already happened once. Hugh Vardy killed his wife and son-in-law. Shot a couple of others also. He . . ." She shakes her head. "He didn't make it."

Chad's shoulders drop. "Hugh was a good man."

"They took our knives too." Bev motions with her hand. "Every single one of them, in case Emma . . ." She tilts her head. "It's been bad. We thought it was a virus, so Kylie had to stay in our room."

"All by myself." She pats her dad on the face. "Alone. I didn't like it."

"I'm sorry." He hugs his daughter even tighter.

"Mommy had to clean everything over and over. She slept on the futon so I wouldn't get sick."

"Poor Doc Sanderson, he's exhausted." Beverly releases her own exhausted sigh. "Everyone is. There are so many sick."

Chad returns Kylie to the floor. "I can see Emma?"

Beverly's smile doesn't reach her eyes. "She's sedated and may not recognize you."

As Chad slips into the bedroom, Bev says hello to Naomi and Nicole, making the appropriate remarks about how they've grown. When her eyes meet mine, I give a slight shake of my head. She embraces me again, telling me how sorry she is as we both cry.

Sometime later, Rey and I are on the futon in the cozy living room while Beverly and Nicole bring chairs over from the table. We share snippets from the last eighteen months of our lives. Naomi and Kylie are sitting on the rug, playing with interlocking blocks, seeming as if they'd played together their entire lives, as only young children can.

There's a big change in Bev since we last spoke. She's always been on the quiet side, calm and serene. But now there's something else. A melancholy. She smiles and chats, but it all seems fake, much like the way I've been since we lost Nate. When we have some time alone, I hope we can have a good talk about everything we've both been through—everything our families have gone through—in the past months.

Chad steps out of the bedroom. "When will they wake her?"

Beverly motions to a chair next to her. "Soon. Thankfully, she doesn't have any of the other symptoms. It's made her treatment a little simpler."

"Am I correct in remembering there's no antidote for ergot poisoning?" I ask.

"No antidote." She shakes her head. "Stopping the consumption of the ergot and then treating the symptoms is all they can do. For some, the treatment is, surprisingly, small doses of the poison itself. It's . . ." She lets out a noisy breath. "It's just so strange. A poison known to cause death, ergot was developed as a medicine to use for migraines."

"Really?" Nicole asks. "That seems so weird."

Beverly ducks her chin in agreement. "It's been around since the Middle Ages. Saint Anthony's Fire is one of the names for it. I can see why. Some people have screamed out in pain, saying their legs or feet were burning." She gets a thoughtful look.

"Someone said the name wasn't derived from the burning sensations but rather from a group of monks who provided treatment. Anyway, at least with Emma she doesn't have the pain. Not that it was much easier for her. She thought she had bugs crawling all over her. At first, we thought maybe someone had slipped LSD or something in the food. I think that's how they realized what happened."

I shake my head. "I can't even imagine. Who figured it out? One of the military doctors?"

"A history professor. The kitchen staff thought the ergot contamination—the fungus—was mouse droppings. Gross for sure, but with food being in such short supply . . ." Her hands cup her elbows.

I do my best not to shudder. At the Dosen ranch, the pantry was infested with weevils. Also gross, but somehow at a different level. Eating bugs is one thing. Feces is something else.

"It's good the military set up a base in Billings. Otherwise, we wouldn't have the medicine needed for Emma and the others. Well, they don't have everything they need." She meets my eyes and shakes her head. "Besides the hallucinations and sickness, some people developed gangrene. Several lost their toes or fingers, and one man lost his leg." She lifts her hands.

"We've been in here for days, not leaving the apartment. The doc or a nurse stops by, and someone delivers food. I don't really know how bad it is, exactly how many deaths or the extent of the illness."

Chad reaches for her hand. "I'm sure we'll learn more in the coming days."

Childlike laughter carries across the breeze. Naomi and Kylie jump up and run to the open window.

"People are playing with a soccer ball," Naomi declares. "Can we go?"

"Or to the playground?" Kylie adds hopefully.

I glance to Beverly. "Where's the playground?"

"Too far," Chad answers. "The corporal said to stay on our greenspace."

"But . . ." Kylie's eyes fill with tears.

Beverly's voice is soft. "She's been locked in here for days."

Rey squeezes my hand. "We could . . ."

I return the pressure. "We'll take her outside, okay?"

Chad nods his thanks. "I think I'm going to go sit with Emma. Beverly? Join me?"

We spend a couple minutes getting Kylie ready to go outside. Her smile is wide, and she's practically vibrating as I help her into a light jacket. It's still warm, but the breeze can carry a chill. Naomi's wearing the long-sleeved T-shirt I put her in this morning, Nicole and I have button-up shirts over our tanks, and Rey's wearing a blue denim shirt—perfect pre-fall clothing.

As we take the stairs, Nicole whispers in my ear, "I'm surprised the military didn't take our guns."

"I am, too, a little at least. They must feel they have everything under control and the delusions are no longer an issue."

"I guess anyone who had them is sedated like Emma?"

"Likely so. Or locked up. Maybe both."

"Better than being burned at the stake."

With a shake of my head, I choose not to mention a good number of those found "guilty" during the Salem Witch Trials were hanged.

The scene on the lawn is a festive one, with several children kicking a soccer ball and families spread out on blankets. I wish I would've thought to grab something for us to sit on.

Rey gives me a smile. "Do you want to find a spot? I'll go back and get a couple of blankets."

"You don't mind the stairs?" I give a fake shudder at the idea of climbing three flights again.

He puts his hand on my cheek. "For you, I'd climb twice as far."

I let out a laugh as my heart fills with love. "Why thank you, my prince."

Nicole gives an exaggerated eye roll before muttering, "So embarrassing."

The slight lift at the corners of her mouth doesn't escape me. She may pretend to be embarrassed, but I know she's happy things are better between Rey and me—with all of us. Our fractured family is repairing itself.

"Can we play?" Naomi motions to the soccer game.

"Yes, go see if they'll let you in."

"I know them." Kylie waves at one of the boys. "They'll let us play."

The girls joining the game is seamless, with one of them moving to each team. The children are all laughing and enjoying themselves, even occasionally managing to give the ball a good kick. Nicole and I stand at the side, discussing how things are here and what might happen next. We clap and cheer for the players until she eventually asks, "What's taking Dad so long?"

"He probably got to talking with Chad. You know how the two of them are."

"Brothers from another mother?" She raises her eyebrows. "A bromance?"

"Please." I lift a hand and let out a low chuckle. "Don't let them hear you say that."

"They're funny together. Dad's usually so calm, sedate. But when he gets around Chad, he becomes more like him, more excited about things. But Chad . . . maybe now that he knows his family's okay, he'll lighten up a bit."

66

"I'm sure he will. I'll run up and grab the blanket. You keep an eye on the girls?"

She waves a hand, then let's out a cheer. Naomi manages to pass the ball to another player, who then kicks for a goal attempt. It isn't successful but is still very exciting.

"Way to go, Naomi!" I call out as I stride toward the apartment building. She responds with a beaming smile and a thumbs up.

Chapter 11

Kimba

Stepping inside the apartment building, I stand at the doorway a moment to allow my eyes to adjust. A scratching noise comes from somewhere nearby.

Movement in the common area ahead of me catches my attention. A man with a head of thinning hair, jutting out in all directions, rubs something against the wall. When the door clicks shut behind me, he turns.

He rubs a hand against his jaw, leaving chocolate pudding behind. How odd . . .

As his eyes meet mine, a realization hits me. That's not chocolate pudding.

It's blood.

The sadness on the man's face draws me in. I take a step forward and rest my hand on the butt of my gun. "Did you cut yourself? Can I help?"

He lifts his hand up, studying his palm. "I don't . . ." His eyes go wide. "Get it off! Get it off!" He lets out a high-pitched wail.

I take another step forward. "Please, let me help you."

His keening continues as he intersperses unintelligible words. I want to go to him, to help him, but I hold back. Something isn't right.

"Dr. Sanderson?" A woman exits one of the first-floor apartments.

"What's happening?" someone else asks.

"Oh, no." The woman pales. "Doctor . . . no. Are you having the visions?"

The man screams even louder. Soon, the entire space fills up. A man goes to the doctor and yells out to get help.

The door to the staircase opens, and a teenage boy yells, "Help me! There's an injured man here. He's been stabbed."

My stomach drops. I rush toward the boy. "Who?"

"I don't know him. He doesn't live in this building."

"Show me!" I motion him to move, then yell to the group gathered around the fallen doctor, "We need help. Find us a doctor."

Someone responds, "This *is* the doctor. He's sick!"

My feet pound the steps behind the boy. *Please, Lord. Please. Not Rey. Please.*

We reach the second-floor landing, and he yanks the door open.

I see his boots first.

"Rey."

I let out a whimper when he opens his eyes, bright blue against a too-pale face. "Hey."

I sink to the floor next to him. "How bad?"

"Bad enough." Rey drops his chin, motioning to his bloodstained hands at his stomach. His eyes drift to the teenager. "Doctor?"

The boy looks to me and flutters his hands.

I peel off my overshirt. "I'm his wife. They were going after a doctor for, uh, the other gentleman. Go to apartment 312. I need Chad Pitney. Tell him to bring his first aid kit. Then find us a doctor."

"Pitney? I know him. I'll be back." He beelines for the stairwell, letting the door slam behind him.

I press my shirt against Rey's hands. "Knife?"

"Yeah. One thrust. He was . . . I think he has the sickness. The ergotism."

"He does. I saw him downstairs. He's the doctor, the one who was treating Emma, I think, if I remember the name correctly."

"Sanderson. Beverly said Sanderson."

"That's it." I furrow my brow at the amount of blood as I remove my overshirt and press it against his gut. "Are you sure there's only one wound?"

"Mmm." He moves slightly, causing more blood to release.

"Kimba?" Chad bellows from a door at the other end of the hallway as he sprints in our direction.

"He's bleeding out!" I cry.

"Hey, bro." Chad kneels next to Rey. "What'd you go and do this for?"

"Zigged when I should've zagged. Don't think it's too bad."

"Got to move you. Ready?"

Rey grits his teeth and bobs his head. We find a second wound low on his back. Chad pulls out a package of combat gauze from the first aid kit and rips it open.

"Been saving this for a rainy day, friend." Chad pushes Rey's shirt up and begins packing the wound on the back.

69

"Guess . . . it's . . . raining." Rey's voice is hoarse.

"This doesn't look as bad as I first thought. A slashing wound instead of a puncture. A few stitches and you'll be fixed right up."

"You hear that, honey?" I blink rapidly to keep the tears at bay. "You're going to be fine."

His lips lift in a slight smile as his eyes close.

"None of that! Keep your eyes open. You don't get to sleep."

He opens his eyes wide. "Yes, boss."

"How about the stomach wound?" I lift my chin in Chad's direction.

"I don't want to have you take the pressure off. Let's wrap the elastic bandage around the whole kit and kaboodle. Tighten up the pressure and get him some help. The kid didn't say how this happened."

"Someone else is sick. It's the doctor."

"Which one?"

"Sanderson."

"Oh, no." Chad shakes his head. "Gotta shift you again, bro, to get the bandage in place."

As we move him, Chad lets out a yelp. "Found the knife."

"You cut yourself?" I ask.

"Just a papercut." He scoots the knife to the side.

Seconds later, we hear pounding footsteps on the stairs and then the door flies open.

The doctor from the park, Captain Mercer, is followed by several others. "What do we have?"

Rey flutters his eyes at her question.

Chad tells her what we know and what we've done. Within seconds, a stretcher magically appears. They get Rey loaded and wrapped tightly in a blanket before taking him down the steps.

"I'm going to let Beverly know what's happening." Chad wipes his hands on a towel. "I'll make sure the girls are okay, then I'll find you."

"They don't know." I shake my head, wiping my hands on a second towel.

"I sent the boy—Sal—to find Nicole. Told him to have her wait outside with the younger girls."

After thanking Chad and telling him I'll see him soon, I follow the medical team down the stairs. There's still a crowd gathered on the main floor. All are asking what happened and gawking at Rey.

Outside, Nicole, Kylie, and Naomi are waiting near a clump of brush with the teen boy nearby.

When Nicole sees me, she lifts her hands in question. I run over to her.

"What's happening, Mom? This guy— " she throws a hand in the direction of the teenager, Sal "—said Chad said we had to wait here and not move."

"There was another sick person. Hallucinating, I think. But he'll be okay, I'm sure he will. I'm going to the hospital. Chad will be down for you shortly."

"You're going to the hospital? With the sick person? Do you know him?"

"Not the—oh . . ." With there being a blanket over the stretcher, I realize she didn't recognize Rey. "It's your dad. He was attacked."

"What?!" She takes a few steps in the direction of the medical team. "Mom? Is he— "

"They're going to take care of him. I'll be back to the apartment as soon as I know something."

"There's the doctor." The teenager points to another stretcher coming out. The man has stopped his wailing and appears to be asleep. Or sedated.

"I have to go. Stay here. Wait for Chad to come for you. Watch out for . . ." I shake my head. "Everyone." I wrap Nicole and then Naomi in quick hugs before patting Kylie on the shoulder. "Just a minute and your dad will be here." I give her a tight smile.

The stretcher carrying Rey is across the greenway and moving fast. I run to catch up. When we reach the makeshift hospital, with several beds lined up and people sitting in chairs next to them, he's immediately taken to a screened-off section along the side.

"Let's see what we've got." Captain Mercer motions to an assistant, who takes a pair of scissors and cuts off the elastic bandage. A piece of Rey's blue shirt goes with it, landing on the floor. "All right. We're going to surgery. Wallette, you'll assist. And find Dr. Ford."

As they scramble, I stay back and out of the way. When they move Rey, I follow. As they reach a door labeled *supplies*, a man touches my arm. "You'll need to wait out here. We'll keep you posted."

I respond with a weary nod. "How long?"

"No way to know. I'll send someone out when we have more information."

"He'll be okay?"

"We'll be out soon."

Soon ends up being several hours. Chad showed up and found us a couple of chairs to sit in as we wait. When the door finally opens, it's Captain Mercer. I bounce to my feet. Her face is unreadable until her eyes meet mine. There's a slight smile and a nod.

My knees go weak. "He's okay?"

"Doing well."

"Oh, thank God. Thank you, God."

The doctor goes on to detail his wounds—not as bad as I feared but bad enough—and what we can expect for recovery. As always in today's world, infection is a concern. The stab wound to the stomach was low and nicked an intestine. Even before the apocalypse, this could lead to sepsis and death. They've started him on a course of antibiotics.

I send up another prayer to God, thanking him for having the military here—whether people think they *should* be here or not.

"We'll move him to a bed shortly, then you can see him." She gives me a nod. "You should probably get cleaned up first. I'll send someone by with a clean shirt for you."

I glance down at my bloody T-shirt. Chad had passed me a towel earlier, so at least my hands are cleanish.

Shortly turns out to be another hour at least. A woman Chad knows stops by with a Montana State sweatshirt and directs me to a bathroom to change.

There's a jug of water and a few towels. I release my hair from the messy braid and finger comb it before pulling it into a high pony. When I decide I look as good as can be expected, I return to the hard plastic chair next to Chad. My foot bounces up and down, and I rub my index finger against my thumb.

Chad rests a hand on my forearm. "He'll be fine."

"He has to be. I don't . . ." I shake my head.

The door finally opens, and Rey is carried out. I jump to my feet. The man from earlier motions us to follow behind. Walking through the ward, patients and visitors alike stare, point, and talk behind their hands. Rey's taken to a far corner with a screen set up around his bed.

He's still groggy from surgery but manages a weak smile. "Hey." Then he closes his eyes and goes back to sleep.

The sun has fully set, and Chad has returned to the apartment before Rey comes around enough to ask for water. "What'd they give me to knock me out?" He asks after a long drink.

"I . . . I didn't ask."

"Feels like I have a hangover."

"More water?"

He lifts a hand to wave it away. The movement causes him to grimace.

I rest my hand on his face. "That was too close."

"Seems like old times, huh?"

"Not in a good way." I flare my eyes and feign anger.

He gives me a courtesy smile.

"Seriously, Rey. That was . . . I was afraid I might lose you."

"With our line of work, we'd always— "

"This is different." I shake my head. "Then, I knew it was dangerous. Now it seems . . . I can't explain it. After losing Nate, I don't know what I'd do if . . . I don't know if I could handle it."

"You're strong, Kimba. Losing a child is hard on anyone, but you're doing better."

"Thanks to you."

"Not just me."

I let out a sigh. "No, not just you. I know God's with me again. He always was, I just didn't see it. Sometimes, even now, it's hard to know. I don't feel Him, and I'm . . . I guess I'm like Thomas. I want proof. You've been my rock. If you were gone . . ."

"I'm still here." He closes his eyes. "Tired, but here. You're stuck with me." He lets out a sigh. "Don't forget."

I lean back in my chair, wondering how long he'll sleep this time.

"You want a cot?" Captain Mercer comes around the screen.

"I can stay here?"

"Can't promise how comfortable you'll be."

"How long will Rey need to be here?"

She lifts a shoulder. "We'll see how he does."

"The doctor? The one who . . ."

"He's sedated. You know it was the ergotism, right? He wasn't in his right mind."

"How'd he get it? And how didn't anyone know he had it?"

"I'm not sure. He was working and . . ." She lifts her hands. "I don't know. He may have just thought he was tired. Exhausted. It's been a difficult few days for those quarantined in the college."

"You haven't helped here?"

"I arrived from Billings after the lockdown was initiated. We sent a few people in to help, but I stayed on the outside, communicating via radio. Another medical team arrived a short while ago to provide relief. And we're trying to get the word out about this, in hopes of preventing it in other areas. The conditions were perfect for C. purpurea, a hard winter followed by a wet spring during a time of food shortage. It's classic."

"Will there be many more deaths?"

"Some, yes. There's no cure, so all we can do is what we can do. Please try not to think too badly of Dr. Sanderson. He was aware enough to know what he did, and . . ." Her bottom lip trembles slightly. "While I hadn't met him until today, we spoke on the radio often. He'd never purposely cause harm."

"Where can I find a cot?"

Chapter 12

Beverly
Friday, September 11

"C'mere." Chad reaches for me in the early morning light. He holds me for many minutes and tells me how sorry he is he wasn't here to help me when Emma was at her sickest.

The familiar anger builds in my belly. In twenty-five years of marriage, he's rarely been around. Why should this be any different? The longest he's ever stayed home has been during the time since the EMP. A few days off hunting is nothing compared to his military years as he cycled in and out of whatever hot-spot country needed his special skills. I'd hoped when he started working as a contractor with Rey and Kimba, he'd be around more.

And he was, in some ways. Many of their jobs lasted weeks instead of months. But if he wasn't working, he wasn't making money. We were almost ready for him to hang it up and stay home for good. He had some great computer skills that would've translated to a new business—a business that would keep him home. I'd started my own venture, which would help too. Plus, we had many good investments that were paying off.

I let out a sigh.

"You okay?"

"I don't know. I can't believe Doc Sanderson was sick. He seemed so . . . normal. Tired. That was obvious, but . . ." I shake my head and bite my top lip, thinking back to the last time he was here.

I'd noticed his hands shaking when he stopped to examine Emma. And he was more melancholy than usual. I didn't say anything about it, thinking it was just from the exhaustion of working too hard.

He said they knew what the problem was, the ergotism, and we were being released from quarantine. Emma couldn't make me sick. I couldn't make Kylie sick.

Not wanting to be away from my little girl even another second, I raced to Kylie's room—this room I'd come to think of as her prison cell—and scooped her up. Holding her close, I awkwardly carried her to Emma's sick room.

Doc Sanderson gave me a wobbly smile. "Good, good. And Miss Emma will soon be well enough for you to hold and hug too. And how are you today, Kylie? Happy to be able to leave the bedroom?"

"Can I go outside?"

"Not yet. Soon, though. We're going to have your mama and you stay here with Emma. Later today, the people outside the quarantine zone will be allowed back in."

"Is Chad with them?" I asked.

He shrugged. "As far as I know. The Army doc that's our contact on the outside said the hunting group is there. As well as others who have been traveling, trying to get home for who knows how long."

"People who were on vacation when everything happened?"

"Some, I guess. Although, I'm sure most of them won't be happy at what they're coming back to with so much of our town destroyed. She said there're also relatives. With the buses moving now, people can be reunited. Has me wondering . . ." He let out a rattly sigh.

"You know, my wife and kids were doing the whole tourist thing with her folks, going places each day. I don't even know exactly where they were on the day of . . . the day it happened. I'll admit, with the buses moving and things seeming like they might start returning to normal, part of me wonders if they might just show up. Could they be with the people camping and waiting?"

It was hard to hear the longing in his voice. With the bombs destroying so much of the East Coast, it isn't realistic his family survived, whether from the initial blast, the radiation, or the long, cold winter. Plus, with the high-density population in those areas, everyone vying and scrambling for the same limited supply of food . . . I can't even imagine.

Chad pulls me tighter, crushing me against him. I move my head to keep my nose and mouth from being covered. I can't handle anything over my face. Not after . . .

"Rey's going to pull through. He'll be fine." Chad's voice vibrates against my cheek. "I'll tell you, I was sure amazed when I went around that outfitters tent and ran smack into Kimba Hoffmann. I gave up on them showing up long ago. Sad about Nate."

"More than sad. Devastating. When Emma . . . I wasn't sure she'd . . ." I shake my head. "I was so scared."

"I'm so sorry I wasn't here with you. That's the last time I'm leaving you. They can find someone else to lead the hunting expeditions. I'm staying home."

I move a finger to his lips. "I think we both know that won't happen. You'll do what's needed, go where you're needed. I may not always like it, and it may make me mad enough to spit tacks, but it's you. I know it and accept this about you."

His sigh fills the room. "You're the reason I can do the things I do. Knowing you have everything handled at home, with the girls. But this—this is almost too much, to think you had to deal with it on your own. I'm sorry, Bev."

We lay together for many minutes, listening to the sounds of the former college campus drifting through the open window. Tomorrow, I'll return to my duties in the goat barn and cheese house. Chad will return to his security and maintenance work. Emma's doing well enough that Nicole Hoffmann can watch her and the younger girls while we do what's needed.

Kimba will be in and out too. Most of her day will be spent with Rey in the hospital, but she won't be far from her children. I've noticed a big change in her since the last time we spoke, a few weeks before the attacks. To be honest, I'd never really thought much of Kimba's parenting skills.

She was always too aloof for my liking, choosing to put the business and her own needs ahead of the children, to the point that sometimes I thought they may be neglected.

Oh, she loved them, I'm sure she did. But she wasn't attentive. Nicole was at an age when she needed her mom more than ever, but Kimba was giving her way too many freedoms. She'd let her go out with friends whenever she wished and did little to prevent Nicole's teenage misbehaving. Even over Zoom calls, I could see the eye rolls and hear the cheeky tones.

I wonder if things changed when Nate died, or before? Did she show him the love he deserved, or is it just since his loss she's become more demonstrative? I've noticed now how she'll easily pull Naomi close to her, hugging her tight. Nicole, too, though Kimba's plenty respectful of her almost adult age.

It's obvious Nicole has been taking on adult chores and responsibilities for some time. I've even heard of the times she's had to fight for her life. Even just a few days ago, on their way here, she and Kimba were attacked. This world we live in . . . is it safe anywhere?

"I'm going to go see him today."

"Rey?"

"Dr. Sanderson." I say, feeling my husband stiffen. "You think they'll let me?"

"I think he needs a few days of sedation or whatever before he has visitors."

"He's been good to us, Chad. The way he let me help people with my breathing classes. You know he wasn't— "

"I understand. But still. Really, Bev? You want to put yourself in danger?"

I bristle at his words. "I'm not. Surely, it'd be safe to visit him. The sedation— "

"Exactly. He won't even know if you're there or not. Give it a few days. Wait and see if . . ." His voice fades before he swallows loudly.

My movement is abrupt and jerky as I get out of our bed. "I don't want to wait and see if he lives or dies. Doc Sanderson has been a friend to us. We should be a friend to him. Whether he knows I'm there or not, I'm going to visit him."

With three extra people in the small apartment, we're almost tripping over each other as we get ready for our day. Chad and I are standoffish with each other, using civil tones without any warmth.

I'm not really mad at him, just hurt he doesn't understand my need to visit Doc Sanderson. He has truly become a friend over the past year as we were all forced to move to the college when most of the town was destroyed. He even went with Chad and the group he formed when we realized we'd been duped. We were forced out of our homes under false pretenses, and our things stolen before our homes were torched, forcing us all to live at the college.

Why we'd all been moved to the college was something I didn't understand at first. Not until Chad and the others found the people responsible. There was a shootout, and when they captured a few of the survivors, they learned the entire story.

One of the miscreants was someone Chad new from his time in the military and then their private work. After being captured, the man, Jankins, told Chad he should be happy they didn't just kill us all. Letting us live and form a society at the college was his act of benevolence.

There was a struggle during Chad's interrogation of Jankins, and Chad shot him. Doc Sanderson rendered first aid, but there was no saving him.

There were some issues between Chad and Doc Sanderson for him shooting Jankins—truly, Chad and many others. He was accused of murder by one of the city commissioners, Mason, who wasn't even part of the team looking for the bad guys. Mason called for Chad to be exiled from the college, the town even. Another commissioner, one who was part of the group that found Jankins and the others, said he saw the whole thing and Chad did all he could do. It was a kill or be killed situation.

Besides, what could we do with him? Keep him locked up, hoping he didn't escape and kill someone in the process? Feed him from our limited food? That ended the debate and got Chad out of trouble. At least officially. There were still glares and whispers of Chad being a murderer, plus many stories going around about my husband and the terrible things he supposedly did while in special operations.

When our town came under attack by a large group a few weeks later, Chad stepped up and did what was needed, even helping Mason out of a jam of his own doing and saving his life. They're still not friends, not by a longshot, but at least the rumor campaign stopped.

The situation with Jankins led to Chad being asked to lead the security team. Partly because he'd proven himself, but mainly because the only official law enforcement we had left in the town was now dead. Chad declined, saying he'd be happy to help but he didn't have the skillset or organization to schedule patrols and sentries. He was a doorkicker.

He may be a doorkicker, but he certainly has the skillset needed to do whatever is necessary. I know the main reason he didn't take it was he was worried about the time it would take away from us.

He may have traveled all of our marriage, but things were different now. The hunting trips were all he would agree to, and only because he knew we needed the food. Even with the livestock and gardens, last winter was rough.

You'd think with the livestock, we'd be fine. But someone was smart enough to realize if we killed off all our stock, we'd be doomed. We were put on such strict rations that most of the adults ate only one meal a day. Those eating more than one weren't faring much better.

Knowing our children were hungry each night as they went to bed and each morning when they woke was awful.

We almost had a revolt when a group stormed the livestock shed with guns and knives. They were hungry and taking what they wanted. They couldn't understand the animals we were keeping were for breeding and, if we could make it through this winter, the summer and next winter would be better.

Things got better in the spring, when goats and cows started dropping their young and we had milk in abundance. Chickens sat on nests and soon hatched out dozens and dozens of chicks. When the gardens started producing, MSU became Eden with its abundance.

This winter will be better, thanks to our sacrifices last winter. We'll have less people to feed too. Not only from the losses last winter, but now with the ergot.

It's midmorning when Chad gives me an embarrassed smile. "I was thinking, maybe I could walk with you to Swingle. I think that's where he is, the health center instead of the hospital ward."

Kimba's eyes travel to us. "Rey's still in the ward. I'm heading over there shortly if you want to come with me."

"I do. I'm, uh . . . I'm also going to visit Dr. Sanderson."

Kimba's face pales as she straightens her back. "The man who stabbed my husband and nearly killed him?"

"He's— "

Kimba lifts a hand. "Yes, yes. I've heard it wasn't his fault." She stomps out of the living room and into the bathroom, shutting the door much harder than necessary. The three younger girls all have wide eyes.

Nicole shrugs. "She'll get over it. She knows he's sick, it's just . . ." She lifts a hand. "With Nate dying and now Dad hurt, she's scared. Mad, too, but mostly scared."

Chapter 13

Beverly

"And how do you know him?" The sentry at the door wipes the back of his hand across his nose.

"We're friends." I give the man a smile and nod. By my side, I feel Chad move into an attentive position with his hands behind his back. He asked if he could not only walk me but also stay while I visit Doc Sanderson, saying he wouldn't feel good about me being gone and not knowing what was happening.

Nicole offered to stay with the girls and monitor Emma. She's no longer under heavy sedation but is still sleeping and improving. Kimba's at the hospital next door, visiting Rey. Even though she told me she isn't, I know she's still angry. She thinks I'm betraying her.

"Sorry, ma'am. Dr. Sanderson is under deep sedation. He isn't accepting visitors."

Chad takes a half step forward, his posture even more erect than it was. "Can we get an update on his condition?"

I watch as the young soldier's eyes flare. It's obvious he's one of the new Army, what people call the volunteers. But new or not, he recognizes an authoritative voice when he hears it.

"Uh, how about I see if Captain Mercer is available?"

"A fine idea, Corporal."

After the young man leaves, I turn to Chad. "You enjoy that a little too much."

"What?" He flares his eyes in mock innocence. "Seeing all these young 'uns walking around with their rifles—and chips—on their shoulders . . ." He shakes his head.

"You wish you were part of it? You want to join the volunteers?"

Chad's whole body gives a shudder. "Volunteers? No. Not even. But if they'd take me in the regular Army . . ." He raises an eyebrow.

"But they wouldn't, right? You're too old."

"I'm not *that* old." He puts a hand to his chest and feigns insult. "But, well, probably. There's a provision that with prior enlistment . . . never mind, Bev. I wouldn't do it anyway. Not unless I could be sure they'd let you and the girls stay with me."

I feel the anger in my belly again. I know it isn't his fault Emma became so ill and almost died while he was gone, but him even suggesting he's interested in reenlisting . . .

The door opens with a squeak. A very crisp-looking woman gives us a nod. "You're here about Dr. Sanderson?"

"Yes." I give her a weak smile. "He's a friend."

She looks to Chad. "Weren't you with Mrs. Hoffmann last night?"

"That's right, Captain. Rey's a friend too. It's a sad situation."

"Indeed. I don't know what you know about the ergotism, but the doctor didn't do this of his own volition."

I lift my chin. "My daughter has it—*had* it. He was assigned to care for her while we were in quarantine."

"I'm sorry. Did someone check on her this morning?"

"Yes, a man named Roscoe. He's a . . . nurse?"

She gives a dip of her head. "Your daughter is Emma?" The surprise must show on my face. "Roscoe had only one young female on his rounds."

"Oh, yes, of course."

"The report on her is encouraging. I'll be by later today to give her a full examination, then we can discuss prognosis."

"Prognosis? She'll be fine, right?"

The smile Captain Mercer gives is patient and cautious. "From what I know, I do expect that to be the case, yes. With this illness, there can be some lingering effects. We'll know more as time goes on."

"Thank you, ma'am." Chad dips his head. "We're thinking of going to Billings before winter. Will that be possible?"

I spin toward him, my mouth open and my eyes wide. This is the first I've heard of this. Chad sees my confusion and gives a slight shake of his head as a tinge of pink creeps up his neck.

Captain Mercer clicks her tongue. "Let me examine her and then we'll know more. Now, as far as Dr. Sanderson, he's under complete sedation."

"Will he be all right?" I run a hand through my hair. "Will he recover from this?"

"We're hoping for the best. It'll be several days before we know how he's responding. There's no cure for the fungus, so all we can do is treat his symptoms."

I wait for her to say more. When she doesn't, I clear my throat. "Okay, then I guess we'll see you this afternoon when you check on Emma. Maybe you can give us an update on the doctor then?"

"Perhaps."

"You know about his family?"

"I do. Without any next of kin here, we're doing what we believe is best. Believe me, he'll be well taken care of. As far as I'm concerned, your doctor is a hero. That said, I am terribly sorry for what happened to your friend, to Mr. Hoffmann. I'm sure— "

Chad lifts a hand. "I've known Sanderson for years. When things were normal, we knew each other enough to say hello and visit. But now, you're right about him being a hero. He's done so much for our people. We know he didn't do this of his own accord. Glad they sent you to help."

Captain Mercer gives Chad a long look, one I can't quite interpret. With a curt nod, she moves to the door. "See you this afternoon, probably around 1500 hours."

"That's fine," Chad says.

We've gone only a dozen steps from the health center when I ask, "Billings?" My voice is tight.

"Sorry, Bev. With everything happening, I completely forgot we hadn't discussed it."

"Discussed what? You want to move to Billings? Now?"

"Well, Rey and Kimba are— "

"Rey's fighting for his life. You really think he's going to up and go to Billings? You said before winter. With the chill already in the air, that could be any day. Emma's in no shape to travel."

"I know, I know." He reaches for my hand. "While we were camping and waiting for the quarantine to lift, Rey and Kimba told me about their plans, about the things they've been doing and how they want to help with the reconstruction efforts. We could make a difference."

"I'm not interested in *making a difference*. All I want is to get through this with our children safe and healthy. With *you* safe and healthy. We've heard enough stories about Billings to make me positive I don't want to go there. It's a war zone."

83

"It's better now. The Army and Marines, plus all the volunteers, have really cleaned it up. They're taking on specialty workers, and even offering lodging and food."

"We *have* lodging and food."

"Do we, Bev? Remember what last winter was like? How many days did you go without eating?"

I lift a hand. "Not many, thanks to the supplies you had hidden at our house. But that doesn't matter. We made it through, and with the crops and animals, we're better prepared this year. You had a good hunt. How much jerky did you make?"

"Not enough. We gave about half the meat to the cook staff at the quarantine setup. There are thirty thousand people here, all competing for the same limited supplies. And we've lost all of the rye and a good portion of our wheat. We were counting on those grains to feed us and our animals."

"The Army is here."

"And they may help, but it still won't be enough. I think we can get a good thing set up in Billings. We can have enough food each day. Our girls can have enough food. And while we had the cached food last year, and there's still a little left buried at our old house, it's not enough. We need something reliable."

I shake my head. "I don't want to leave here." As the words leave my mouth, I wonder if they're really true. In some ways, leaving would be a relief. Maybe the bad dreams and memories would stop. Maybe I wouldn't be taken back to that day every time I go into the milk barn. And I'd never have to see *him* again.

"We don't have to decide today. Like you said, neither Emma nor Rey is well enough to go. And they may not be before winter hits and the bus service stops."

"When?"

"They haven't set an actual date. Just playing it by ear . . . um, by weather." He gives me a quirky grin. There's always been a fun-loving side to my husband. When I first met him, I had no idea he was military. I mean, I should've known with the way he carried himself and how fit he was, but he was just so easygoing and loved to laugh.

He told dad jokes well before he was a dad. He was even a bit of a dork. His looks are terribly unique and probably not what most people would think of as handsome, but he had such a kindness about him. I was smitten from the start. Then life happened and things changed.

Now we have baggage and issues. We still make it work, but some days it's a struggle. Especially with secrets between us.

This thing with Billings is nothing new, not really. Chad does this. He gets big ideas, makes plans, and I am expected to adapt. That's how we ended up in Bozeman. He met a guy at a survivalist convention. I didn't even know those things existed, but somehow Chad ended up at this big show with everything a person needed to survive the end of the world.

He got to talking to a guy about the American Redoubt. I had no idea what that was, neither did Chad when he met the guy. Apparently, it was a relocation movement where likeminded people— like those at the convention—were moving to places like Idaho, Wyoming, eastern Washington and Oregon, and Montana in preparation for societal collapse.

Chad even tried to join a housing development in Northwest Montana, but it required us to be Christians, which was a no-go. Ending up in Bozeman was his second choice.

Although, if I understand the American Redoubt movement, Bozeman's probably not a good place to be. We've had a huge population growth over the last few years, which is something touted as concerning for the Redoubt, and it should be conservative. With Bozeman a college town . . . well, college towns have a reputation as a whole.

We cross the campus hand in hand. I focus on breathing while we walk, oxygenating my lungs and releasing the anger.

When we reach the greenspace, Chad squeezes my hand. "Terrible about Nate."

"Awful."

"Rey told me Kimba didn't handle it well."

I scoff. "What would he expect? She lost her son."

"Right, no. I understand. She almost lost herself, though, too. I never would've thought . . . Kimba's always been so strong, so good at compartmentalizing. I think you could help her."

I shake my head. "I don't think so. Remember how she was when I told her I was getting my breathing coach certification and starting a business? She wasn't very supportive."

"She didn't understand what it was or how much you could help people."

"She laughed at me, made fun of me for *teaching* people to breathe."

"Well, that's in the past. I think Kimba would be more welcoming to it now. Besides, she knows the power of breathing."

"You mean for when she's sniping?"

He flips his palms up. "It's important. She's always used the box breathing technique. It's not terribly different from what you do."

"Um, it's very different."

"Yeah, maybe. But if you present it to her— "

"I'm not going to force her into something she doesn't want to do. Besides, she's still mad at me, remember?"

Even though I said I wouldn't force her into it, when Kimba returns from seeing Rey, I decide to test the waters. She's much calmer and not at all angry at me—or doesn't seem to be at least.

Emma's asleep in her room, Nicole has taken the younger girls outside to play, and Chad's checking in with his work crew to make sure of his assignment for tomorrow.

"Rey's asleep, so I thought I'd get away for a while." Kimba gives me a smile as she relaxes on the sofa.

"Did you see the doctor? Mercer?"

"She was there. Said she met you this morning. Please forgive me for being such a snot. I do know it wasn't Sanderson's fault. And I understand he's your friend. I'm sorry."

"Please." I wave my hand. "Think nothing of it. I may have acted the same way."

Kimba shrugs and then redirects her gaze to stare out the window. "I can't imagine losing him too. I'm not sure . . . I just don't know what I'd do. What the girls and I would do."

I chew the inside of my mouth as I consider Chad's suggestion of offering to help Kimba with breathwork. She'd been so negative about it the one time I told her what I was doing, calling it new age hooey. I never mentioned it again. Not after I got my certification. Not after I rented space in a therapeutic massage studio. Not even after I started an online practice, making more money than I'd ever dreamed possible.

I know Chad had mentioned it to Rey on some of their missions; he'd been very proud of my success. Rey even congratulated me on a streaming call we all had. But not Kimba. She smiled, in what I took as a condescending way, but said nothing.

"Would you . . . I could maybe help you."

She turns to me and nods. "I know you would. But he'll be okay. I'm sure Rey's going to be fine."

"No, no. I didn't mean . . ." I let out a breath through my nose. "With everything that's happened over the last year and a half, plus losing Nate, you're exhausted. Stressed."

Kimba's eyes fill as they meet mine. "I'm doing better, learning to be still and know He is God." She gives me a watery smile. "He's helping me find peace. Unfortunately, as we experienced this morning, I'm still a work in progress." She lets out a slight laugh.

Rey and Kimba weren't religious before. They'd go to church sometimes, but it didn't really carry to their lives. Kimba had a mouth on her that would make a sailor blush. Chad had said something last night about them finding Jesus.

"Well, that's . . . nice. I was thinking maybe I could help you too. We could do a breathing session to help you relax."

She furrows her brow. "I don't think so. Thanks, but no."

"Okay." I dip my head. I knew she'd say no.

Kimba stares out the window again. After a couple of minutes, she turns back to me. "Does it really work?"

"It does. We spend so much time in our fight or flight nervous system that our stress hormones are working overtime."

She snorts. "Well, that's for sure."

"Yes, especially now. But even before, when the lights were on, people had work stress, marital stress, family stress. We were a nation of stressed-out people. Then, when everything fell apart, our stress hormones went through the roof. Many people couldn't cope, so they . . ." I clear my throat.

"One of the reasons Doc Sanderson and I were friends was because he saw the value in breathwork. He had me doing group sessions and working with people who were really challenged with our new way of life. People who had relied on antidepressants before. There are several we were able to help. Not everyone, but many."

"The doctor thought it was useful?"

My shoulder goes toward my ear. "He was hesitant at first, but when we started to see results, he got on board. So much so, he started seeking out other alternative medicine practitioners. We have massage therapists, yoga instructors, an acupuncturist, Reiki, and more. Without pharmaceuticals, he was willing to look at other options.

There're several people in Bozeman who know about wild plants—both edible and medicinal. Definitely a benefit of a college town. We found people able to think outside the box, look at alternatives to the norm."

"Good. That's good he was willing to explore other options." She lets out a loud sigh. "Maybe I'll try it, but not today."

Chapter 14

Kimba
Friday, September 18

Under a darkening sky, the woman sitting next to me sniffles into a handkerchief. The pastor leading the service seems to be winding down his message. Families and friends of the dead already gave their eulogies.

As of yesterday, thirty-six have died as a result of the ergotism. Well, a few not directly from being infected by the fungus but from being attacked, like my husband was.

It's been just over a week since the doctor stabbed Rey. If Sal Reese hadn't found him when he did . . .

I straighten my back and try to shoo those thoughts away. Sal *did* find him.

In the days following the stabbing, I found out a few of the details from Sal. The teen said he heard Rey call for help, but with so many people being delusional, it was nothing new. He figured someone living in the building was affected. He knew better than to confront them after the guy who worked in the livestock barn freaked out and started shooting.

When Sal started hearing knocking, that also did little to attract his attention. Knocking, tapping, scraping, convulsions—all of it has been normal since the sickness started. Just a few minutes before, he'd been hearing scraping noises and then voices, so he didn't think much of it. Then he heard a pattern. Three long knocks. Three short knocks. Three short knocks. Three long knocks. Three short knocks.

"I was a Boy Scout," he said with a sheepish look. "Figured I should check it out. I didn't think someone in the middle of a hallucination would be tapping out SOS in Morse code over and over."

I lean forward slightly and look to my right, where Sal's sitting on the other side of Beverly. Since he found Rey, he's been spending a lot of time with us. His mom is one of the many being memorialized today; she was the first to die, before they even had a clue what was happening or how many were infected.

At the time, they thought she'd had a seizure, which then caused a heart attack. Maybe it is what happened. It's not like they're doing autopsies now. After the lockdown was lifted, Captain Mercer went to Sal and asked him some questions. After her interview, she said she thought his mom might have been an early casualty.

Sal said it didn't change anything. Dead is dead. His dad died earlier in the year, leaving Sal on his own. Orphaned.

Rey's no longer in the hospital, instead he's recovering in the Pitneys' apartment. While he still spends much of his time resting, he's doing better but is not yet well enough to be out and about. Neither is Emma. Chad stayed with them and the younger girls, while Nicole, Beverly, and I attend the service in support of Sal and many others who were friends of Beverly's and Chad's.

There've been no new cases since Dr. Sanderson attacked Rey. Those first few days Rey was recovering, when severe infection was a worry, I felt myself sliding backward, returning to the dark place I'd been after Nate died.

Nicole and I were sitting at Rey's bedside, quietly talking with him, when Mr. and Mrs. Kingsworth padded over. A man around Rey's age was holding Mrs. Kingsworth's elbow.

"How ya doing, Rey?" Mr. Kingsworth asked.

"Fair to middlin'" my husband said, making sure to use his Midwestern cadence—not much of a problem any longer. I can't even remember the last time I heard him use his regular voice, what he often calls the Queen's English. Even though his accent was slight before, thanks to living in the US for so many years, it was still there. Especially when he got wound up about something.

Since leaving the ski lodge six months ago, he works hard to keep his tone even and fully American. Probably a good thing since Bozeman is a rumor mill, and I've heard more than once about how foreigners were the cause of the apocalypse.

"Good, good." Mr. Kingsworth smiled, showing a crooked front tooth. "We wanted you to meet our son, Adam."

After introductions all around, I said, "Adam, do I remember correctly you're a professor and a pastor?"

"A church pastor with a ministry here on campus too. My church, along with my home, was destroyed early on. My parents thought you'd like us to pray with you."

I start to say no but then glance at Rey. "Please. We . . . we'd appreciate it."

The words the pastor spoke were exactly what I needed to hear at that time, a reminder I wasn't alone. God was there with me, helping me—helping all of us—through our trials. Not just helping. *Carrying us.*

Forcing my attention back to the present, I look to the front at Pastor Adam Kingsworth. "Let's bow our heads in prayer as we not only conclude this memorial but also ask for a blessing on the food. You can make your way from here to the picnic tables for today's luncheon. Perhaps the weather will hold out long enough for us to enjoy a little fellowship."

After the prayer and amens, we join the food service line.

As we walk, Sal asks about Rey and Emma.

"Both are doing well," Beverly answers. "Captain Mercer was there yesterday. Emma's been having a little numbness in her fingers, but the doctor thinks it'll go away on its own. Would you mind helping us take food back to the apartment for them?"

Sal smiles and says he'd be happy to. He knows we plan to leave for Billings as soon as Rey is well enough, and he's dropped a couple of hints he wants to come with us. Rey and I've talked about asking him to come along.

Bev insists Sal was amazing during the quarantine, helping out where he could, showing much more maturity than his years. But I have to admit, part of me wonders if Sal wants to go along because of Nicole. I've caught a few glances in her direction, suggesting he's interested in her. The last thing she needs is a boyfriend. Not now. Not with everything happening. I couldn't bear to worry about . . .

"Hello, Mrs. Hoffmann, Mrs. Pitney, Nicole, Sal." Mr. Kingsworth bobs his head. "Did Adam tell you his weekly Bible study is in your building this evening?"

"He did." I dip my chin and smile. "And Captain Mercer has even given my husband permission to go."

"That's excellent." He turns slightly to Bev. "And will you and your husband be able to join also?"

"Perhaps another time." Bev's response is amicable.

Bev and Chad have made it clear they believe Rey and I may have lost our minds. On more than one occasion, Chad's reminded Rey about the "religious nutjobs" they've encountered over the years. Beverly has her own, more personal reasons. Sad reasons.

We're talking and visiting as we eat our lunch at the long tables. "This weather . . ." Bev says, zipping her jacket to her neck. "I suspect we'll see another winter like last year."

"Maybe." I nod. "I'm hoping for less snow and cold. We just— "

"Hello, Beverly."

Bev straightens her back and purses her lips. "Gary." She gives a crisp nod.

"Heard your daughter was afflicted. She doing better?"

"She's fine, thank you."

"Great, great. S'pose Chad'll be going off with the hunting group then, huh?"

"Um, I . . . uh, no. I don't believe he will." Beverly drops her gaze back to her plate.

"Hmm. He's one of our best. Surely, they'll ask him to go along. We'll need the food for winter." His eyes travel toward me. "Who's your friend?"

I give him a polite smile as the hair stands up on the back of my neck. "I'm Kimba Hoffmann."

"Nice to meet you, Kimba. You come to town recently?"

"Not long ago." I return to my plate.

Bev's still staring down at hers, not eating and not looking at the man.

"Oh. Well, then, I'll let you get back to your meal. Give my best to your daughter, Beverly."

After he walks away, I whisper, "Bev?"

She shakes her head. "Not now."

As we walk back to the apartment, balancing plates of food for the rest of our family, Sal asks about the Bible study.

"I only went to the one last week. It was held outside since the weather was so good." I look at the rapidly darkening sky. "The theme is unlikely heroes and heroines of the Bible. It's designed so you don't need to attend every week to know what's going on."

"Do you think the preacher would mind if . . ."

"Of course not. Please join us."

Back in the apartment, Rey invites Sal to stay and chat while they eat their lunch. Rey, Chad, and Emma are at the table, while Naomi and Kylie sit on the floor, picnic style.

We'll all be crowded together in this small space for only a few more days—until an apartment or dorm can be found for us. With so many of the homes destroyed by Jankins and his ruthless gang, the college was filled to capacity with all the apartments and dorms in use—or as MSU calls them, Residence Halls. The recent deaths have changed things, but it takes time to make the arrangements.

Nicole and I are on the futon, and Bev brings the other dining room chair in to sit near us. Sal's near the younger girls, leaning against the wall. It all feels so normal, so comfortable.

Chad, who usually digs right into meals, seems to hesitate as he looks to his wife. She shakes her head and gives him a slight smile.

He tilts his head from side to side and works his neck, releasing the tension. Then he clears his throat. "Mercer said she thinks Emma is going to be fully recovered soon. Maybe another couple of weeks, a month on the outside."

Although we'd heard this yesterday after the doctor left, I bob my head. "Yes?"

"Uh, yup. Probably about the same time Rey's healed up. You all are still planning on going to Billings, right?"

I look to my husband, who tilts his head.

"That's right." Rey nods. "Doc says I'm about on the same timeline as Emma."

"Exactly what we thought. Beverly and I've been talking, thought we might go with you and see if we can help with the reconstruction too."

"We're still talking about it." Bev's voice is soft, patient. "Our final decision hasn't been made yet."

I look to my friend. Her face is a mixture of sadness and something else. Hope, maybe. "They're doing quite a bit here also. With the Army setting up— "

"Oh, we know." Chad waves a hand. "And it'd be easiest to stay. Really, we should stay, with the gardens and livestock. But . . ."

Bev sets her shoulders. "We've been talking about the opportunities in Billings."

I glance to Kylie and Naomi. "You know it's not . . . it was bad before the Army went in. It should be better, but . . ."

Rey sets his fork on the table and leans back in his chair. "We'd be happy for you to join us. We just want to make sure you know what you could be in for. When we traveled through Billings in the spring, food was scarce."

Chad waves his hand. "Food was scarce everywhere in the spring. Even here, with the greenhouses and ag buildings, we didn't have enough. Winters are harsh."

Rey raises his eyebrows. "And we're leaving at the beginning of winter."

"We'll take things with us. We have a few things put aside. Plus, Captain Mercer said things are much better in Billings than they were. She didn't think it was a bad idea for us to go."

"It's like a third world country in some ways. Chad, you've seen what those were like, but Bev and the girls . . . Billings was like that when we came through, with gangs controlling certain areas. But it certainly could've changed in four months' time. I'd like to think it's safer now."

"We know what we're in for," Chad says as a clap of thunder sounds in the background.

Rey leans in. "You know they're not taking old guys like us for the volunteers, right? Even if you're retired military."

"Mm-hmm. When I talked with Mercer, she said there's still plenty of work for us. Better that way with the family. Once you enlist, they can send a man anywhere."

Beverly clears her throat.

"Sorry, dear. Man or woman. Mercer said there are almost as many females enlisting with the volunteers as males."

All the adult eyes drift toward Nicole. She visibly straightens. "I haven't decided yet, not for sure. It's still about six weeks until my birthday."

"And two days." I swallow around the lump in my throat. "But who's counting?"

"Right. And unless you sign a waiver, I have to wait until then."

My heart pounds in my ears. I don't want her to join up but know it's a decision she must make on her own. "If it was something you truly wanted, we'd sign."

She lifts a shoulder. "I just don't know. I know I want to help and be a part of this. But like Chad said, they could send me anywhere. I don't know if I'm ready. I've always thought we'd do this together, as

94

a family. But with Nate . . ." Her voice turns thick. "With him gone, everything feels different."

There are several minutes of quiet as rain splatters against the windows.

"I'm joining up." Sal seems to sit a little taller. "Since my folks are dead, I don't have to wait until I'm eighteen. I just need three letters of reference."

Chad and Rey share a look, and Chad shakes his head. "When will you turn eighteen?"

"Um, well . . ."

"Wait." I hold up a hand. "How old are you now?"

A blush starts at his ears. "Fifteen, but my birthday is coming up, the twenty-third of October."

Nicole crosses her arms and narrows her eyes. "I thought you said you were eighteen?"

"Um, no. You said, 'What are you? Eighteen?' I just didn't correct you."

She chuffs out a response.

"They'll take you at sixteen?" Beverly asks.

Sal lifts a shoulder. "With the letters of reference and a few tests, I think so, yes."

Chad looks toward Rey. "I suspect you and Emma will be well enough we may already be in Billings by then."

Bev shoots her husband a look. "*If* we go."

"Right. Like Bev said, we're still discussing."

Rey and I share our own look. There's little doubt in my mind the Pitneys will be going to Billings with us. I just pray it's the right decision—for all of us.

Rey bobs his head several times. "Seems a shame to miss Sal's birthday. Kimba?"

I smile at Sal. "We've been talking, Rey and me. Thought maybe you'd like to come to Billings with us, join us in whatever it is we'll be doing there to help the city—our country—get back on its feet."

Tears cloud Sal's eyes. "You're sure?"

"Maybe you'll even want to wait until next summer to enlist? See how the winter goes?"

Chapter 15

Beverly
Wednesday, September 30

I lean against the large sink, washing the final milking bucket. My crew is in the barn, getting the goats settled and performing other needed tasks.

While the Hoffmanns are here, Kimba's on the goat crew with me. She took to the hand-milking easily and is surprisingly good with the does. Part of the crew is gathering the goats we turned out on pasture to browse after their milking, and Kimba is at the well pump refilling water jugs for our cleaning room's storage tank.

Our lives are so much like days of old, hauling water and tending the herd while they eat their fill. Browsing the goats for fifteen minutes, four times a day, gives them most of their nutrition. We supplement with cut alfalfa hay put up to get us through the winter, especially for the pregnant does, and also add in surplus vegetables and green scraps.

The fall harvest is coming to an end as winter threatens. I've decided Chad is right. Even though it seems we have an abundance, it's likely not enough for all of us. Captain Mercer told me a few days ago that she thought us going to Billings was a good choice. While there are more people in Billings than Bozeman, most are military.

The civilian casualties the days before and after the EMP were numerous. So numerous, Mercer says our losses were considerably less. Bozeman and its surrounding area is at nearly half the population it was before. Billings is a mere quarter.

All the little towns between Billings and Bozeman have also suffered. Mercer said the population of the entire state is estimated to be somewhere around half of what it was. Half! It's hard to imagine a state once home to just over a million people was so decimated.

Even with very few direct attacks from the terrorists prior to the EMP, there were plenty of casualties from those events. A railway station was targeted and caused some nearby deaths, but most of the losses came from the violence and looting that started during the cyberattack.

In Bozeman, the first of the fires started then, burning out some of our downtown area and killing hundreds. At the time, we thought it was an accident. But after we discovered our neighborhoods being purposely destroyed, maybe the downtown destruction was also intentional. We'll never truly know.

Kimba said it was a blessing the attackers wanted our supplies and came up with the ruse to get us out of our homes. They came across many places where supplies were taken by force, leaving families dead in the wake.

She'd leaned into me and said, "There're some bad people out there, Bev. I always knew there was evil in the world, and of course I'd seen it firsthand, but now people feel they have nothing to lose. Even people who may have once been decent, upstanding citizens. They take what they think they need. Or just what they want."

Kimba didn't need to tell me that. I already knew. I glance to the cot in the corner of the cleanup room. I should've taken the thing out and burned it. But it's there for the overnight watch to rest his or her eyes during kidding season. The cot isn't to blame for what happened to me.

Gary Searle is to blame.

My stomach clenches at the thought of his name. I knew Gary before the EMP. We'd met when I first started thinking about opening my breathing and relaxation studio. He worked for the city and knew about all the licensing I'd need.

In those early days, I was thinking big; I'd have an entire building. I'd already found the perfect place, and not only would I do individual and group breathwork sessions, but I'd also offer an oxygen bar, a therapeutic float tank, a luxury massage chair, yoga classes, and more.

My hope was it'd be the first of many buildings and I could even do a franchise option. Chad was close to retiring, and he could help with the business end and all the computer stuff. We could open up new buildings all over the country and live in different areas throughout the year. It'd be a new life for the four of us.

Gary was very helpful with detailing the obstacles I'd face from the city, county, and state. During the process, we became friends and would meet for coffee or lunch. He was newly widowed after losing his wife to a short illness. The doctors were never able to discover exactly what was wrong with her, which added to his grief.

Chad was gone a lot during that time. He and Rey were working a long-term job in South America and would only make it home every few weeks. I'll admit, I was lonely. Gary was lonely. One thing led to another and . . . I let out a sigh.

While I never completely broke my marriage vows, it was certainly an emotional attachment. An emotional affair. It went on for weeks before I came to my senses and knew what I really wanted was my husband and children. That's when I took the easy route and rented space in an already established studio and decided to focus on building an online business in addition to local. With an online business, we could still live anywhere at any time.

Gary didn't take it well when I broke it off. He essentially became my stalker. It wasn't until I threatened to tell his employer and his church, where he was a deacon, about everything that he finally backed off.

Church.

What a terrible example of a Christian he is. Not only because of our relationship, but also . . . my eyes travel to the cot again. Like so many others, Gary Searle has decided he can take what he wants during the apocalypse. I didn't even hear him enter the cleaning room that day. As is so often, I was alone and finishing up.

At first, he was friendly and asked how things were going. I was short and abrupt with him, telling him I needed to finish my work and get home. It was then he overpowered me and threw me down, covering my mouth and . . .

A shudder runs through me as tears sting my eyes.

A noise at the door causes me to turn quickly, dropping my metal bucket with a clang into the sink.

With a five-gallon bucket in each hand, Kimba steps inside the small room. "You okay?"

"Um, yes, I . . . sorry. You startled me. I was lost in thought."

She sets down the first of the buckets, which will help refill the thirty-five-gallon holding tank. "You don't just look startled. Have you been . . ." Her voice drops. "Were you crying?"

My face scrunches as I try and force the tears away. I'm unsuccessful and can only nod as I drop my gaze to the floor.

"Oh, Bev, what happened?" Kimba's quickly at my side.

I shake my head and cover my face with my hands. "N-nothing it's . . . it's nothing. Please just . . . just give me a minute."

"Come. Let's sit on the cot."

"No!"

Kimba stiffens and takes a step back. "Bev?"

I let out a ragged breath. "I don't want to go anywhere near that cot."

Her arms circle around me as she pulls me close. The tears come hard and fast, my whole body shaking. Kimba makes soothing noises and pats my back. Finally, the worst of it subsides and I take a step away. I wipe my nose on the sleeve of my sweatshirt, getting a strong whiff of goat in the process. I stink. Kimba stinks. Goats stink.

Kimba offers me a slight smile. "What happened on the cot?"

I lift my gaze to meet hers. "Nothing good." My voice is hoarse and croaky. I clear my throat. "You can't . . . Chad doesn't know."

"You were . . . forced?"

I scoff. "Look, just forget it. It's in the past. I'm almost finished cleaning up. You have the water?"

"Who was it? Someone . . ." Her eyes go wide. "The man from the memorial service. Gary something. I just saw him." She spins on the ball of her foot.

I grab her arm. "No! It doesn't matter."

"Doesn't matter? Of course, it matters. He hurt you. I'm going to hurt him."

I drop my gaze. "It was my fault."

"What?" Kimba steps closer to hear my whispered words.

"You can't go and do whatever it is you plan to do. I didn't want to, but there's . . ." I look up at her piercing blue eyes again. "We have history."

Several expressions cross Kimba's face. Confusion, surprise, anger, then finally understanding. "Oh. You and he . . ." She tilts her head.

"We didn't . . ." I shake my head. "But we were close. Too close. *We almost . . .*" I lift a hand. "I ended it. He wasn't happy, and there were issues. Then, when we got here and everything was so bad, I stayed away from him. Last spring, Chad went out with the hunters, and I was working here. We were running behind that day. I'd sent everyone else away to their next jobs while I finished up. He must've seen them go since his— "

"Since his job is so close. I saw him at the greenhouses on the way here. He *waved* at me."

An ugly snort escapes me, releasing much more than air. "He waves at me every time I see him. I've taken to going around the backside of the barns so I can avoid him. It was too much."

"Why don't you sit in the chair?" She motions to the straight-back kitchen chair near the cot. "I'll finish the dishes and then get the water filled."

"I'm fine. I'm close to done. The water is cooling, so I need to get back at it. I'd hate to have to heat up more. Soon, we'll keep a fire going in here while we milk and do the chores. That'll help keep the water hot." I realize I'm babbling and talking much too fast. I take a deep breath and then release it. Kimba's watching me closely.

"That's why you stopped."

"Pardon?"

"One of the ladies was telling me she used to take your breathing classes. She said they were amazing. You did individual stuff with them. But then you said no more individual sessions, just group. And those became infrequent. I thought it was because of your busy schedule." Kimba motions around the cleaning room.

Chewing the inside of my mouth, I think about how to answer. "The individual sessions relax me too much. I can't let my guard down, or else I remember."

She nods. "But the groups?"

I lift a shoulder. "I can mostly keep it together during the groups. Breathwork was such a help to me, to so many of us, during the early days of living here. We'd all lost so much. I know you think it's nonsense, but it really is amazing. Many people have used it to help heal from trauma. I've seen it, experienced it."

"But not this trauma?"

"No. No, I can't let myself go, not on my own. If I had someone to help me, to breathe with me, maybe. But no, not alone. Plus, it's . . ." I blink rapidly and shake my head. "I'm scared, Kimba. Scared I'll get too relaxed, and he'll suddenly appear. I need to be on my guard all the time. I never know where Gary Searle is going to show up. He has a knack for appearing out of nowhere."

"Does he, now?" Something resembling a smile crosses my friend's face. "Let's get our stuff finished. I don't have another crew until after lunch. You?"

"Uh, no. I'm in the cheese house this afternoon."

Kimba gives me a nod and picks up her buckets. I step back to the sink as she funnels water into the cistern, which uses a hand-pump system to give us running water from the faucet. Cold running water, but it's still helpful to add to the hot water for cleaning up.

As we return to our chores, I attempt to put all thoughts of Gary Searle from my mind. If we move to Billings, will I forget about him? Will I stop always looking over my shoulder and being afraid. Will I finally be able to relax? To breathe?

When I've finished the dishes and wiped everything down, Kimba's done filling the water tank and has put away the large utility wagon we use for hauling water from the nearest well pump to the barn.

She locks arms with me. "Today, we're taking the direct route. Together. We're putting an end to this."

My body trembles as I shake my head. "No, please. Let's just— "

"He will not continue to terrorize you. Today is the day this ends."

"But he said he'd tell Chad and make it sound like I was willing."

"He won't. I promise he will understand it's in his best interest to leave you alone. But, Bev— " she looks at me square on "—secrets are hard on a marriage. This has been made exceedingly obvious to me since Nate died."

"Chad would hate me."

"Hate? No. Never. This wasn't your fault."

"But before—when we were friends . . ."

She lifts a hand. "Let's take care of that scum sucker Searle."

I'm shaking as Kimba locks arms with me again. She takes a couple of steps, then stops. "I, uh . . . let's pray."

Chapter 16

Kimba

Beverly doesn't even try to stifle her groan at my suggestion we pray before going to confront her attacker, to confront Gary Searle.

She waves a hand. "You know how I feel."

"I know, and I respect what happened in your past. I know you blame your dad— "

"Because it's his fault. He did it."

"You've said yourself he was mentally ill. What he did was related to his mental condition, not to him being a preacher."

"Humph. Maybe he was a preacher *because* he was mentally ill."

"Do you really believe that?"

"I don't know, Kimba. Maybe. I mean, look at Gary Searle."

My brow crinkles. "Is he a preacher?"

"A deacon at his church."

"Okay, I get it. And he's a bad guy." I clear my throat. "But do you think Rey's a bad guy? Do you think I am?"

"That's not the same."

"Bev, I know you've been hurt, terribly. Your dad wasn't a good role model for you of what a Godly man can be like. I'm sure he tried, and you've said yourself he wasn't always bad."

"Not always, but enough of the time. The way he was with his congregation, expecting everyone to behave just so, and how he was with my mom and me . . ."

"And it became worse over time, right? To the point after you left for college, he was relieved of his duties?"

"He was fired. The church fired him. He couldn't handle it. Killed my mom and then himself."

I know her story. Originally, Chad told us, but Bev and I also talked about it once before. She was the same then, relaying the details like she was a newscaster. I'm surprised when I look at her and see her eyes shimmering.

She lifts her chin slightly before shaking her head. "The breathwork, it helped me so much. Helped me relieve some of the anger and grief. I was getting better. It wasn't easy. You know the first time I tried it, the breathing, was a lark. You know my friend Becca?"

"Your sorority sister?"

"Right. She convinced me to go with her on a girls' weekend to a swanky spa. I was so out of my element there." Bev lets out a nervous laugh.

Where Chad is vivacious and outgoing, she's quiet. Maybe a little awkward. And very plain. I'd suggested a mani-pedi day once and she quickly begged off, saying that wouldn't really suit her.

"We were there a few hours, having eaten our sprout salad for lunch, and I was thinking why in the world did I agree to this? There were a variety of classes scheduled over the weekend. You know, yoga mostly but also gong baths and other things. Breatheology was the first class, and it . . . it changed my life. In that class, surrounded by six other women, I faced my demons. It was so powerful.

"That's when I knew I had to help others the same way I was being helped. I was learning to forgive my father. Forgive the church. Maybe even forgive God. Chad and I had even started talking about going to Adam Kingsworth's services. But now that old anger is back. Not like it was, but it's still there."

"Because of Searle, because of what he did to you."

"Maybe."

"A few months ago, I probably would've had something very profound and churchy to say to you." I arch an eyebrow at her, which elicits the slightest smile. "But now, after losing Nate, I just about lost myself. Rey and I had just come to know Christ over the winter. I thought He'd put a hedge of protection around us, and that made us . . . immortal, I guess. That He was behind our journey and would keep us safe.

"I first started thinking maybe I was wrong when another boy in our group, Asher, was killed. When Rey and I used to go to church before, when we lived in Denver, it was *understood* once we had Christ in our lives, our troubles would disappear. Rey and I used to tease that if we'd give ourselves fully to God, all the world troubles would end and our business would no longer exist.

"When I actually learned about God and who He is, that wasn't part of the equation, and I never heard anyone preach about that in our Bakerville community. But I guess it still stuck with me. I'd forgotten just how much evil and sin are in the world. I mean, really, it's how we got where we are, right?"

"Evil and sin? Yes, I suppose so."

"When Asher died because of that evil and sin, I was still shocked. Then Nate was taken from us by a freak accident. I was such a mess. I'm still a mess somedays, but now I'm able to allow God—and my family—to help me through my mess. God never promised us an easy life as Christians. In fact, Jesus says just the opposite. He said we'll have trouble in this world, but we should take heart because He has overcome the world."

"John 16:33."

I clasp both of Bev's hands in mine. "What your dad did was terrible, the way he treated you and then taking your mom's life before his own. I don't blame you for being angry. You should be. But is God the right recipient of your anger? You grew up in the church. You obviously know your scripture verses."

"Knowing is different than believing. Even the devil knew scripture, or at least how to paraphrase it."

The word paraphrase hits me hard. *Is that what I do?* "Paraphrase it . . . you mean like I did? Hmm. That's a good point. Even though I paraphrased it, you knew what verse I meant. I'll admit, though, too many times Rey and I'll be talking and I'll say something like, 'Doesn't the Bible say blah, blah about that?' Then I'll paraphrase the verse." I shake my head.

"Wow, Bev. What am I missing by paraphrasing? Am I piecing scripture together to suit my own needs instead of *really* knowing what the Bible says?"

"I . . . I don't know."

"Well, I think I do. Thank you, Bev."

"For?"

"For helping me see this. Now I'm going to pray God will help me. I plan on making sure Gary Searle is no longer a threat to you, but I'm going to need God's help and guidance to do it." I give my friend an exaggerated wink.

Still holding Bev's hands, I bow my head. I softly ask God to give us a true hedge of protection and guide me. "God, if this is really what You want me to do, help me do it in a manner You approve of. You know, if it were up to me, that man wouldn't . . . well, he wouldn't be walking away from our conversation."

I feel Bev stiffen.

"Help me make him know he will no longer bother Bev, or any woman, in this community. I pray these things in Jesus' holy name, amen."

"Amen," Bev whispers. "What are you going to do to Gary?"

"Not what I originally planned, I'll admit that. I'm going to let God lead. I'll try and follow."

Gary Searle is alone in one of the greenhouses, hand-watering plants with a little metal waterer. This is one of the winter garden greenhouses, filled with greens and other fast-growing items.

A large pile of compost, mostly waste from the livestock barns, is in the corner by the door we enter. At the other end is a small woodstove, the heat-powered fan on it barely moving from the small fire inside.

The surprise on Searle's face is evident. This quickly turns to concern as I drag Bev with me and we move toward him.

He takes a step backward.

I look him in the eyes, he seems to wither. I quickly and concisely tell him he will leave my friend alone. If I even suspect he's bothering her, we will have a problem. He opens his mouth, but I raise a hand and repeat my orders.

He must realize I will follow through on my promise because his eyes go wide. His shoulders drop and the water container in his hand trembles. "I understand. I'll . . ." He swallows and then looks at Bev.

"Don't even look at her. That time is done. She wants nothing to do with you. Truthfully, you should be thankful she told me about this and not my husband, or her husband. And you should be thankful I asked God to help me before coming in here, because my first instinct . . . well, you don't want to know what it was."

He moves the shaking water jug slightly in front of him, covering his belt buckle. I'm surprised to see a wet spot form on his jeans.

Bev and I are out of the greenhouse and walking quickly away from it when she whispers, "He wet his pants?"

"Um . . . the way the water jug was shaking, I think he just spilled it?"

"I've never seen anyone look so scared. You only talked to him. You didn't even hit him or anything."

I shake my head and lift a shoulder. "I don't know. I wanted to hit him, but I guess that wasn't God's plan. I just don't know."

"In their hearts, humans plan their course, but the Lord establishes their steps."

I can't help but smile. "That doesn't sound paraphrased."

"Proverbs 16:9. Thanks, Kimba. Do you think he'll really stop?"

"We'll make sure of it."

That night, in our new apartment down the hall from the Pitneys, Rey and I are in bed as I tell him about meeting Searle. I'd asked Bev for permission, telling her it was important Rey knew in case my talk didn't accomplish what we needed. She reluctantly agreed but asked he not tell Chad. She'll tell her husband herself.

When we reached the building, she'd pulled me tight and said, even if Searle didn't completely leave her alone, me going with her to confront him gives her courage to change things. It's time to move past this, to tell Chad. He'll be angry, not about the rape but about the near affair a couple years ago. And it may change things, too many things. But it's necessary. Secrets have no place in a marriage.

"Bev said something about the devil knowing scripture enough to paraphrase it. That really struck me."

"How so?"

"I realized, although I may have an idea of scripture, I may not be using it properly. If I don't know the actual words and only think I do, am I taking things out of context? Distorting the Bible to say what I want it to say instead of what it truly says? I mean, really, I could just put things together and make it claim whatever, not what it truly intended. I need to make a point to memorize scripture. This is one of those times I wish the internet was still up."

"To help you memorize?"

"To help me find verses I think I know so I can memorize them the way they're truly written. And so I can read the verses before and after so I have context."

"Hiding the words in your heart."

"Yes, exactly. Now . . . do you know the actual verse and where to find it? It's a good one to start with, I think."

Rey lets out a soft laugh. "I don't. Psalms, maybe. Guess I'm just as much of a paraphraser as you. This would be a good thing for all of us. And I can definitely see how having the internet would be helpful. A few keywords and we'd find the verse and go from there."

"Bev knows scripture."

"Really? How? Oh, I forgot about her father being a preacher. Makes sense, even though she walked away from church years ago."

"It's hidden in her heart." I poke him in the arm.

He laughs and then winces.

"Oh! Sorry, Rey. Did I hurt you?"

"No, I'm fine. Moving sometimes causes a pinch. You've heard Mercer. I'm right on track for my recovery. We'll be off to Billings before you know it."

"Did Chad tell you if they made a decision? I was going to ask Bev today, but then this whole thing with Searle came up."

"I don't think they've fully decided. They're waiting to see if Emma's well enough."

"She's doing very well. And there are doctors in Billings, right?" I adjust so I'm snuggling closer to him.

"Right. Do you think Bev would help?"

"Help with Emma?"

"No, sorry. Help us with scripture. If there's one we remember and want to learn, could she find the actual verse?" He rubs his hand on my back.

"Hmm. She might be able to. I don't know how much she remembers."

"But do you think she'd be willing? I know she's an atheist."

"I don't think she's actually an atheist." I shake my head. "Not that she calls herself anyway. She's just been so hurt. She told me her breathing stuff helped her get over some of the anger she had toward her dad. Wouldn't it be amazing if she could combine her breathing work with God and . . . and something. I'm not sure what. But what if she focused on God while doing it? Do you think she could get over that anger too?"

"Maybe. I don't know much about what she does, but I did get the impression it's more of an Eastern religion thing, kind of like meditation."

"Isn't there meditation in the Bible?" I lean up on one arm so I can look into his face. The moonlight's shining on him just right, highlighting his blue eyes and the silver at his temples. Mercy, he's handsome.

"Prayer, sure. But meditation . . . I'm not sure. Guess we do need more Bible study and verse memorization."

He motions me to snuggle back in, and we lay quietly for many minutes. I'm about to continue our conversation when I realize Rey's breath is even and he's softly snoring. I curl up next to him, thanking God for healing my husband and asking Him to help Beverly with her hurts and heartache.

Chapter 17

Kimba
Tuesday, October 20

"I guess that's about it." Chad takes a final look around. "Glad this was well hidden and undisturbed. It should stay this way, should we find ourselves in need of a resupply."

"Well done, old friend." Rey claps him on the shoulder. "I take back all those teasing remarks I made."

Beverly reaches for her husband's hand. "There was plenty to tease about. You weren't the only one who thought he'd gone off his rocker." The look her deep brown eyes send Chad takes any sting out of the words.

"The teasing was relentless, but who's laughing now?" Chad throws his head back and gives a whoop of laughter.

"*Dad*," Emma mutters and shakes her head.

That only causes Chad to make more of a scene, which soon has everyone but his embarrassed daughter chuckling. I'm glad to see some of the fun-loving Chad back. He's been so serious since we first saw him at the pseudo campground, I'd forgotten just how goofy he can be. And his wife, quiet and meek, is a true saint to put up with him and his antics for all these years.

Of course, her relationship with Gary Searle shows just how human Bev is. She came clean with Chad over it—over *all* of it. He was understandably hurt. Bev came to me after she told him and said she thought he was leaving her. He'd stormed out and spent the night in the men's dormitory. The next day he returned, saying he wanted to work it out. They're better now. Not perfect, but I can see a lot of improvement in their relationship.

As far as Gary Searle, the day Bev and I confronted him in the greenhouse, he left his job and went to his room. He cleared out all he could carry and took off for parts unknown. The last weeks we've been here, Bev has finally started to relax.

When she and Chad got past the worst of their issues, Rey and I asked her if she'd help us with finding Bible verses we wanted to memorize. She said she'd do her best. We started with Psalm 119:11. *"I have hidden Your Word in my heart that I might not sin against You."* It seemed like a perfectly fitting first verse to memorize.

Bev also gave us a Bible dictionary and concordance she found at the book trading center. I'll admit, I didn't know something like that even existed.

Arriving at Chad and Beverly's burned-out home yesterday, we set up camp well away from any debris. While there were very specific things Chad wanted to get for beginning their new life in Billings, we were a little sidetracked by the remnants of their old life.

The house was destroyed and, prior to the fire, scrubbed of valuables by the group our former associate Jankins was with. Thankfully, not everything of value was taken. Chad took inventory of the place in the weeks following the assault on his neighborhood, choosing to leave things where they were should they need them in the future. On a few occasions, he came over and found cached food for them during the long winter.

The prepping was just one of a long line of obsessions Chad engaged in. He'd get a niggle of something and go all in, spending time and money on various collections. At least the preparedness phase is beneficial today. His old coin collection may also have a use in today's world. Not so with the antique beer can or banana sticker collections.

Weapons, food, his old coins, and a large assortment of other supplies went undiscovered. He had a hidden, fireproof safe room in the basement, plus a variety of buried caches around the yard and even on the edge of his neighborhood. The beer cans had been in the basement family room, now charred beyond recognition. I have yet to ask about the banana peel collection.

"What time is your friend showing up?" Rey asks as he hefts his backpack into place.

I help Naomi with hers before telling her to button up the neck of her jacket and pull her cap over her ears.

"It's not that cold, Mommy."

"If the wind comes up, you'll be glad for the hat. You can take it off when we're on the bus."

After adjusting my own knit cap, I snap the chest belt of my backpack and look at the brand-spanking-new pack Chad is helping his wife with. My pack is faded and dingy. Even after scrubbing and letting it air out for the past several weeks, it has a decided reek to it. The girls' and Rey's are no better. Sal is carrying a duffle bag—not ideal for being on the road, but we don't anticipate needing to do much walking.

Chad's friend, someone who has an old Toyota pickup from the '70s, dropped us off nearby yesterday. The destroyed neighborhood hasn't fared well over the winter. There're several burned-out shells of cars on the roads and debris from the houses scattered about by the wind, making driving the roads hazardous.

Even walking isn't completely safe. I've watched the children intently to make sure they stay well away from any dangers. The last thing we need is a cut that becomes infected. Even with the military and their medical supplies, avoiding infection or illness is the best choice.

The friend with the Toyota will drive us to the bus depot, then it's a nice, easy ride into Billings. At least that's the plan. We could use easy. So many times, our plans go awry and what we think will be a cake walk turns into trouble. Trouble does seem to find us.

When Captain Mercer was at the apartment last, clearing Rey and Emma for travel, she surprised me by asking, "So what's your deal? It's obvious Pitney is military. The way he carries himself, I'd say Marines maybe, or some sort of special forces. But what about you two?"

With a benign smile, I told her neither me nor my husband had been in the military.

"Mm-hmm. So, were you spooks then?"

Her frankness not only surprised me but caught me off guard. Thankfully, I was sitting down. Maybe I should've adapted the Kim persona for our time in Bozeman. No, I'm glad I didn't. I'm done with that. No more shows. No more operations. I just want to do what we can and live in peace.

"Never mind." She waved a hand. "I don't expect the truth about it anyway."

When Rey looked her in the eye and arched an eyebrow, she nodded. "I knew there was something about the two of you. Pitney also, but not Beverly. She's not one of you, is she?"

Rey shook his head. "She's one of us, but not in the way you mean. She's the one who keeps us steady. Together."

"Sane," I added.

Mercer pushed her glasses up her nose. "You said you were in Billings a few months back? Things have changed after the pronouncement of the Wastelands. With so many states declared uninhabitable, Billings is now a major operating base for the west. The training for the Volunteer Unit is done there, and all sorts of people have converged from all over the country. Not all for honorable reasons."

"Sounds about like most towns with military bases nearby."

"Yes, well, you'd do well to keep your head down. And maybe have a few friends." She pulled a notebook out of her pocket. She spent a few minutes scribbling, then thrusted it toward me. "Give this to Colonel Ellis. He's operating out of the old Moss Mansion."

I took the note and folded it a couple of times before tucking it in the front pocket of my pants without reading it. "Why'd you leave Billings?"

"The sickness here."

"Is that all?"

She gave me a sly smile. "That's enough."

After she left, Rey leaned into me. "Well, let's see it."

I pulled it out and unfolded it enough to read. *Calling in one of those many favors. Do what you can for these friends. Sparrow.*

Chuffing, Rey said, "I'd say we weren't the only spies in this room."

Rey and I walk hand in hand toward the meeting point where Chad's friend will pick us up. The two youngest girls are chattering, excited about the bus ride, staying clear of the hazards on the road. Emma and Nicole are more subdued as they talk quietly. Sal's grin spreads across his face.

"I hear an engine." Chad motions in the distance.

A few minutes later, we're piled in the bed of the small pickup truck. Before going to Chad and Bev's place yesterday, Chad had his friend drive Rey and him to the bus depot to secure tickets. We're all set for the 3:00 p.m. bus to Billings.

In the weeks since we were last on the public bus, the route has changed. While it still travels Interstate 90, they've dropped their service to only one day per week, with the Missoula to Billings route now taking two days instead of just the one. Because they only drive during daylight hours and the days are now much shorter, they're only stopping in larger towns, and just long enough for people to get on and off, with an overnight stop in Butte.

More private bus companies have sprung up along the way as more of Interstate 90 is cleared and the military expands with westward service all the way to Coeur d'Alene, Idaho, and service east into South Dakota and beyond. Billings may now be training the Volunteer Units, but Ellsworth Air Force Base in South Dakota has long been a fixture. Clearing the roads between Billings and there was given a high priority.

I'm mildly surprised by this, considering South Dakota declined help from the regular military operating as their police force. But the reality is, transportation is important to get things back to normal. The open roads will give us opportunities for trade and more.

The road clearing has benefited enterprising individuals who are willing to transport travelers. Rumor is, one of the bus companies is going completely old school and bringing back stagecoaches. While they don't have the speed of the biodiesel buses, it still beats walking.

When the snow starts, the transports will stop for the winter, but the stagecoach folks are saying they'll put sleds on the wagons and keep going. I love the idea and know how well it will work. When we left the ski lodge last March, PJ Cameron's wagon was turned into a sleigh for the journey off the mountain.

My eyes shoot to my eldest daughter. Her eighteenth birthday is fast approaching. She has yet to announce if she's going to join the volunteers then. I think she'll wait, spend the winter with us and then see what the summer brings.

Sal, who'll be sixteen in just a few days, no longer talks about joining. I'm glad. He's so young. Sixteen in this world isn't the same as sixteen was before the EMP, but if he can try and hold off on needing to do the full adult things a soldier does, it'd be better.

However, there's no denying everyone grows up fast in the apocalypse. With Emma's recent brush with death, she's well beyond her thirteen years. There's a quietness about her that wasn't there before. Her recovery is nearly complete, without any physical issues, but she's haunted by nightmares. Mercer said it's probably residual from the hallucinations and should fade over time.

Beverly's doing individual breathing sessions again, hoping to help her daughter with the dreams. She even met with a few others at the college who are having the same troubles. She told me that confronting Searle and coming clean with Chad made the difference for her.

She's asked a few more times if she can help me, breathe with me, but I'm still not interested. Would it help? Maybe. I do know the power of breathing for times of high stress. I've used box breathing for years to slow my heartrate when shooting or at other necessary times. But lying on a camping pad or yoga mat and breathing for an entire hour? Too weird.

Rey has also fully recovered, at least physically. While he doesn't have nightmares like Emma does, there's still something going on. I've asked if he wants to talk about it, and he says he does but he can't put his finger on exactly what the issue is. He thinks getting to Billings will help.

Dr. Sanderson, the man who attacked Rey, is still recovering. The ergotism hit him hard. Not only did he have delusions, but he also got gangrene on one of his feet, which had to be amputated. Even over a month after he attacked Rey, he's still in the medical ward. I don't know if he'll pull through.

When we reach the bus depot, with an hour to spare until our boarding time, Sal's grin has yet to fade. "Never thought I'd be so excited to go to Billings."

"We'll get there today, before your birthday too." Naomi's smile covers her face. "Maybe we can have a party. I like birthday parties."

"I wish we knew where we'd be living." Nicole shakes her head. "Didn't Captain Mercer tell you anything?"

I scrunch up my face. "Not much." Neither Rey nor I told the children about Mercer identifying us, but we did share the info with Chad and Bev. Chad seemed surprised, but Bev said it made sense, that the three of us have a way about us.

The bus seems to be the same one we were on before, with the widely spaced seats for our packs to tuck in at our feet. An hour later, we're pulling into Livingston, the first stop since we boarded. Several people get off here. After the last person exits, there's a slight delay and a clunking sound as someone boards.

A few seconds later, an elderly woman steps on, her cane thumping along the floor. She's followed by a red-haired woman several years younger than me. Our eyes meet, and she gives me a nod and a sad smile before helping the aged woman into a seat a few rows in front of our group.

Several hours later, as the sun is just beginning to set, we take the downtown Billings exit and pull into an old Cracker Barrel restaurant. When we were in Billings before, it was on the eastern side. This time, we approached from the west. What we can see of the largest city in Montana looks just as I expected: ramshackle and worn down.

There're windowless buildings from being burned out or vandalized, along with mere shells and piles of rubble. It was easy to see when we were getting close to the city by the increase of vehicles in the ditch. Will the owners ever return to these cars? Will they ever run again? Like the buildings, they've also been vandalized, with windows busted out, tires removed, set on fire, and more before the military moved them into the trenches to clear the road.

With our feet on the pavement and a definite crispness in the air, Rey takes a deep breath. "Let's find a place to sleep tonight, then make our way downtown to meet Colonel Ellis tomorrow."

"We need to check in." Bev recites the instructions from the bus conductor to register. The rest of the bus passengers, including the red haired lady and her elderly companion, are already making their way toward the guard station.

At the end of the check-in line, we're quietly talking when a voice booms at us. "Well, well, well. I should be surprised to see you, Pitney. But, somehow, I'm not."

The hair on the back of my neck stands up at the familiar voice. Rey drops a hand on my shoulder. We turn together.

The shock on Eric Bohm's face is quickly masked. "Should've known the three of you would be together. Now we can really get this party started."

Chapter 18

Kimba
Tuesday, October 20
Billings, Montana

With a tightly clenched jaw, Rey dips his chin. "Bohm."

"Great," Chad mutters.

Sensing the situation, Bev takes the younger girls by the hands and motions for Nicole and Sal to keep moving.

"No hello from you?" Eric "Doc" Bohm squares up, facing me head on. "Maybe a hug for an old friend?"

I set my shoulders. "We're not friends." My eyes travel to the man I was once more than friends with. He looks almost exactly the same as he did when we met twentyish years ago, but with a sprinkling of gray peppered throughout his dark hair. I expect he probably has wrinkles around his eyes, but his dark shades—unneeded in the fading daylight—hide the evidence.

He's dressed essentially the same as the last time I saw him. Eighteen months into the apocalypse, and he's wearing dress pants, a button-up shirt, suit jacket, and a necktie. Even in the chill of the October day, he's forgone a coat. At least his shoes fit the occasion: heavy hiking boots with considerable tread.

The edge of his lip lifts. "Sure we are." His gaze drifts to Rey. "Right, Hoffmann?"

"Who you working with here?" Rey asks. "Military or . . . someone else?"

Bohm lifts his shoulders. "You know how it is, whoever needs me. I'm actually surprised to discover the opportunities in this new world. Where have you three been holing up?" He turns toward Chad. "That's right. You live in Montana. The college town, right? Missoula?"

"Nice seeing you, Bohm." Chad gives a dismissive wave. "Hope we don't see you again."

The three of us quickly walk away as Bohm calls out, "Oh, we'll see plenty of each other. Count on it."

Rey reaches for my hand. "You okay?"

"He's . . . he's trouble."

"Yeah. Wonder what he's doing here?"

Chad claps Rey on the shoulder. "Spreading joy wherever he goes? Just like always."

I chuff out a laugh. "Joy? Is that what he does? Torture isn't my idea of joy." Eric Bohm, known as Doc by many, is a trained interrogator. The techniques he's learned and created are ruthless. He'll do whatever is necessary to get the answers he wants. Not necessarily the truth, but what *he* views as the truth.

In addition to his interrogation skills, he's a master manipulator. He has a way of getting into people's heads, turning them so upside down they no longer know the truth. He uses a variety of psychotherapy treatments to twist and change a person—treatments that are beneficial and healing when in the hands of a trained, *sane* person, but something awful with Bohm.

I can imagine even Beverly's helpful breathing sessions would be something Bohm could use to corrupt a person into what he needed. And what he usually needs, or wants, from people is evil. Pure evil.

When Eric and I first met, I fell into his trap. His charms. He manipulated me from the start. At the time, I thought it was a purely personal relationship, but after I ended it, I wondered if he wasn't set on me—given me as an assignment in order to . . . to what I don't know. But I did feel I was being used in some way.

It wasn't long after I broke up with him when the mission I was on with Meagan Wright's fiancé happened, and everything fell apart. I lost my career and was almost tried for treason, threatened with prison . . . or more.

The time we spent in Bakerville with the person formally known as Meagan and now called Doris was an eyeopener as far as Doc Bohm was concerned. Doris also thinks he may have been involved. She told me she thought that, at the time of her fiancé's death, Bohm and I were in cahoots. We'd worked together for the mission to fail for our own gain. She knew we were dating but didn't know I'd dumped him.

During one of the many conversations Doris and I had, where we tried to hash out our past and move on to a friendship, we'd talked about Bohm in depth. I remember telling her how grateful I was I'd never have to see the man again. And now here he is, still looking quite the dandy and considerably out of place in this new world.

We catch up with Bev and the children in the check-in line. Bev raises her eyebrows at Chad.

He gives her a nod and a slight smile. "I'm beat. I hope we can find a place to rack out."

While standing in line, we hear the spiel. We'll be able to stay in temporary housing, a former hotel, for three days while we get settled and find a work crew. Work crews have housing included in areas fitting for the jobs.

The older lady with the cane, who got on the bus in Livingston, causes a bit of a stink, saying they're moving on to South Dakota but not until the rest of their group arrives on horseback. That will be more than three days from now, so what are they supposed to do?

The patient private assures her she and her traveling companion can return and register for a second three-day pass if their friends haven't arrived.

"I certainly hope so, young man. Come, Merissa. I need to get off this ankle."

"Yes, Mother Pearl." The younger woman dips her head before shooting me an apologetic smile.

We're given two connecting rooms with double queen beds in each and a third room across the hall for Sal. We're on the third floor of what was probably a nice hotel at one time. Now it's little more than a hovel, with serious cleanliness issues.

"Bed bugs?" I ask after Rey checks the mattress.

"Doesn't look like it. They put a plastic mattress cover around it. And we'll use our own bedding since the room doesn't have any." He raises his voice to call into the Pitneys' room. "How's your place look, buddy?"

"Disgusting." Bev's voice leaves no doubt what she thinks of our accommodations.

Rey strides to the door. "I'm going to check on Sal."

I look around the room and take it all in with a feeling of dread deep in my gut. Eric Bohm in Billings. Jankins was on his way here. Captain Mercer, also known as *Sparrow*, said we'd need a friend here and gave us a note—a pass of sorts—to ensure Colonel Ellis was that friend.

Maybe we should keep moving? Get on another bus and make our way to Denver? Back to our condo where I can find a few pictures of Nate and we can regroup?

We know the buses are running on I-90, at least as long as the weather allows, but I don't know if there's anyone running down I-25. I haven't even heard if the military's working on clearing Interstate 25 and rebuilding Denver.

I'd asked Captain Mercer if she knew anything about Denver. Her eyes went wide before she muttered, "Nothing good."

When Rey returns a few minutes later, Sal's by his side.

"How was it?" I ask.

"It's fine." Sal's smile is pleasant, as always. "Rey said you might have a cleaning cloth? I thought I'd give it a wipe down."

Bev responds from the other room. "I have a bottle of disinfectant spray. I'm just about finished with it and then you all can use it."

Rey claps his hands together, then rubs them. "After that, we'll eat and then have Bible study."

An hour later, we've cleaned as best we could and had our dinner—jerky and dried zucchini we were given as a going away package by the organizers at the college—and are settling in for a Bible reading.

Even Chad, Bev, and their girls join us in our room as Rey reads from 1 Corinthians 13. I find it to be an interesting choice, considering its focus is on love. With just having ran into Eric Bohm, who I know neither Rey or Chad—and especially me—have any love for, why is Rey reading this?

When Rey finishes the chapter, I discover I'm not the only one with questions.

"What's that about, bro?" Chad asks.

Rey cocks a brow. "Meaning?"

"We run into that nutjob Bohm, and you choose a passage about showing love?"

"I'm not sure it means love like you think, Chad." Bev smiles at her husband. "I've always understood Paul is talking about agape love."

"And?"

"Uh, well, it's different. It's not like love in a marriage or friendship—not really. It's a love given whether or not it's returned. It's a sacrificial love."

Chad snorts. "Well, I'm not sacrificing anything for Eric Bohm."

119

Rey grunts out a laugh. "Honestly, I wasn't even thinking of Bohm when I found this. I was thinking of the women on the bus, the lady with the cane and her daughter."

I scrunch up my face. "I think maybe daughter-in-law. She called her Mother Pearl. That would be more of an in-law phrase than her own mom's title. A southern thing?" I look to Bev, who gives a nod.

"Whichever, I just thought it was obvious they cared for each other, and they reminded me of this passage."

"I'm impressed you knew where to find it." Bev gives him a smile.

"The concordance." Rey motions to the tome sitting near his leg. "That thing's amazing."

"I guess you won't need me any longer." Do I hear sadness in Bev's voice?

"Not true. While it was perfect for finding this, we still need you for when we just have an inkling of what a passage or verse says. I hope you'll continue to help us and join us for these readings."

"We'll see."

"What do you think it means that we'll have housing near our work crews?" Sal asks. "If we're on different crews, will we be in different parts of town?"

"Sounds that way." Chad makes a face. "Not what I thought we'd be getting."

"Well, we just make sure we get on the same crews." Rey turns toward Sal. "And we listed you as part of our family. I believe we'll be able to stay together if that's still what you want."

"It is. Thanks."

Nicole clears her throat. "I guess now's as good a time as any . . ." She looks at the stained carpet. "I've made my decision. I'm joining the Army or the Marines if they'll take me."

I close my eyes and swallow the lump in my throat.

"The volunteers?" Sal asks.

"I'm hoping I can get into the real Army or Marines. I talked with Captain Mercer. She wrote me a letter of reference."

My head shoots toward my oldest child. "She did? Why didn't you say anything?"

"I wasn't sure yet. I was still trying to decide if it was what I wanted. And it's a long shot. She said they aren't really organized enough for actual enlistment, unless it's a former military person who has proof they were honorably discharged."

"DD-214?" Chad asks. "They're taking those for reenlistment?"

She nods, her eyes still on the carpet. "Do you have yours? Or did you lose it in the fire?"

"It was in a firebox along with other important papers. I have it."

"So, you could get back in if you wanted, I guess."

Bev looks at her husband.

Chad reaches for her hand. "Not in my plans."

Nicole finally looks in my direction. "Mom, are you . . . are you mad at me?"

I blink the tears away. Mad? No. Scared, concerned, and a myriad of other feelings, absolutely. "I'm proud of you for doing what you think is best. I do wish . . ." I let out a sigh. "We know if things were different, we'd be planning college for you, but with the way things are, I understand this is the choice you feel is best. I truly do."

Nicole bobs her head several times. "It is. I feel good about it, especially if Captain Mercer's letter helps. Then, when things start getting back to normal, I'll have the benefits of regular service. Maybe colleges will start up again and I can even get financial aid."

I give her a smile, not wanting to admit I don't think those things will happen any time soon. And if college does start again, it's not likely to be anything like what we had before.

And financial aid isn't necessary when we don't have money. Of course, some form of currency must be in the works. We can't truly rebuild without having an active trade system. The importance of that has been shown over and over throughout history. "I'm sure it will work out fine."

"Thanks, Mom. I'm kind of excited. I hope they'll let me stay here and not ship me out right away. Captain Mercer said they do most of the training in Billings, but that's only like three or four weeks and then . . ." She lifts a shoulder.

"Three or four weeks?" Chad shakes his head. "Not nearly enough. Good thing you have some training already."

"I think that's the theory. Most people have been forced into survival training, so what more do they need?"

"Plenty. More than you can even imagine."

Chapter 19

Beverly
Friday, October 23

Moving day. The morning after we arrived in Billings, I stayed with the youngest girls and Sal, while Chad and the Hoffmanns went out in search of work.

Well, Rey and Kimba were in search of work. Nicole went to the recruiter to join up. She wasn't successful in getting into the regular Army or Marines but was happily accepted to the Volunteer Unit with a promise that, if she lived up to the glowing letter written by Captain Mercer, things could change for her.

Kimba's in a funk. She's so torn on how to feel. Pride for Nicole but also fear and worry—what any parent would experience. The day after Nicole's eighteenth birthday, she'll report for training. Kimba's hope is she'll winter in Billings before being shipped anywhere. There's a good chance that'll happen, since winter travel will be difficult.

Today is Sal's birthday. Sixteen. How different it is being sixteen in today's world than what it was just a couple of years ago. No real school. No driver's license. He can't even sneak a beer or smoke with friends. Not that I think he'd do those things; he's definitely more on the straight and narrow than many boys his age.

Still, it's staggering to think about the things he'll miss out on, the things my daughters will miss. I try not to dwell on the stuff they're being deprived of. This new world is what we make of it, and I'm determined it will be good for the children.

One way is celebrations. Today we'll celebrate Sal's birthday. Nothing fancy, of course, but something. And in just over a week, we'll celebrate Nicole turning eighteen. We'll put aside our sadness over what may come and just be happy in the moment. That's all we can do.

I'll admit to being as surprised as everyone else about Sal's age. Chad and I met him and his parents a few weeks after we were all forced into the college housing. At the time, I estimated Sal to be college age.

Physically, he's tall yet on the scrawny side, lanky like so many young men before they fully mature. His demeanor was mature and calm. He isn't a handsome lad, but he isn't unattractive either. He spent the bulk of his time working on different crews. When his dad died shortly after the new year, in a freak accident while cutting wood, Sal really stepped up and made sure his mom was taken care of.

When his mom died, I wasn't terribly surprised. In the time we'd known her, she was often ill. I think it was more of a broken heart than anything. She didn't really bounce back after losing her spouse, and her body couldn't handle the grief.

I tried to help her with a breath session, but she couldn't get through it. We'd barely began, with her lying flat on a yoga mat with a bolster under her knees and pillow under her neck, when she started crying.

Emotions are typical during a session, and I'll usually just guide people with breathing and encourage them to take three deep breaths. But for her, she just curled up and cried. Not a terrible thing since emotions are necessary in humans, but she wouldn't move from there to try anything different. We spent the hour with her in a fetal position and me rubbing her back.

I wanted to try again, but she came down with a cold. When she was better, she kept putting me off. Then, after Gary Searle attacked me, I was done with private sessions. I just couldn't do them. One-on-one, it was too easy for me to relax, to let my guard down. And I couldn't do that. Not safely, at least not in my mind. And Sal's mom was in no condition for a group session.

When I heard she died, I felt like I'd failed her. I truly expected to discover she'd taken her own life. I'll admit to feeling a weird sense of relief when I learned it wasn't suicide. Not that it made her death any easier on Sal, but at least it wasn't at her own hand.

Emma's been responding beautifully to her breathing. The nightmares are almost completely gone. During the day, I'll catch her doing a few deep breaths. When I ask her if she's okay, she just says, "I'm practicing not holding my breath."

I'm not sad to be moving from this hotel. It served its purpose to keep us out of the cold and weather, but it's not overly comfortable.

Too many people are crammed into this place with paper thin walls. As I return from taking out the small amount of trash we've accumulated in our short stay—the few things we can't reuse in some way—I bump into our next-door neighbor.

"Oh! I'm so sorry. I wasn't paying attention."

"It's fine. You found a place?" Merissa Weaver asks. She's the red-haired woman who we first saw on the bus to Billings. She's staying here with her mother-in-law while they wait for the rest of their group.

"We did. My husband and the others will be back soon, and we'll get out of here. Your friends aren't here yet?"

"Not yet. Today is really the earliest I'd expect them. They won't push the horses too hard."

"And then what?"

"Then my mother-in-law and I will take the next bus as far as it will go, they'll ride, and we'll repeat the waiting and then traveling pattern."

"And you're going to . . . ?"

"South Dakota. Mother Pearl has family there. Although, I am a little concerned the weather will become an issue. The flurries last night had me worried."

"At least it isn't sticking yet. Last year, we already had snow on the ground by now. Maybe we're back to our normal weather of snow on the ground and then it'll warm up and melt. I heard the buses will run whenever they can."

"I heard that too. The wind is more of an issue. If it snows and blows, we won't be able to travel." The woman gives a weary smile. "I'll be happy when we get there. What's your new housing like?"

"Oh, well, I haven't seen it yet, but we're staying in the YMCA building."

"Is that where the military is staying?"

"They have the houses in the area. They're working out of a historic mansion."

"I've heard."

I tilt my head. "Were you military?"

"Well . . . it depends on who you ask." She gives a small smile. "I was Coast Guard."

"Ah, okay. I think that counts."

"To you maybe, but not everyone. Your husband, he's a Marine?"

"Is it obvious?" I choose not to tell her he was special operations.

"My husband was Army." Her eyes cloud.

"Oh, I'm so sorry. Is your loss recent?"

She nods. "Not long. Our town was attacked. That's why we're going to Rapid City. My husband and his brother died, and our houses were shot up. With the mail running again, we'd heard from Pearl's sister, and she said to join her anytime. So . . ." She lifts her hands. "Here we are."

"I'm so sorry. I hope— "

"Do what I say!" a man's voice carries from down the hall.

Merissa shakes her head. "Those two again. They were going at it in the middle of the night. I won't be upset to leave this place."

A high-pitched wail comes from the room. "Stop! You're hurting me."

Merissa lets out a sigh. "Well, we can't have that." She walks toward the sound of the commotion, her semi-automatic bouncing on her hip.

I scurry to catch up. "Wait!" I reach for her arm. "Let's . . . we'll get help." The sounds of something breaking, followed by another scream, causes me to release her arm. "Okay. I'll help you."

Sal sticks his head out the door. "Beverly?"

"Run, Sal. Go get one of the guards. Ask Emma to watch the girls."

Sal quickly relays my message to Emma, then takes off in the other direction as Merissa and I reach the open doorway.

A man is holding a woman against the wall. His hand is in a fist as he calls her terrible names.

"Stop." Merissa's command leaves little doubt she means it.

The man turns slightly. His eyes widen before he sneers. "None of your business." He tacks on a colorful word at the end.

"It is when you're abusing her. Release her and step away."

The man narrows his eyes as the woman lets out a whimper.

I'm standing behind Merissa, lifting on my toes to look over her shoulder, as her lean body fills the doorway.

Whatever the man sees in Merissa's face must convince him she means business. He drops his hands and takes a step back.

When the woman moves, his head snaps in her direction. "Don't even think about it."

Merissa stiffens.

The next thing I know, in a blur of movement, the man punches the woman, and she goes down.

Merissa is also moving. She reaches the man, her elbow connecting with his nose. A knee to his gut—or lower. When he bends forward, the heel of her hand hits his chin.

The woman screams and covers her face.

With the man on the ground, I rush to the woman's side. "C'mon. Come with me."

"No! Stop! She's hurting him."

The man is on his side, curled up and blubbering. "My nose. You broke my nose."

"Oh, baby." The woman squats next to him. "Are you okay?" The woman lifts her gaze and gives Merissa a hateful look. "How dare you! This was none of your business."

"No problem." Merissa strides from the room. I scurry behind her. Footsteps are pounding down the hallway.

"We're going to report you!" the woman yells. "They'll kick you out of here."

"I hope they do," Merissa mutters.

Down the hall, we meet Sal and two out-of-breath guards. Merissa gives a brief account of the situation, ending with, "I broke his nose and put him on the ground."

"Where's the lady he was hitting?" one of the guards asks.

"By his side, mad I put him down."

The guard shakes his head. "There may be more questions. Which room are you in?"

After we give our room numbers and I tell them we're moving today, the two head off down the hall.

"Thanks for the assist." Merissa lifts one side of her mouth in something resembling a smile. She turns to Sal. "And thank you for being so quick to get the soldiers."

"She was really mad at you?" Sal shakes his head.

Merissa lifts a shoulder. "People being abused make excuses for their abusers."

"That makes zero sense."

"I'm sure there's a good psychological explanation for it, but I don't know what it is. Anyway, thanks again. And I wish you well. I hope the new housing is better than this."

"So do I," I agree. "Safe travels. God bless you." *Where did that come from?* I smile to hide the shock of my statement.

Merissa pauses. "God bless you too." She wraps me in a sisterly hug before, again, telling me goodbye and moving off to her room.

When we're back in our room and have assured the girls everything is fine, Sal asks, "You think there'll be trouble?"

"From the couple? I don't know. The woman was pretty bruised up, so the guards should maybe . . . I don't know."

"We won't have loud neighbors at our next house, right?" Kylie asks.

"I'm not sure. You remember how your dad and Rey said we're staying in what used to be the YMCA? Our apartment will be in one of the racquetball courts."

"I've never seen a racquetball court, so I don't know what it looks like."

"I know. And I've never seen this one, so I don't exactly know. But it is probably just a big room with our beds. The bathrooms are outside, and there's a well outside where we'll get water."

"I'd rather have a house."

"Maybe later we will. Right now, this'll be fine. We'll all be together, and that's what's important."

Chapter 20

Kimba
Saturday, October 31

There are no costume parties or trick-or-treating. No bobbing for apples, cake walks, or any other popular harvest festival events. I don't even think the younger children know it's Halloween.

With this being the second year without acknowledging the day, at her young age, Naomi may have little recollection of what Halloween used to be like. I'm okay with that. I've never been a fan. Dressing up and scaring people hasn't ever been something I've considered fun. Especially since I know people can be scary without a mask.

An image of Eric Bohm immediately comes to mind. We've seen him way too much, since he also lives here at the Y. He keeps a calm smile on his face, and the sunglasses are often in place—his mask to attempt to portray a normal guy and not the sadistic torturer he is. A killer.

Seeing Bohm takes me back to times past. Times I'd rather forget. Rey notices it, I think. Since we've settled here, he's seemed to be more intense, more like he was when we were both working for the government. Different governments, of course, me the US and him the UK.

When we first met, Rey was so uptight. I thought he might break when he walked! But as I got to know him, I realized it was one of his coping mechanisms, a way to keep up a layer between the real Rey—or Reynard, as he was called then—and the business Rey. I was pregnant with Nicole before I started to see some of that layer chip away. When she was born, whatever was left was gone the minute he looked at her.

While Rey and I had an okay marriage, he truly shined at being a father. He still does, but I can see some of that layer of protection again. He's uptight and on edge more than he's been in years.

When we lost Nate, Rey was sad—more than sad—but it was different. Something is definitely off since we've arrived in Billings. I'd like to chalk it up to starting something new. A new job, new housing, so much all at once. And then there's Nicole.

Tomorrow, our oldest child turns eighteen. We're planning a small party during lunchtime. Then, as soon as we're finished, she'll move to the nearby Volunteer Unit barracks. They're training a fresh batch of recruits beginning on Monday.

At least she'll have several weeks of training before being given a new assignment. I'm hoping her new assignment will be in Billings. The weather should be in full force by then and keep her close by.

At the moment, winter's still mostly holding off. We've had a few light snows, but they didn't really stick. Within a day, the ground is bare. The I-90 bus is still running but has made it clear they will stop without notice depending on the weather, even if that stop is somewhere along the route. They may or may not be able to go again. I'd hate to be the drivers or conductors.

Without meteorologists and the twenty-four-hour news cycle, we're without weather reports . . . to a degree. There are plenty of people who claim to be able to forecast the weather based on the clouds and the way the air feels, but no one seems to have the talent our friend Atticus Dosen did. He was a true marvel.

There's another group using the *Old Farmer's Almanac* books preserved in the library to glean their weather predictions. They insist, if it snowed on a certain date for a certain percentage of days in the last fifty or one hundred years, it's likely to snow on the same date this year. There's a forecast written on a dry erase board in the cafeteria. So far, it's been right most days.

I'm trying to push Nicole joining the Volunteer Unit out of my mind. She, Sal, and I are spending time in the gym. When the YMCA was converted to housing for the Civilian Defenders, the official title bestowed on the nonmilitary shooters and doorkickers, most of the rooms and classes were modified to housing.

All the workout rooms with electric treadmills, stair climbers, elliptical trainers, and spin bikes were emptied of their nonworking machines. But the weight room and anything else not requiring electricity was preserved.

Like the Army, Marines, and new Volunteer Units, physical training is a necessary part of the Civilian Defenders' day. Chad and Rey are required to work out five days a week. Families are allowed to use the weight room and equipment during specific hours. I'll admit, the fact I'm relegated to family member status and not one of the Defenders was an issue.

When we went job hunting the day after arriving in Billings, Chad, Rey, and I presented as a team to see Colonel Ellis. Unfortunately, the colonel had fallen down a flight of stairs a few days earlier and was out on convalescent leave.

We weren't comfortable going to the major taking his place, so we went through the regular channels of finding work. We still presented as a team, but I was quickly rejected as a Defender on the basis of Naomi. As a rule, any woman with a child under the age of fourteen can't be a Defender unless her spouse or suitable family member is in a COS—Civilian Occupational Specialty—that is deemed safe.

Rey and I were not even given a choice on which of us wanted to be on the Defenders. Instead, my COS is Culinary Specialist. That's right, I work in the kitchen.

I rarely do anything special. More often than not, I'm really the dishwasher and not the cook, but it's fine. And at least we have what is considered premium housing and a desired duty system.

In many ways, Billings has set up a caste system. The official military—those in the actual Army, Marines, and even a scattering of Air Force and Navy, along with the Montana Guard Units, are at the top of the class.

Maybe even slightly higher in standing because we need them so much are the engineers and electricians working on the power stations. Getting the lights back on is a nationwide priority. The military is here to assist in the efforts by keeping the workers safe and ensuring they're fed.

Next in class are the Volunteer Units and Civil Air Patrol, which was up and running in Billings before the collapse and expanded in the very early days of the rebuilding effort. Then the Civilian Defenders and farmers or ranchers. Below that are a few different degrees of COS. It takes everyone to make this new world work, but it's clear—at least in Billings—not everyone is equal.

Nicole's doing dumbbell flies on a weight bench across the room when a man walks up to her and starts talking. She sits up and spins, causing him to move enough I can see his face.

Eric Bohm.

My heart's beating in my ears as I set down the medicine ball I've been working with and make a beeline for my daughter. I'm steps away when Sal calls over to her from a nearby location, asking if she can spot him while he does bench presses. She quickly agrees and moves from her bench and Bohm.

I start angling a different direction, not wanting to get any closer to Bohm than I already am, when he calls to me.

Squaring my shoulders, I turn to address him. "Yes?"

At least he's not in his stupid suit and tie today but is appropriately dressed for working out. He still looks incredibly crisp and clean. I resist the urge to look down at my faded tank top and cut-off yoga pants.

He gives me a smarmy smile. "It's nice seeing you again. Your daughter—she's the spitting image of you."

My nod is curt. Dismissive. I spin on the ball of my foot.

"Kimba?"

"Yes?" The question is also curt and dismissive. I have little use for Bohm and zero desire to converse with him.

"Let's find a way to bury the hatchet. In a small place like this, we're bound to see each other regularly."

"That's fine. We can see each other. I see people daily, but I don't talk to most of them."

"When you're working in the kitchen? That must really get to you."

I narrow my eyes.

"I mean, someone like you, with your skills relinquished to KP . . . you should be a Defender. Why didn't your husband give up his spot?"

"You are aware my husband has his own skills, right?"

He waves a hand. "Maybe so. I suppose you're right. The chauvinism in this newly formed base is apparent. I heard your daughter is joining up, tried for regular Army but was relegated to the volunteers."

"She tell you that?"

He shakes his head. "Just scuttlebutt going around."

"Rumors about my daughter?" *Why is anyone talking about Nicole?*

"Not much is kept secret around here. My guess is, if she's anything like you, they'll be changing their mind really quick and move her to one of the regular units. She'll advance quickly, just like you did. 'Course, we'll hope she doesn't flame out just as quickly."

"Like I did?"

He lifts a shoulder. "I wouldn't say that. You were railroaded . . . mostly."

"*Mostly*. Yes. Look, Bohm, I agree we'll see each other from time to time, and when we do, I'll be cordial, but— "

"Thank you. That's what I want. To move past any wrongdoing you think happened."

" *Think* happened? Right." I straighten my back. "I'm well aware of exactly what happened. I know your part in it too."

"My part?" He flutters his hands. "You should be throwing blame at that handler of yours. What was her name? Meagan Wrong?"

Knowing full well he knows Meagan's last name was Wright, I ignore him and turn away.

He grabs me by the arm. "I don't allow people to walk away from me."

With my heart instantly pounding, my adrenaline shoots to the top. I stare at his hand until he removes it, then continue walking.

"Kimba, I mean it. Think long and hard about what you are doing."

My strides are strong and purposeful as my heart beats a rapid and loud staccato. Twenty years ago, Eric Bohm was not only a deadly interrogator, but he was also a black belt in more than one martial art discipline. He used to brag he could kill a man with one finger. I believed him. Him touching me at all feels completely wrong.

I've calmed down only slightly when I reach Nicole and Sal.

"Mom?" Nicole lifts her eyebrows.

Sal sits up on the weight bench and looks past me. "We leaving?"

I force a light tone. "If you two are ready."

Sal's quickly off the bench and grabbing his hand towel to wipe it down.

Nicole steps to my side. "Sal said that was the Bohm guy we saw when we got off the bus. I didn't recognize him. Is it?"

"It's him."

"We're going to let him drive us out of the workout room?"

"No. I thought . . . aren't you finished?"

Nicole gives me a patient smile. "I wasn't, but I can be if necessary."

Back in our room, Bev and the younger girls are in the tiny sitting area consisting of a loveseat and a couple of kitchen chairs placed on an area rug. The twenty by forty-foot space, with its incredibly high ceiling, will never be used for its original purpose again, at least not without a major remodel.

The hardwood floors are hopelessly marred and scarred from the addition of wall dividers nailed into place to form sleeping rooms. Instead of providing real privacy, the thin walls only reach a height of eight feet and give the illusion of separation.

With a sitting area on one side by the front door, there are three rooms on that side and four on the other, connected by a central hall. No doors, just old curtains or sheets spread across rods.

Our beds are a mishmash of twin, full, and cots rounded up from who knows where. Rey and I squeeze together on a full-size mattress in our small room, while Bev and Chad have two twins in their space with barely enough room to walk between them. Kylie is next to them, then Emma, and Sal's at the end.

On our side of the hall, it's us, then Naomi, and then Nicole. When Nicole moves to the barracks, we've been told we may be given another roommate—someone we don't know that needs a place.

I've tried to be gracious about the idea, willing to accept a stranger living with us—near my little girl. But I don't like it. I totally get we're at the mercy of those above us, the ones who are tasked with the rebuilding efforts. They've given us the converted YMCA for housing. It's not like we own the space where we are living. *But still.*

Part of me wants to rant about this, declare to everyone who'll listen how unfair it is that a stranger will live with us. How it's bad enough we have paper thin walls and two families. Before, that's exactly what I would've done. I would've used my powers of communication to change minds, convince them of a different route. If that didn't work, I would've gone to management and lodged a formal complaint.

In the world we live in now, there's no avenue for communication. There's no way to protest. By agreeing to the work crews, which really wasn't a choice as much of an assignment, we agree to the rules of the housing.

133

In many ways, we've joined up just like Nicole will be doing. Rey and Chad may not really be part of the Army, but we get the same rules and regulations. The only difference is we can't be forced to move to a different town.

But Nicole will go where they say, when they say. At least we'll still have time together. I'm holding on to the fact this is winter and travel will be difficult. I'll have my little girl until early spring at least.

That's my prayer.

Chapter 21

Beverly
Thursday, November 12

Even though there are serious challenges with our new life in Billings and living at the Y, I do have to say, the choice to move here was right as far as food is concerned. The Civilian Defenders aren't on rations. Not what I would consider rations, anyway. Officially, they are, but they're extremely generous. More than enough to maintain weight and energy, even if people won't be getting fat.

Potatoes and turnips are a huge part of our meals, which means peeling is a huge part of my day. Often Kimba will be at my side, and we'll peel and talk as we sort out the world's problems, or at least those we see in Billings. Quietly, of course.

It's been made clear our husbands' positions aren't just about the skills and talents they bring to the cause. We're expected to contribute also. And not just by peeling potatoes and washing dishes. We're the moral fortitude, standing behind and beside the Civilian Defenders. We're to be a cohesive unit.

We may not be an official unit in the Armed Forces, but we follow many of the same rules. Contemptuous speech will not be tolerated, by the Defenders or their family. Kimba and I are very careful not to criticize command or the president's plan.

Not that we really know what the plan is. His speeches have become increasingly like sound bites or cheerleading sessions during his weekly Wednesday addresses that started a few weeks ago.

The Fireside Chats, as they're called in reference to similar addresses delivered by FDR during the Great Depression, are supposed to provide comfort and confidence in what we're going through, to encourage us to stand fast and help with the rebuilding efforts—to obey authority.

Last night's presidential address actually consisted of more detail than the previous ones. He listed Billings as one of the main hubs for reconstruction, along with Rapid City, South Dakota; Cleveland,

Ohio; and Tulsa, Oklahoma. He said all efforts will be concentrated in these locations in order to bring our country back to what it once was.

Better than it was, even.

The evacuation of the Wastelands continues with the help of the Volunteer Units. There's a rush to get as many people to safety as possible before the height of winter hits.

The president also made a special plea to anyone listening in the designated evacuation areas to move on their own to the nearest Clear Zone aid station. The Wasteland and the Clear Zone. No longer do we think of our country as the United States of America.

In fact, even the president seems to be going away from our country's official designation. Did he even say "God bless America" in last night's speech? I know he has before, but did he? I'll pay better attention next time.

The president's speech did spark quite the discussion in our small apartment, a discussion that caused enough division Kimba's still mad at me this morning. She'll shoot me a look every so often, but our usual banter is missing.

"Mom?" My head snaps to the door of the kitchen, where Nicole is leaning in. "Can I . . . is it okay to come in?"

Kimba sets down her peeler and scoots back her chair. "What's wrong?"

"Nothing. Well, it's not wrong. I'm just . . . we're going. They're sending us out."

My friend visibly deflates. "Now?"

"We're going to one of the aid stations near the Wasteland. We'll finish our training there."

"Where?"

"I'm not sure, not exactly. I do know we'll stay in the west. Another unit is heading east. At least, that's the rumor. You know they don't really give us more information than we absolutely need."

"But your training— "

She gives a partial shrug. "They think we're ready, enough at least, and they'll teach us more once we get where we're going. It'll be fine, Mom. Don't worry."

Kimba blinks several times. She's soon on her feet and wrapping her daughter in a tight hug. "I'm sure I'll still worry. You'll write?"

"As soon as I can. The others should be writing, too, all our friends we traveled with and Doris. I've sent them all letters to let them know they can find us at the Y."

"You, Nicole. Just you. That's . . ." As Kimba's eyes fill, she again pulls her daughter in tight. Kimba mumbles something into Nicole's hair.

"Today, after lunch . . . er, *chow*. I already stopped by the room and said goodbye to Naomi and the Pitney girls. Saw Sal hauling water on the way. I'm going to find Dad next. You know where he's working today?"

"I never know." Kimba steps back only slightly and turns toward me. "Bev, did Chad mention where they'd be today?"

"There's a food delivery arriving. I think they're providing security for it."

Kimba blinks at me a few times before turning back to Nicole. "Maybe you'll be able to find him."

"I'll try, but if I don't, please tell Dad I came to tell him goodbye. Make sure he knows. And I'll write as soon as I'm settled. Be safe, Mom. I love you all."

They embrace again. Nicole ends it and announces she has to hurry if she's going to find her dad.

After Nicole's gone, I go to my friend and wrap her in a hug. Kimba cries for several minutes before briskly declaring we'd better get the stupid potatoes peeled or our people won't get any *chow*. She lets out a small, weepy laugh. "Please tell me she'll be safe."

I take her hands. "You want me to pray with you?"

At her nod, I start us off. I'm rusty in conversing with God—like thirty years rusty. My words are awkward and trite in the beginning. I take in a deep breath through my nose, and something changes.

While I'm certainly no great Christian orator, my words become heartfelt and true. God is making a way in the desert . . . the desert of my heathen heart. When I'm done, tears are streaming down my face. Instead of adding her own words, Kimba croaks out an amen.

When our eyes meet, her own are rimmed in red. "Thank you, Bev. I never . . . your prayer was so . . . please help me get through this time of Nicole being gone."

"Yes, yes. I will."

After lunch is served and cleaned up, we trudge back to our room for our couple of hours break until we start the supper prep. As Nicole corrected herself, most everyone here calls it chow. Chad got a good laugh out of this, declaring that's just playing Army, and not recent Army either but the Korean War version. But it persists nonetheless, to the point my supervisor got after me for calling it lunch and not chow.

The girls are at afternoon school. The handful of children are taught by one of the wives, a former educator. It's only a few hours, three days a week, between lunch and supper so that it works around the teacher's full-time crew job. It's little more than the basics, but it does provide the girls something.

Kimba melts into the loveseat, pulling her feet underneath her. "I thought we'd have more time. What if a storm comes in while they're on the road?"

"Didn't she say when she visited last time they were training with the New Cavalry? They had horses and buggies . . . um, wagons?"

Kimba lifts her hands. "I guess. But Nicole isn't learning how to ride a horse, is she? She didn't mention that."

"No, maybe not. But I thought she said they'd be using them and wagons for transport. If so, then a little snow won't matter as much as if they were taking trucks or buses to get where they're going."

Kimba leans back and drapes her crossed arms over her forehead. "I'm ready to do the breathing relaxation thing with you."

Hiding my smile, I ask if she's sure. A few minutes later, she's stretched out on her camping mat with a cushion from the loveseat tucked under her knees and a sweatshirt behind her neck to act as a pillow. I'm sitting cross-legged beside her, leaning against the loveseat. Once I confirm she's comfortable, we begin.

As I instruct her to take in and let out three breaths, a feeling of peace and calm comes over me. I have a very specific script I follow and know what I should say next, but instead, I surprise myself.

"God loves you, Kimba. Neither death nor life, neither angels nor demons, neither the present nor the future, nor any powers, neither height nor depth, nor anything else in all creation, will be able to separate us from the love of God that is in Christ Jesus our Lord."

Kimba opens her eyes and turns her head to look at me. "I didn't . . . I thought these sessions were secular. I didn't know you used scripture."

"I . . . I don't. Not usually." I giggle self-consciously. "Go ahead and settle back in."

138

"What is that? Can we add it to our memorization list?"

"It's from Romans, and yes. Now relax. God breathed life into Adam. He is the source of all our breath. While we breathe and relax, I'll help you focus on Him. The peace of God, which surpasses all comprehension, will guard your heart and mind in Christ Jesus."

After an hour of deep breathing and prayer, I encourage her to roll to her side when she's ready to sit up. "How do you feel, sweet friend?"

"Exhausted . . . and exhilarated. Was that meditation?"

"Some people view it that way."

"Is that Biblical?"

"The Psalmist tells us to delight in the law of the Lord, to meditate on it day and night. Meditate means to reflect on something, to ponder it."

"And we've been reflecting on God. Pondering—ruminating— over His love for me." Her eyes meet mine. "For us."

"I hate to rush you, but we'd best get moving. Time to peel more potatoes."

She lets out a laugh as she rolls to her feet. "Thank you for this. I'm still concerned about Nicole, but you're right. God's peace is guarding my heart and mind."

"Remember that. When the worry starts, take three deep breaths, let each out slowly, and think of the peace from today. Remember the verses that offer us peace, love, and hope. We'll do this again next week."

At supper, Chad and Rey sit with the children at our usual table, far against the wall away from the three doors entering the room. The children have their backs to the doors, while Rey and Chad sit side by side facing out. No surprise there.

As soon as Kimba and I are finished serving food, we take our plates and join them at the table. Rey looks beaten down. In the food line, as I'd plopped mashed turnips on his plate, he said Nicole had found him.

Now, as we sit together, he says he asked around and she's definitely heading west. He thinks somewhere along the Idaho-Washington state line where there's been some trouble with people clashing.

Chad leans back in his chair, crossing his arms behind his head. "Seems odd they'd move them out now. We could use them here."

My fork pauses halfway to my mouth, a soggy carrot falling off. "Why?"

"It's nothing." Rey waves a hand. "We'll take care of it."

"Take care of what?"

My husband clears his throat and then leans forward. He lowers his voice. "There're rumors of a rebellion brewing. Seems some people think they're being treated poorly in the rebuilding efforts. There're always people who think they should get more than they deserve."

"Deserve?" I don't leave the Y often but have seen deliveries come in, and some of the delivery folks look like they've missed way too many meals. "You mean because they don't want to be hungry?"

We were hungry last winter, very hungry, but we heard food was better here, that the workers were being fed and treated well. It's true, no one goes hungry in the Y. But what about the other workers? Are they being taken care of?

Chad's entire body shrugs. "Hard telling. I'll agree there is some . . . disparity. But it's the way things are for now. We'll get it rebuilt and then it'll improve. They just need to be patient."

Sal stares at his plate. "Hard to be patient when you're hungry."

I shift my gaze toward him. "Do you know something about this?"

He gives a slow shrug. "Some. I heard people talking when I was filling the water. Did you know that in parts of the city, some of the housing assignments have to walk a mile to the nearest well? There're a few places they tried to drill but couldn't hit water there, so . . ." He shrugs again. "I don't even understand why they set things up the way they did. Using an old casino as a livestock barn is weird."

Nodding my agreement, I put down my fork. "It is weird, but bringing some of the livestock to the people makes sense." I turn to Chad. "It's, what, a few milk cows and goats, chickens for eggs, and rabbits for food?"

"Some chickens get butchered too." Rey nods. "But, yeah, just things for daily use mainly. It does make sense to have the milk nearby. Without refrigeration, we don't need to be transporting it from the edge of town where they've set up the farms. The converted casino is just one of the buildings turned barns or processing plants in the city."

"Wherever they're housing people, they're setting up similar operations," Chad says. "The downtown one, though, that's where we're hearing most of the grumbling. Especially considering the widows and orphans are housed nearby in an old antique mall. It's a sore spot.

"They sent a group to meet with the colonel, to try and get more aid for those who most need it. But Ellis is still out of commission, and the acting major, a guy named Dudrock, said he isn't negotiating. I haven't met Ellis yet, but from everything I hear, he'll get it worked out when he's back. Rey?"

"Maybe." Rey shakes his head. "They do have a point, and they feel like they're being ignored. But I'm not sure they really have the expertise to put much of an uprising together. I think they're just grumbling about things, hoping someone will listen."

Chapter 22

Kimba
Wednesday, November 25

There's no post office, at least not like there was before. Here, in our section of Billings, we take any outgoing mail to what used to be the post office and leave it in a wooden box set up in the front section, trusting our letters will end up where we want them.

An incoming box is also set up. With no postal workers or letter carriers—that's not part of this phase of the reconstruction efforts—mail is taken by travelers. An individual, family, or group heading out of Billings will check one of the wooden boxes scattered about town and see if any of the addresses are along their route. It's purely a trust thing.

There is a rumor postal service is planned for the spring. As is getting the trains running again. The Downtown Station Post Office will likely be one of the first to set up official business. The historic building, constructed in the early 1900s, is near the railway and gives a prime location for receiving mail. I'll be surprised if it happens, considering mail and trains are secondary to electricity. There's no ETA for electricity here in Billings.

During last week's presidential address, he said Cleveland is once again leading the nation on lighting. Just like in 1879, when Cleveland inventor Charles Brush lit up their public square, they're being called the City of Light. It's minimal, and only a few blocks are working, but in the race for electricity—the race for a return to normalcy—they're making great strides.

Cleveland's success has the crews in Billings increasing their efforts. There's even been a push to add more workers. Not necessarily engineers, though they'd like those, but laborers and helpers. Several of the Civilian Defenders were poached for the electrical crew. I was talking with one of the wives, who was almost giddy over the change. While the Defenders is a respected and well-cared-for group, the electricians—or as they're commonly called, the E-Crew—hold the key to our future.

One of the Defenders said he heard from someone on the E-Crew that Denver was making strides toward getting their lights on. I'd be lying if the idea of Denver being rebuilt didn't make my heart beat faster.

Whether it's true or just a rumor is the question. As far as I know, the president has never mentioned Denver in any of his addresses, but the electrician said it was all over the amateur radio transmissions in the spring. But he also said he hasn't heard anything more about Denver lately. Still . . . could we someday return to our home?

When we first lost Nate, all I wanted was to get back to our condo. To have it the same as we left it, with pictures on the walls and photo albums in the drawers. To see my sweet son's smiling face. If Denver is being rebuilt, and if the road between here and there is safe and secure. My want could become reality. Maybe not immediately, but perhaps next summer.

Or maybe not. When we'd asked Captain Mercer about Denver, it didn't sound like it was being rebuilt. Who knows what the truth is? These days, rumors and innuendos seem to be more common than facts.

Rey and Chad have had quiet and easy duties so far, not yet getting into the thick of any issues. Not so for all the Defenders. A sentry post on the south side of downtown was attacked a few days ago. One man was killed before the attackers were neutralized. The assailants were unknown and weren't believed to be Billings residents, but it still shook us up.

While I'm under no illusions Billings and this assignment is safe, it's still difficult to know my husband has a target on his back when he's doing his job—his job to keep the rest of the Billings's workers safe. He and Chad are often assigned to the nearby power station as security. While we don't think it would happen, it's possible some misguided folks might decide turning the lights back on isn't a good idea.

The lights, the trains, the mail . . . all of it is at the mercy of the weather. While winter held back long enough for my daughter's unit to leave town, that's no longer the case. It started snowing a week ago, dumping enough snow to throw us full into winter. The roads are now impassable, and the buses have officially stopped running until spring. It's unlikely we'll receive a letter from Nicole until the buses start up once again.

Even so, there's a break in the weather today. I plan to trudge the mile between here and the Downtown Station Post Office to see if there's anything with my name on it. Tomorrow is Thanksgiving, and I can't think of anything better than to receive a letter from my daughter.

Rey said there was a group of travelers who arrived from the west a couple of days ago, coming in just like an old-fashioned wagon train. It's a long shot they were anywhere near where Nicole has ended up, but I can't help myself. Just as soon as we get the lunch service finished and the cleaning done, I'm going.

While Bev and the other women fill plates in the serving line, I work on the dishes. I asked Sal to bring me extra water before lunch started so I wouldn't be slowed down waiting for it.

The old-fashioned wood cookstove, used for heating water and cooking, along with providing nominal heat to the building, was found in one of the many antique shops in the area. When the Army decided the Y would make a good place for housing, it was brought here along with a couple other woodstoves.

Why they decided to turn the YMCA into housing, I'll never understand. In some ways, it seems letting each family fend for themselves in individual houses would've been smarter. Chad laughed and said that's not the Army way.

While the higher-ranking officers do have their own homes, most everyone else is grouped together. It does make it easier for food. The deliveries are brought here, and we prepare food for everyone. It reminds me of the phrase "many hands make light work." It was the same thing we did in Bakerville last winter.

A popping noise sounds from the dining hall. Another pop is followed by a scream. My vision narrows as I dry my sopping hands and simultaneously drop to a crouch. *Naomi.* She's at our table with Emma, Kylie, and Sal.

My hand is still slick as I unholster my Glock. Not slick enough to stop the motion, but it's noticeable. I quickly move the weapon to my other hand while I dry my right on my sweater sleeve.

The chaos in the dining area has increased, with more gunshots and screams erupting by the second.

Like me, Bev and Sal are also wearing sidearms. We put them on each day, same as our shoes and socks. It's become part of who we are.

I peak around the doorway, into the hall. The dining room isn't connected to the kitchen but rather down the hall at the other end of the building.

There're three men between me and where I need to be, their faces covered with balaclavas or ski masks. One's at each exit door from the dining room, blocking the escapes as they lean against the door jamb and rhythmically squeeze the triggers on their tactical rifles. With the room closed off, it's like shooting fish in a barrel.

With a split second to plan, I launch myself from my crouch to a full run with my Glock at the ready. I'm only a few feet from the nearest guy before he turns toward me. I react by squeezing the trigger three times. He goes down on the second.

The next guy spins and starts shooting wildly. My heart's pounding as I dart into the doorway the guy I killed was guarding. Inside the dining hall, I move behind the nearest cover: an overturned chair.

"Let's go! Retreat! Retreat!" someone yells.

As I search out the voice, the man I think was yelling lets out a scream as he grabs his shoulder. Another man, wearing a bandanna over his face, helps the injured man to the door, firing wildly as he goes.

I line up my front sight on the man and pop off two rounds. He flinches and stops shooting but doesn't go down. A miss.

Another of the assailants calls out for retreat.

Within seconds, the shooting stops as the crying and screams continue. I check my area before scooting forward to an overturned table. A woman is lying there, pressing both hands to her stomach.

I'm not wearing my daypack, having gotten out of the habit in the building. I frantically search for something to stop the bleeding and find a cloth napkin balled up nearby.

"It's . . . bad." Her eyes are unfocused. "Too . . . much."

The growing puddle of blood surrounding her agrees with her assessment. She sucks in another breath. It rattles on the way out, then stops partway.

"Report!" a voice calls out.

The next few minutes are chaotic as the reports come in. People call out their names and room assignments, along with their condition and the condition of those around them.

145

I want more than anything to get to the table my family always sits at, but I know better than to move when people can still be jumpy and have itchy trigger fingers. It's a good way to get shot by friendly fire.

When there's a lull in the responses, I call out, "Kimba Hoffmann, Racquetball Court Three— "

"Mommy!" Naomi calls. "Mommy, Sal's hurt!"

I suck in a deep breath. "Kimba Hoffmann, moving from cover. Do not shoot. Repeat. Do not shoot."

"Copy that!" several voices call out.

Our table is flipped over. Bev's already there. Sal's leaning against the wall, his eyes closed as Beverly applies pressure to his arm. Thankfully, the blood is considerably less than the lady who was shot in the gut.

Emma and Kylie are huddled nearby, wrapped in each other's arms. Naomi's sitting near them, her legs pulled to her chest. She gives me a tearstained smile when she sees me. "I knew you'd come soon."

"I'm here, baby. You're not hurt?"

"Not me. Just Sal."

"I'm okay." His voice is weak.

Bev tightens the dishcloth around his arm, causing him to wince. "Not much more than a scratch. He'll be fine." She gives him a smile.

"Kimba?" I swivel my head to look at Eric Bohm. "We'll have medical here shortly."

"Who were they?"

He shakes his head. "Townsfolk. I recognize a couple of the dead."

"They had their faces covered, Mommy. Then they just started shooting."

Bev leans back on her heels. "How'd they get in here? What about the guards at the door?"

"Dead. Took them out quietly. They knew when to hit us, when we'd be at lunch."

"Lunch is mostly the women and children." Bev pales. "Why?"

Bohm purses his lips and touches his chin. "Making a statement, I'd guess. Plus, they probably figured it'd be easier."

I pull Naomi close. "There's a lady by the other entrance. I can't remember her name, but she didn't make it."

Bohm shakes his head. "We lost too many. It's terrible what they did, but in some ways, I can see it."

146

"You can see them attacking women and children?" My voice is tight.

"I can see them wanting a change. They're treated as second- and third-class citizens in most cases. The haves and the have nots. You've seen it before, right? These types of rebellions are nothing new. Not only are they not new, they're necessary."

I flare my eyes at Bohm, then turn to Bev. "Do you want to take the girls back to our place? I'll stay with Sal."

She gives Bohm a pointed look. "Yes, good idea."

I pull Naomi into another quick hug and tell her I'll see her soon. Bev hustles the girls out of the dining room, instructing them to keep their eyes on the ground and not look around.

I turn my attention to Sal. "You doing okay?"

Bohm squats next to me. "Looks like it's just a scratch. You'll be fine, kid."

Sal responds with a hesitant nod. "Hurts."

"Yeah, bullets do. Even just a skim. Right, Kimba?"

"You want to lay down?" I take my sweatshirt off to form a pillow. Once Sal's reclining, I turn my attention to Bohm. "There are others who probably need help."

"Good thing the medics will be here soon."

"Do you need to go, Kimba? It's okay. I'm okay." Sal's eyes are wide as he shivers.

I should've put the sweatshirt over him. He's looking shocky.

Bohm notices and peels off his suit jacket. Even in here, in the dining hall of the former YMCA, he's wearing a tie and jacket. His shoes are out of place, though. Instead of dress shoes or even loafers, he's in well-worn work boots with heavy tread. "You've always been a patriot, Kimba. At least you were. Did things change when you married the Brit?"

"Nothing changed."

He leans in closer to me. "Then I'm sure you can see how wrong this is. How the rebuilding efforts are going to put us right back where we were. How they're doing nothing but separating people. The changes we've had in the last year and a half were necessary. Needed. Well, to a point. The nukes, though . . ." He lets out a noisy sigh. "Those weren't needed, but here we are. It's time to make a stand. These men, that's what they were doing."

"You sound like you admire them."

147

"I don't agree with attacking women and children."

I push a lank of hair away from Sal's eyes and send him a smile. "I should hope not."

"I don't agree with it. But sometimes it's necessary." Bohm effortlessly rises to his feet and strides away.

Chapter 23

Beverly
Saturday, November 28

The massacre left a dozen wounded and took the lives of seven people, including one child and her mom, along with two of the attackers.

Sal's wound was cleaned up and given a couple of stitches. Even though the military has medical supplies and medications, including painkillers, he's only using the tincture Kimba has for pain, along with raw honey and garlic oil to ward off infection. Sal's injuries are relatively minor compared to some, allowing the Army docs to save their limited meds for others who need it more.

The number of people killed is likely to increase in the coming days.

We're all a wreck. Emma's nightmares have returned. Kylie and Naomi are also having bad dreams. Yesterday, I had the girls, Sal, and Kimba all stretch out for a group session. I'm not in much better shape than they are, and we needed the time. I should've done a second session for the men when Chad and Rey returned home from work.

They are mad. Chad's jaw is continually clenched. I've warned him he's going to break a tooth if he doesn't relax. And that's all he needs. While we do have some medical care, I'm not sure there's an operating dentist in Billings.

The planned Thanksgiving feast was on a much lesser scale. With the dining hall out of operation, we're making food and lining it up on tables in the hallway, serving there so people can go and eat wherever.

Our family has decided we'll take our meals in our small apartment. It isn't ideal without a dining table, but hopefully it's safer, at least until the people behind the attack can all be found and brought to justice. Then maybe we can be assured this won't happen again.

Today's my half day off. I did breakfast prep and service this morning and am now done for the day. Chad's also on a half day, not because it was planned—requested days off aren't something that happen for the Civilian Defenders—but it's just how it worked out.

The weather is decent, so we're taking our girls and Naomi for a walk. Chad found an old pamphlet depicting a walking tour through historic Billings. While I'm sure it's not nearly the same as it was, it might be fun. When he first suggested it, I said no, that it'd be too dangerous. Keeping Kylie and Emma locked up in their room seems the only way to keep them safe.

Chad gave me a patient smile. He understands how I feel but also knows it's not reasonable to keep them under lock and key. One of the dead attackers was recognized as being a worker in the sanitation department from a crew near the MetraPark Arena—on the other side of Billings and well away from where we live and plan to walk. But it still concerns me. They knew our schedule.

Kimba said that creepy Eric Bohm told her he can understand how something like this could happen, how women and children could be attacked and killed.

I don't understand it at all. If the attackers have a problem with the way things are, why not go after those making the changes? Go after the military, not the innocents working and just trying to get by— same as them. I can't say I particularly like the way the rebuilding efforts are going either. There's a definite class division and separation between the people.

"When will Dad get back?" Kylie asks.

"Soon. Anytime. Then we'll go for our walk. You know where your coat is?"

She gives me a look before pointing to the pile nearby. The organization in this small place is terrible. There's one closet for all of us to share and a handful of hooks at the end of the hallway.

We each have a small dresser, which doubles as a nightstand. The only good thing is we don't have many clothes, just what we carried with us and what we've been able to get in the free store with our ration coupons. At least we have decent winter gear, thanks to Chad's insistence and the things he'd stashed and collected.

Soon turns into over an hour. I've just about given up on Chad coming home in time for our walk when the door squeaks open. He gives me a tired smile. "Looks like snow. We can still go if you all are ready. How's Sal?"

150

"I'm good," he calls from his bedroom. There's no such thing as privacy or quiet conversations in this place. We adults have taken to stowing away in a supply closet down the hall when we need a private chat. That or what we're doing today, walking outside.

"Feel up to a short walk?"

The pause is several seconds. "You know, I think I do. Give me five?"

"It'll take that long for everyone to get their coats on."

Chad's wrong. It took ten minutes to get coats and gloves on. Kylie could only find a single glove. The second was under the book they'd been reading. How it got there is a mystery for the ages.

Outside the Y, Chad reaches for my hand. As we pause to wait for Emma to adjust the lace on her boot, I whisper to him. "Are you sure this is okay? Safe?"

He nods and pulls me close. "We're fine. I promise. We need this."

We walk hand in hand while the children trudge along in front of us. The several inches of snow make their boots essential. Sal lets the girls walk ahead, the two youngest chattering and Emma more solemn. Chad noticeably slows our pace and puts distance between us and the kids.

I tilt my head at him and raise my eyebrows. "What?"

He lets out a rattly breath. "I'm glad we're out of there. Those walls are really starting to close in on me. Seriously closing in."

Snorting out a laugh, I shake my head. "You leave every day. Try having your work and homelife all in the same place."

He bobs his head several times and mutters an agreement. "I needed to talk to you. How would you feel about leaving here?"

I scoff. "And go where? It's winter, remember? You said— "

He increases the pressure on my hand. "Shh. I know. I thought . . . this isn't what I thought it'd be. The reconstruction, it's . . ." His head swivels back and forth.

My anger is quick and hot. I feel like screaming. We left Bozeman to be a part of this, and now . . .

"Do you see what's happening, Bev?"

"You mean with the massacre? Yes, I definitely saw that. I was right there, remember? Our *children* were right there. They knew the little girl. She was the same age as Kylie. They had classes together."

He works his jaw. "I shouldn't have brought you here. We should've stayed in Bozeman."

"It's a little late for that."

"Can we roll down the hill?" Kylie calls, pointing to a slight slope.

I force my response to be light. "You'll get wet. Maybe on the way back, so you don't get too cold." I lower my voice. "Did you bring the map for the walk?"

"Oops. Sorry. I forgot. Let's just . . . this is fine, right? We'll just walk and then we can turn around and come back this way and let them play on the hillside. Yeah, this is fine."

Chad's still holding my hand. I want to pull it away and pout. We could've stayed in Bozeman. With Gary Searle gone, it would've been much better.

My stomach lurches as I remember the days after I told Chad about the trouble with Searle. Finding words wasn't easy. And, probably to make myself look better, I started with what happened in the cleaning room. How he raped me. Chad almost lost it, wanting to go after the man. It was when I confessed to our relationship a few years earlier that things changed. He was rightly hurt over it.

He still wanted to kill him for what he'd done to me recently, that didn't change. Chad understands there's a big difference between being willing and not. Searle and I had come close to a physical relationship in which I was a willing participant. By the grace of God, it didn't happen, but our emotional ties were still very wrong. When Chad found out Searle had left Bozeman, I think it took a weight off him just like it did me.

Coming clean about the relationship with Searle has changed things between us. We're better than we've been in years. The terrorist attacks and EMP brought us closer but removing the secret between us made us whole again. Chad's desire to move to Billings, to be a part of the reconstruction efforts, wasn't really what I wanted, but being with him was. But now . . . "You want to go back to Bozeman?"

He works his jaw again. "That's not what I was thinking. You know Eric Bohm?"

"The creepy guy?"

"Why do you call him creepy?"

"Have you looked at him? Who in the world wears a suit these days? And a tie? Seriously. That is creepy."

Chad coughs out a laugh. "Maybe so. You know we knew him from before?"

"Kimba told me. She told me *lots* about him."

152

"About how they dated?"

I dip my head. "And how they broke up, the things she learned about him, and the way he was. He is not a nice guy. She said he tortured people. That was his job."

"He got information out of people. Needed information."

"Kimba said he enjoyed it."

"Well . . . it was his job."

"Why are you asking me if I know him?"

Chad sucks in his top lip, chewing on the hairs of his scraggly mustache. The facial hair doesn't really suit him. There're several clean-shaven faces in Billings. The bulk of the officers shave, as was the standard before our world fell apart. Now they're allowed to wear a beard, but it must be kept neatly trimmed, not wild like my man's.

I asked Chad how they shave since disposable razors have gone the way of the dinosaur, just like disposable everything. He said the old-fashioned way, with a straight blade of some sort. "I think Bohm's part of the resistance."

My head is swimming as I try and absorb what he's saying. "The resistance? The ones who attacked us?"

"I don't think so. I think those were . . . someone else. A different group. Not as organized. And maybe the resistance isn't the right thing to call Bohm and his bunch. I think maybe . . ." Chad lets out a breath. "I'm going to sound crazy."

I squeeze his hand. "I'm used to your brand of crazy."

"Yeah, well, this is a doozy. I think he's been a part of it all along."

"A part of it . . . a part of what?"

"*All* of it."

I watch the girls. Kylie and Naomi are farther ahead than they were. Sal's with them as they stop and look at something in one of the trees. Even Emma seems interested as she points to a branch. I slow to a stop and turn to look at my husband. "The terrorist attacks? The EMP?"

His body shudders. "I think so. You know how Jankins said they were meeting up in Billings? It makes sense they'd both be a part of it. They worked together. But there's more. I don't think it went as planned or started when Bohm expected. He said he was on an assignment. Freelance work, not with Jankins.

"He'd known it could start but expected it to be later. When the planes went down, he knew it was *on* but thought he'd have more time, so he tried to finish the assignment. He ended up stuck and couldn't make the rendezvous, which wasn't supposed to be Billings. This was a surprise."

"A surprise. But Jankins was coming here too?"

He tilts his head. "I guess they saw certain signs and figured this was as good a place as any to meet up."

"I don't understand. Bohm was part of the attacks?"

"Mom? Are we stopping?" Emma calls.

My mind is going in a hundred different directions. I attempt a smile. "No, we're still walking." Chad and I resume a slow pace, staying well back. "How do you know?"

"He pretty much told me. Rey too. Said there's more happening here than we're aware of. And it's not what the plan was. He hinted the president was supposed to do things differently. The reconstruction efforts we're seeing aren't what was planned."

"The president of the United States was part of this? Part of millions dying?"

Chad takes off his stocking cap and runs a hand through his too-long hair. "Sounds like it. Maybe."

"All the talk of conspiracies, they were true?"

"I don't know, Bev. Bohm was cryptic, but yeah. I think so. I think there was a group pulling the strings. Rey and I, we'd been approached last year by another guy we worked with. He'd hinted— "

"You knew about this? Last year?"

"No, no." He crumples the cap between his hands. "Not really. He said something big was coming and we should get on board. But the guy was always a blowhard. And we didn't really know what he was talking about. Now I wonder . . . I don't know, honey. I don't know."

"Why is Bohm telling you this now?"

"To get us on board. To bring the country back to what it should be. Not the way it's been going, but the plans they'd made to start fresh."

"By killing almost everyone?"

"I think something may have gone wrong."

"You think? Really, Chad? Something may have gone wrong?" My voice is coming out like a squeaky door. I take a deep breath and let it out slowly. Tears sting my eyes. "You're saying Eric Bohm, and not just him but a group of people including the president of the

United States of America, knew about this and were a part of this. You may have even known about it— "

"No, no. I didn't know. Not then. I've wondered if maybe . . . but really, until Bohm pulled us aside, I didn't put it all together."

"The prepping. Was it because you thought this might happen?"

"Well, yes. But not in the way you think. I started after we infiltrated the group down south. Remember? The ones calling themselves the End of the Line?

"The ones Kimba was undercover with."

"Right. That was years ago."

"But you got more serious about it recently. About, what, five years before the planes were shot down?"

"Because of everything happening, the way our country was going." He straightens his cap and shoves it back on his head.

"It just didn't seem sustainable to keep going down the path we were on. And if getting a well pump from that guy in Belgrade could give you and the girls water, I wanted to do it. If stockpiling food meant you didn't starve . . . I didn't know, Bev. I worried but didn't know anything. I wasn't a part of this. I promise you. If I was, do you think we would've lost our house? Our supplies?"

The sun peeks out from behind a cloud. As it lights up the sky, the dark band to the west seems to increase. It will snow again. Whatever it is Chad is thinking we should do, wherever it is he wants us to go, that's not going to happen anytime soon. We're here in Billings until the snow's gone. "What do you have in mind?"

Chapter 24

Kimba
Thursday, December 3

"You can't trust him."

"Kimba, please." Rey rests a hand on my arm. "He helped the kids during the massacre."

"Helped? He was there. He didn't help. Sal is the one who flipped the table and made sure the girls were behind it, not Bohm."

Rey screws up his face and lifts a hand in the air. "Naomi says he did."

I shake my head and narrow my eyes. "This is the first I've heard of Eric Bohm doing anything to help our family. Don't you think Bev would've said something?"

"I don't know. You know how things can get in times of stress. Bev's focus was probably on her girls and Naomi, even Sal. She might not have seen what was going on around her."

"Either way, no. Just no. Eric Bohm only does what's good for Eric Bohm. Not to mention, what he's suggesting is treason. I've been accused of that before. I'm not doing it again."

I watch my husband's face for what feels like a very long time as he stares over my shoulder. A puff of steam trails from his mouth. "According to Bohm, Colonel Ellis is the treasonist." Rey doesn't meet my eyes, just keeps looking off in the distance. A slight smile forms on his face.

I turn on the park bench in time to see Naomi throw her hands up as she reaches the bottom of the playground slide. From the top of the slide, Kylie calls out, "Watch me!" Emma's nearby swaying slowly on a swing, her feet touching the ground with each pass. The only way to have a private conversation with my husband is well away from the YMCA.

This conversation is one I could do without. What he's suggesting, what Bev and Chad want to do . . . I breathe in through my nose and instantly regret it as the cold burns my nostrils.

Winter is still mild in comparison to last year. The snow's been off and on, dropping a few inches and then retreating and warming up until a day or two later. I still check the mail, waiting and praying for a letter from Nicole.

Rey nudges my shoulder with his. "What time do you need to be back?"

"I still have time. I'm only serving dinner tonight. You?"

"All-company meeting after dinner."

"What you're suggesting . . . I don't think I can do it."

"I know, it's a lot."

"A lot? That's the understatement of the year. You want to take the word of a known liar, a person whose job it was to manipulate people."

"Well, in fairness, his job was to get the truth."

My grunt is very unladylike. "Using any means possible. How many times did he get the *actual* truth? You know the statistics on torture to get reliable facts. It's low. Besides, did you ever get a clear answer from him as to why he is here? What's he doing in Billings?"

"He said he was in the region on business. Look, Kimba, I still think you should talk to him directly. Ask him the questions if it's bothering you."

"It is bothering me! All of it. He knows too much. And you didn't hear him the day of the massacre. Naomi may be right, he may have helped them. But he said sometimes women and children need to die."

Rey looks at his boot before tapping it lightly on the ground, knocking off a chunk of snow. "Pretty sure I've heard you say something similar before."

"No. No." Memories of a conversation about a long-past war we had no part in play through my mind like a movie reel. I may have said something similar, but it's different now. "That's not the same."

A trill of laughter carries across the cold air. I reposition so I can watch the girls as they run and throw little snowballs at each other. Emma's still on the swing, a contented smile on her face as she watches them. She's made a good recovery from the ergotism, but she still gets tired easily.

"He was part of the original nationwide attacks. Somehow, he knew about them all, right?"

"I'd say that's a fair assumption." Rey nods.

"Start again, at the beginning. You and Chad have been cooking these plans up for days now, right?"

"It's not like that, Kimba. We weren't— "

I raise a hand. "Save it. You brought Bev into it. You think I haven't seen the looks and whispers? I knew when you asked me to go for a walk and when you wanted the kids to stay back in the room. I knew then."

At least he has the decency to look guilty. "I'm glad you said we should bring them. The outing does them good too. Plus, you were right about not letting them out of our sight."

"Exactly, Rey. Don't you see? We aren't safe at the Y. Look what happened! The thought of leaving them there when we are gone . . ." I shake my head a little too vigorously.

His sigh is loud. "The beginning, huh? Everything blends together so smoothly, it's hard to tell exactly where the beginning is. Bohm came to us a few days after we started on the CD. Chad and I were in our all-day training, the one where they introduced us to the rules and the job." He looks to me for confirmation.

I nod to indicate I remember the training day.

"Right. So, he asked if we knew what was happening here, if that's how we ended up in Billings. Right then, I figured there was something going on. I told him we knew the reconstruction was focused here, and we thought our skills might be useful."

I snort. "Yeah, my dishwashing and potato peeling skills are what's going to put this country back on its feet."

He gives me a tight little smile. "Bohm point blank asked if we were here for the assemblage. I started to say no, we didn't know anything about the gathering. Chad jumped in and said, all huffy like, 'What do you know about that?' Turns out he knew plenty, and he was happy to tell."

I shake my head again. "I don't buy it. Bohm wouldn't just tell you. No, that's not how he operates. He told you what he thought you should hear and nothing more."

"He knew things, Kimba. I think he really was a part of the attacks. It was an inside job, forces within the US who turned against our country. And I think the president was part of it, but then he got cold feet and couldn't follow through.

"One thing, Bohm did tell us he didn't know in advance about the assassinations of the US Senators and Representatives. He waved it off as a piece that was performed by another group within his group, but he did seem . . . " Rey screws up his mouth. "Let's just say, I'm not entirely sure he believes the assassinations were his group's doing."

"So the deep state Donnie McCullough used to rant on about is real."

Rey lets out a soft laugh. "Donnie did have some passion, didn't he?"

Rey and I share a smile as we remember our former traveling companion, hopefully living happily ever after with his new bride Leanne Monroe and her two children in Lewistown. If the mail ever starts working as it should, maybe they'll receive the letters Nicole wrote them and we'll get a response.

"Not the deep state, though, at least not as Donnie understood it. Bohm said over and over they were patriots."

"He used the same word with me. 'You've always been a patriot, Kimba.' That's what he said." I choose not to add how he asked if marrying a Brit made me less committed to my country.

"I know you love this country. So do I. One main reason we've ended up here in Billings is to get the United States back on its feet."

"Not this way, Rey. I'm telling you, if Eric Bohm is involved, it's not right. He's a snake. Not to mention, how in the world can he and his group think the way to save the country is to destroy it?"

"He said they needed a big shakeup."

"Ha! I guess an EMP and killing more than fifty percent of the US population is a shakeup. Not to mention nuking both coasts. Yeah, way to shake things up."

"Also a mistake."

I narrow my eyes. "What do you mean?"

"The nukes, they weren't supposed to happen. Or if they were, he didn't know about them. And I— " He lets out a long breath. "I think I believe him."

"Why?"

"Because . . ." Rey licks his lips before wiping his nose with the knuckle of his gloved index finger. "Because they had a plan for the port cities, a plan they can no longer use after the ground detonations."

The air rushes out of me as I lean back on the bench. "An invasion?"

"Yes."

"And you think they are patriots? What I don't understand is how could Eric Bohm know so much about this? He was a . . . a nothing. Sure, he had a special skillset that caused people to cringe, but to be involved in a global conspiracy? I mean, that's what this is, right? Global?"

"Shh. Keep your voice down. I don't know how he knows. Like you, I thought he was a hired man. That's why he was here, in the Rocky Mountain states. He was on a job. I think things got messed up. He said it started early and he wasn't where he was supposed to be."

"I want to talk to him. Look him in the eye when I ask him questions."

"Would it do any good? You've said yourself he's a trained liar."

"Exactly. But so am I. So are you. Between us, maybe we can . . . look, I don't know. I don't even want any part of this. Rey, this isn't who we are. We shouldn't even be talking about doing something that may slow the return to some sense of normalcy. That's what Bohm wants, right? To oust the military and . . . and then what?"

"And then start a recovery that puts people on equal footing. He says by segregating out the groups, we'll be right back where we were. What they're doing here in Billings, maybe in other cities, too, is doing nothing but provoking people. It's causing people to distrust the military, to distrust the police, our group of Civilian Defenders. It's . . ."

"It's nothing new. The same thing happened for years. People were being turned against each other. One race against another. Civilians against the police or military. The rioting with no consequences for the mass amounts of destruction those riots caused. But again, Rey, this is not who *we* are. Have you prayed about this?"

He screws up his face again and stares off at the girls on the playground. His voice is a whisper. "No. Not really."

"That might be the place we should start, don't you think?" I cringe at the scolding tone of my voice. "I mean— "

He lifts a hand. "You're right. That should've been the first thing I did. Let's talk to God about this. Then we'll talk to Bohm?"

"Pray first. Then *maybe* talk to Bohm. Maybe God will give us a burning bush and we'll know exactly what to do."

He snorts out a laugh. "Wouldn't that be something? I could use a divine manifestation."

"I know God has a plan for us. We just need to listen to Him. I can't believe . . ." Tears sting my eyes. "I can't believe we came all this way. Lost Nate, and now Nicole has gone to who knows where. I want to trust God. We need to go to Him. We may not have our answers today, Rey, but we have to listen and be still."

Rey takes my hand and bows his head. He gives me a few moments to adjust before he begins his petitions. "Father God, I want to thank you for . . . for being You. And for my wife, who has been growing in You and seems to hear Your voice much more clearly than I do." He gives my hand a squeeze.

"All I really want, Lord, is for my family to be safe. My friends to be safe." Rey's body relaxes next to mine as he releases a breath. "The rest is all secondary. You see all. You know all. You know this situation much better than we ever could. I don't want to follow any man but to follow You and Your plan. It's so easy to get caught up in *things*, to think what is going on around us is unfair.

"When all this started, with what seemed to be an isolated event, we didn't really know You. Not in the way we do now, the way we should. Even though I feel like I know You, there's still so much I need to learn. Trusting You and going to You first to start with. We live in a fallen world. We always have, but it's become increasingly apparent in these last couple of years.

"I now see it was that way even before the attacks started. We were going down a path of destruction as things seemed to change around us. The strife and food problems. The division between people. And now . . . losing our son . . . it's all too much. Too much on our own.

"We need You to carry us through. Help us to know what is right. Men like Eric Bohm will always be fallible. They may think they know what's best, but it's You who truly knows. Kimba may be right—*is* probably right. Bohm can't be trusted, *shouldn't* be trusted. Our trust should be in You and You alone. Please, Lord, guide us through this. We pray these things in Your Son's holy name, amen."

I blink a few times before giving Rey a smile. "That was . . . good. Very good."

"I think He did give us a burning bush."

161

"Yeah. Me too. Eric Bohm can't be trusted. But God can. We know this from His Word and our own understanding. Rey— " I shake my head.

"We can't be a part of Bohm's plans. But more than that, I think . . ." Rey drops his shoulders and lifts his chin to the sky. "We need to get out of here, out of Billings. None of this is for us."

Chapter 25

Kimba
Thursday, December 3

We gather up the children and start the short walk back to the YMCA. Rey has a calmness about him I haven't seen in weeks, not since we arrived in Billings.

I had zero idea Eric Bohm had been working on Rey since we got here, convincing him to join the insurrection Bohm and his cohorts are planning. After we finished praying and Rey declared we were done—done with Bohm, done with Billings, done with all of it—he stopped being diplomatic and trying to convince me Bohm isn't a bad guy.

I know the truth about Bohm. And somehow, during the short time we spent with God, Rey's eyes were also opened. Doesn't the Bible have a verse about that? About the eyes of the blind being opened? I'll need to use my fancy concordance or ask Beverly to help me find it. Another good one to add to our memorization.

With as much Bible studying and praying as we've been doing, I'm surprised today was such a revelation. I thought Rey and I had been doing well—talking with each other, sharing time together. And things were so much better than in the dark days after we lost Nate. Maybe even better than we'd ever been.

While we'd always put on a united front and did our best to look the part of a happily married couple, there were things between us. I'm sure nothing different than most marriages—work, kids, household stuff, money . . . all the normal. Maybe a little resentment too. I'm not sure either of us were ready to marry when we did, but with Nicole on the way, it was the only choice.

Oh, sure, we may have had other *options*, but neither of us were comfortable with those. We married and made the best of it, building a good business and a wonderful family. We had our ups and downs.

The last few years, before the attacks forced us from our home in Denver, were more down than up, but separating wasn't really an option. Not while the children were at home. Besides, Rey traveled so much with work, we were separated more than half the time anyway.

I thought Rey's change in demeanor lately was just new job and new town jitters, but it was so much more.

It wasn't just an issue between us, but an issue between Rey and God. Rey hadn't gone to God with his concerns. He was relying on his own understanding, his own methods of dealing with issues, with conflict.

The change in just a few minutes time is apparent. There's even a physical change in Rey. Not only is he calmer, but he looks better. The lines around his eyes and mouth have lessened. His smile is true.

He holds my hand as we saunter back to our housing. Naomi and Kylie are still full of energy and bound ahead. Emma's doing her usual young teenager *I'm too cool to be here* way of carrying herself. I've noticed her demeanor changes slightly when Sal's around. I'm not saying she has a crush on him, but . . . well, maybe she does. She definitely seems less cool and more awkward.

Sal has done nothing to encourage her. I've watched, and he treats her exactly the same as he does the younger girls. I think Emma's noticed also and is disappointed, at least a bit.

Sal's recovered well from the bullet trim. He's back to work, hauling water and wood into the building, plus whatever else needs doing. He's what they call a grinder. His official job title is a little fancier, but not much.

Essentially, he's grinding away, day in and day out, doing whatever anyone needs. Not only does he bring in food and water, but he'll often help in the kitchen, with cleaning, in the laundry . . . pretty much anywhere. And he does it with a smile. Out of all of us, and considering everything, Sal's inner joy shines through.

From the day in Bozeman when he asked if he could join the Bible study hosted by Adam Kingsworth, Sal's life has been transformed. He's been passionate about our own readings and studies. He memorizes verses easier and quicker than any of us.

Sal isn't the only one being transformed by God's Word. Bev, who for years has turned her back on God, is also changing. She, too, reads and studies with us. What started as her helping us has morphed into something different. She also encourages Emma and Kylie to memorize the verses with us and participate when we do our Bible studies.

Chad's still a slight outlier, more aloof about God than his wife or the rest of us. I think, for the most part, he just puts up with us Bible thumpers.

Rey's mission today was to convince me Eric Bohm was on the up and up, convince me we should join forces with him in upending Colonel Ellis, who is finally back on duty after his long recovery from a fall down a flight of stairs.

Not just Bohm either. According to Rey, Bohm has many people in his pocket. Most are part of the Civilian Defenders, but there're also many from the Volunteer Units stationed here, along with a good number from the Civil Air Defense, Marines, and even Ellis's Army. Chad insists Bohm has several thousand people ready to go to battle, to end the class divisions happening in Billings.

And that's not all. Once Billings is conquered, they'll move on to the other base camp cities. The changes Eric Bohm and his cronies thought they were making when planning the original terrorist attacks will finally come to fruition.

It's still a muddy mess in my head, how Bohm thought destroying the country and killing millions would bring about the change he wants. But here we are. I've long thought Bohm and those like him were—to use one of Chad's phrases—nutcases.

I still don't believe Bohm is much more than a trigger puller. No way is he the brains behind any of this. He may be a master manipulator, but it isn't of his own doing. He's always been the type who does exactly what he's told without thinking for himself.

I'm sure if whoever is above him told him Colonel Ellis and the president are on the right path with this reconstruction, Bohm would be like a bobble head tripping all over himself in agreement.

The girls wait when we near the door, kicking the snow off their boots. The guards need us to check in. Once we're all together, Rey holds open the door. He gives me a nod and a confident smile. "Chad should be off duty by now. Bev too?"

"Yes, she should be."

Inside, we begin peeling off gloves and scarves as we trudge to the room. A large mat in the middle of the hallway helps to absorb the remaining snow on our boots. We'll leave them on a carpet just inside the door of our small apartment to further allow them to dry and slip into tennis shoes to wear in the building.

Even with setting our boots out, they never fully dry. It's just not warm enough nor is there enough air circulation. Rey, Chad, and Sal's are particularly affected since they spend so much time outside. At least Rey and Chad have a second pair as part of their allotment. Sal, the girls, Bev, and I have only the pair we brought with us. In order to get second pairs, they have to be ruined to a point of no repair or we need different jobs.

I'll admit, this kind of thing, the limits of what is determined we need, does make me consider Bohm may be right. The allotments are just a way to further divide us. But boots, shoes, and clothes are all in limited supply.

Billings had a rough time of it in the beginning, like most of the cities did. Lawlessness was the norm. Houses and buildings were destroyed, and even unusable goods were looted or ruined. Knowing that, I guess I can understand keeping a tight inventory.

We're none too quiet as we tromp down the hall and open the door to our room. Chad and Bev are both home, sitting on the loveseat hand in hand. It's good to see them getting along so well.

Moving to Billings didn't have the same stressors for them that it had for Rey and me. While Rey became distant—and rightly so, now that he's revealed the truth—Chad and Bev seem closer than ever. The issues their marriage has faced have been dealt with, and they're becoming stronger for it. With the truth about what's been bothering Rey coming to light, I think we'll be fine too.

"Hey, girls." Bev's smile is bright. "Did you have fun?"

Kylie goes into an excited description of the playground. Emma shrugs. Naomi plops on her bottom to untie her boots. Once we're undone and Kylie's chatter has abated, I tell Naomi to go change out of her wet clothes and put on dry socks.

"Can I put my jammies on since we eat dinner in here now?"

I meet Rey's eyes and catch his slight nod. "Sure, why not. Get comfy. We'll get your food for you, and you can just relax in the room."

Kylie and Emma are told they can do the same. With the girls in their rooms, Rey squats down next to Chad. "Maybe Emma could watch the girls for a minute? We could move down to the storage closet and have a quick chat."

166

Chad's smile is big as his gaze travels to me. I work to keep my face emotionless. I can tell he thinks I'm on board. We're going to blindside him, and I hate it. Chad's been a friend for such a long time. More than a friend. He and Rey are like brothers in many ways. They've depended on each other, put their lives in the hands of the other, traveled the world and faced dangers together.

It's likely Chad will be angry. Bev may be angry too. Rey thinks they're true believers, fully behind Bohm and his cause. Chad's been disenchanted with all he's seen and experienced here in Billings. In Bozeman, too, in some ways. While not as pronounced, there was a hierarchy.

Of course, there always is. We'd be foolish to think it didn't exist in the world before. People have either embraced it or spoken out against it.

A guy who attempted a presidential run a few years back did little to hide his desire to expand existing government-funded programs, to move us into full-on socialism. And others embraced the class differences, making more and more money and moving capitalism to a whole new level.

We lived a very comfortable life, with a degree of wealth the majority of people didn't have, thanks to capitalism and being able to build a business charging what we felt we were worth. Our nation did, of course, have many public features reminiscent of a degree of socialism, but as far as full public ownership, we weren't there.

When we lived at the ski lodge last winter, I think we were very close to socialism. Nobody owned anything, not really. Everything was done for the good of all. In many ways, it was just like Billings with everyone working together.

But it felt different. There, people *wanted* to work together. Those who had nothing to their names, like my friend Rochelle Bennet, were treated with respect and admiration.

No different than Zeb and Ellen Frost who owned the ski lodge out of Bakerville and seemed to have an abundance—an abundance they were willing to share. Zeb was the type of guy some may have called a hoarder. He had barns and sheds full of things. And he opened those doors to the community and gave it all. He sowed generously.

The life of abundance Rey and I had ended before we ever reached Bakerville, when our car ran out of gas on a jam-packed, two-lane road between Casper and Shoshoni. We took everything we could carry and started walking. When we finally reached Bakerville, and once we got past Doris Snyder wanting to shoot me between the eyes, we were welcomed and cared for.

Loved even.

That's definitely not a feeling I've ever had here in Billings. It could be because of the size of the city. Even after losing so much of its populace, it's a bustling town, made so by the military using it as a base.

There's little feeling of comradery or togetherness in the Y. All of us live here together, and we still feel like strangers, nodding our hellos but rarely taking time to get to know each other. The shooting could've brought us together, but it's driven us farther apart. Rey's right, we need to get out of here.

After letting the girls know we'll be right back, Bev and I leave first. We take a long, circular route to a storage closet down the hall, checking nearby spaces for people lurking about. When we're satisfied we'll have as much privacy as we can expect, we slip into the little room. I leave the door open long enough for her to find the battery-operated light and switch it on.

As the door softly closes, she gives me a smile. "I'm so looking forward to getting our own place. I've had it with communal living. A place for just the four of us again . . . I can barely stand it I'm so excited." My smile must be lukewarm because she narrows her eyes. "What's wrong?"

"I . . . I agree. Not that you and Chad aren't fine roomies, but a house of our own would be wonderful."

Her shoulders drop. "You're not doing it."

My stomach tightens. The hurt in her eyes is almost too much. "I . . . our men will be here shortly."

"Why, Kimba? You can't *like* this. Living this way, the rebuilding—you must know it's wrong."

"Shh." I motion with my hand. "I don't like it. But wrong . . ." I let out a puff of air. "The men will be here shortly. We'll talk then."

"Why bother? This is like . . . like the Civil War."

I fight the urge to roll my eyes and accuse my friend of being overly dramatic. Part of me knows, though, she may not be wrong. If Chad and Bev insist on joining Bohm and his resistance and we don't—or worse, Rey and I choose to fight against them and fully side with

168

Colonel Ellis—it'll very much be a war. A war between friends. Family.

I reach my hand out to cover Bev's shoulder. She shrugs it away.

Chapter 26

Beverly
Thursday, December 3

"Don't you know what this means?" My voice is too high pitched. Angry. Hot tears sting my eyes. "Rey said . . . he said you'd understand. How can you not get it?"

Kimba drops her gaze to the floor. "Bev, please."

I raise my hand. "Don't. Don't patronize me."

"Patronize?" Kimba swivels her head. "I know Bohm. He's a snake. If he thinks it's a good thing, it's not. Not at all."

The breath from my nose comes out in an unladylike huff. "You don't know. It's been, what, twenty years since you knew him?"

"Men like him don't change."

"Really? All your Bible reading and praying . . . you said *you* changed. Rey changed. But not Bohm?"

Kimba furrows her brow. "Are you saying Bohm's a Christian?"

"Well, I don't . . ." I shake my head. "Not the point. You used to be a . . . a . . ." I lean forward. "You were a killer, right? And now?"

Kimba straightens her back and lifts her chin. "Beverly, understand this. I gave up that life. Not because I wanted to at the time, but because I was forced into it. Rey and I made something good out of the awfulness. But you're right. I was a killer. Even recently. Even now. I'd kill if I needed to. But do not ever compare me to Bohm. We are not the same. He took pleasure in killing." She gives a strong shake of her head. "Not just killing. He took pleasure in torturing. That was his passion."

I cross my arms and lean back against the wall. "Can't you see it's wrong? What's happening here is wrong."

"I know it seems wrong, and it may be. But Bohm wanting to take over isn't any better. He may sound all benevolent in his desire— "

"He's doing the right thing." As the words come out of my mouth, I can hear the hesitancy in my voice. *Is he doing the right thing?*

"You're just . . . your personal issues with him prevent you from seeing just how bad things are here."

"That may be true." Kimba's voice is a low growl. "It probably is true. But I'm right. Bohm is a snake. A murdering, torturing snake."

There's a slight scraping noise at the door. I give Kimba a nod when the scrape sounds again. Our men sure took their time getting here. Once Chad and Rey are inside, Kimba asks them if there was any trouble. When both say all is fine, I blurt out about Kimba and Rey weaseling out.

Chad's chin drops as he turns to Rey. "Really, *bro*? I thought you were in this with us. I thought you were on board."

"I thought I was. Kimba was even starting to maybe come around."

Kimba gives a barely noticeable dip of her head. "Maybe, yes. I mean, I know things aren't great here."

Chad and I make almost identical noises of disgust. *That* is the understatement of the year. Chad works his jaw and shakes his head. "Ya think? You were attacked."

Kimba squares her shoulders, looking ready for a fight. "You think I don't remember? Even you said Bohm wasn't with them. But now he wants to lead his own revolt?"

"Bohm wasn't with the ones who killed here at the Y. But they were after him, after Bohm. Colonel Ellis was behind the attack."

I watch as Kimba's face pales. That was the same reaction I had when Chad told me the man who is supposed to be leading the reconstruction efforts—the efforts to save lives in Billings—was responsible for the deaths of people we knew. Was responsible for my children being in danger. "Do you understand now?"

Kimba seems to deflate, all the fight now gone from her. "Are you taking Bohm's word for it that Ellis was behind the attacks? He was still on convalescent leave, right?"

"Supposedly." Chad shrugs. "There is some question as to . . . we don't know exactly what's happening."

Kimba turns to Rey. "You knew about Ellis?"

"I knew Bohm *said* Ellis was responsible. I don't know for certain he is. *We* don't know for certain, do we, buddy?" Rey motions to Chad, who hesitates before saying it's true, they are going on what Bohm said.

"Wait." I put a hand on my Chad's forearm. "I thought you said Bohm had proof?"

171

The guilt on Chad's face is evident. "Well . . . it's more of a theory than proof."

"You lied to me?"

"I didn't lie, Bev. I tried . . ." He clears his throat, one of his methods for gathering his thoughts—and buying time.

I close my fingers around his beefy arm. "Let's have the truth now." I look to Kimba. "If I'm going to go against one of my oldest friends, I need all the facts."

Kimba gives me a grateful smile. "We all do. Maybe more information will help me too. But I need to tell you, Rey and I prayed about this, and . . ." She shakes her head.

"Well, as long as you've prayed about it." Chad's voice is harsh. "Because, of course, you'll get all your answers that way."

"Chad," I hiss as I let go of his arm.

He raises his hands in surrender. "Fine, fine. God told you not to make our lives better. That sounds about right. I mean, after all, if you do something to improve your lot in life, why would you need to go to God for help? Keep depending on Him, and you'll be right where He wants you."

Sadness is etched on Kimba's face. "You mean with my son? In Heaven?"

At least my husband has the decency to look ashamed. "Sorry, Kimba. That's not what I meant. I'm . . . I'm sorry."

Rey wraps an arm around Kimba's shoulders. "We think we should leave Billings."

"Go where?" Chad shakes his head. "The buses are done for the season. We don't have the equipment and gear you had when you left your ski lodge. Where do you want to go? And when, Rey Hoffmann, have you ever run from a fight?"

"When I knew it was the right thing to do. This is like some of those jobs we turned down. How many times did someone come to us offering a boat load of money to do something we thought would be simple? You'd research it, and we couldn't make heads or tails of what was really happening. This is like that."

"Because God told you?"

Rey tilts his head and runs a hand across the back of his neck. "Partly. But the more we talk, the less things are adding up. Why is Eric Bohm in Billings? Did you ever get a straight answer from him?"

Chad's mouth pulls into a tight line. "He was on a job."

"In Billings?

"Nearby." Chad clears his throat. "Um, Wyoming. Near where you wintered."

Kimba lifts her chin. "Really? Where?"

"A little town called Prospect. Heard of it?"

The myriad of emotions crossing Kimba's face tell a story all their own. "When?"

"He was there when the attacks started. He said they were early. That's why he was there. He knew there was something planned, but after talking to him, I don't think he knew exactly what the plans entailed. He knew there would be disasters—disasters that would be blamed on terrorists. But I don't think he knew exactly what. And I don't think the timeline was what he expected."

"The daily attacks?"

"Right. I think he thought it'd be a more drawn-out assault. The planes first and then a week or two later the bridges. But like I said, he didn't know what the attacks would be, and everything escalated so quickly. The next thing he knew, the town he was in ran out of fuel and he decided to ride it out. He found a way to be useful and stayed until spring. Well, I think there's more to his story, but that's what I know."

"Why was he in Prospect?" Kimba's eyes drill into Chad.

Chad lifts both shoulders. "A job? You know the kind of work Bohm did. I guess— "

"He tortured people, right?" I look to the others in the room. Rey and Kimba are both bobbing their heads. Chad shrugs again. "So, you're saying he was there to torture someone?"

"He was a straight-out killer too," Kimba answers. "Could've been either. Torture or assassin."

"In Wyoming? Isn't that the kind of thing that happens in other countries? Or at least Chicago? But Wyoming?"

"You may be surprised. There's been more than one time a news story made me wonder about what was really happening in Wyoming. Or Montana for that matter." Something changes in Kimba's face, as a look of understanding passes. She turns to Rey. "The school shooting."

Rey rubs a finger against his hairy chin. "Could be. But the shooting was on the other side of the state, near Gillette." They share a long look before Rey nods. "Of course, we know the people involved were in Prospector County when the planes were shot down, don't we?"

Chad asks what they're talking about.

"I'm sitting down for this." Kimba plops herself on the floor. "Sure wish we could find a better meeting spot than a too small, too stinky closet."

I settle on the floor next to Kimba. My anger at her has subsided. I still want out of this place, out of the communal living and lack of privacy. But I can see I didn't have all the facts about the situation. I look to Chad as he, too, settles onto the floor with his back against the door. He gives me an apologetic smile, one I can't bring myself to return.

Rey's across from Kimba and me, his long legs stretched in front of him. "So, you all heard about the school shooting in Grover, Wyoming?"

I give a slight nod. I remember it, of course. Mostly because it happened so close to home and it was quite the tale. A husband and wife were visiting their children's school for some event when it started. They were able to stop the assault before it escalated too much—no kids were killed at least. If I remember correctly, a couple of teachers and maybe the principal died.

"Right." Rey dips his head. "The husband and wife who stopped the shooting disappeared a few days later, remember that?"

Chad leans the crown of his head against the door. "I remember we talked about this at the time, about how it all seemed suspicious. Because before the husband and wife—and their kids, right? Before they disappeared, a couple of other people who were at the school died. You said how hinky it seemed, how there was probably a lot more to the story we'd never know."

"Yeah, well . . . turns out there is more to the story, and I do know about it." Rey then goes into this fanciful tale, with Kimba adding in bits as needed, about this family they met when they were in Bakerville.

It was the husband and wife from the school shooting. They were hiding out, squatting on some land in a camp trailer, when everything fell apart. The husband was a doctor and came clean about who he was when he was called on to keep people from dying. The wife had medical training, too, and they were soon part of the medical team in the little town.

174

While they did try to keep the couple's actual identity secret, even using fake names, it was more of an open secret than anything. Rey and Kimba knew, and so did many others. The husband, Sam Mitchell, said nothing in the school shooting was what it seemed. Plus, the official news story was slightly contorted.

"He said things were definitely hinky." Kimba bobs her head and meets Chad's gaze.

"Right." Rey makes an identical motion. "There were two shooters, both decked out in too much gear and too professional. They seemed to be on a mission. Sam found a third guy, already dead. Turned out to be a local troubled teen. He was wearing jeans and a T-shirt and wasn't at all the same type of guy as the other two.

"A few days later, the gym teacher at the school, who helped Sam stop the assault, died in a car accident. Then the school secretary committed suicide. The official story was she was distraught over the death of the school principal and couldn't handle the stress of the event. Sam said his friend, a deputy sheriff, said her death was staged.

"That's when Sam fled with his family. They had a little help in the beginning, getting new identities and a little guidance. His friend, the deputy, was killed a few days later, and Sam knew they were on their own. When the world fell apart, it helped them stay hidden."

"It makes sense." Kimba nods. "June, Sam's wife, she'd told me she was a nervous wreck once when she'd gone into Prospect for supplies. She thought she was recognized. Maybe . . . maybe she was. Maybe that's why Eric Bohm was there."

Rey runs a hand through his hair. "She was recognized. She had to be. Otherwise, why would Sam have been shot?"

"Wait a minute." Chad leans forward. "You guys were in the middle of nowhere, at the end of the world, without anything—no phone, no internet, no television—and someone recognized *and* shot the guy? No offense, but getting shot in today's world doesn't have to be related to some big conspiracy."

"It does when there are photographs."

Photographs. I lift a hand. "I don't understand at all."

"It's crazy for sure," Kimba agrees. "Sam was shot by an unknown assailant. He lived for a while—weeks. But infection eventually took him. We told you about the shooting in the ski lodge, on the day of the wedding when someone there attempted a coup d'état?"

175

"Yes, of course. Both before and after the shooting here in our *own* dining room."

"One of the insurgents . . ." She looks to Rey. "What was his name?"

"Brad. Brad Quinton."

Chad lefts out a laugh. "Brad Quinton, huh?"

"You know him?"

"Slimy, sweaty guy?"

Rey nods. "Yep. Sounds like him."

"West Coast assassin. Jankins had him on his crew for a few jobs. Called him Q, remember?"

Rey looks to the left and down slightly before shaking his head. "Maybe. I may have heard the name in passing, but I know I never met the guy. He was a stranger to me."

Chad shrugs. "Yeah, well. I know Quinton. So let me get this straight. You and Kimba, along with the former Meagan Wright—all highly trained, um . . . *individuals*—meet up in a little nothing town and another trained killer also lives there?"

Kimba shakes her head. "He didn't live there. His girlfriend did. Ex-girlfriend from like thirty years before. He showed up there, the same day we did in fact."

"Of course!" Chad lets out a laugh. "It's like some poorly written novel."

"Or a soap opera," I offer. It really is. The tale is almost too much to believe. "But where does Eric Bohm come in?"

Kimba lifts her hands. "I'm only speculating. But after Brad was killed, his wife found pictures of Sam and June Mitchell, even their children, plus photos of the gym teacher and school secretary. Newspaper clippings even. It all made sense Brad Quinton was hired to kill them."

"Makes sense to me." Chad nods. "But still, Bev's right. What a soap opera."

"Well, what if Bohm was also in the area, having been tipped off to the Mitchells' whereabouts, and he was part of the whole thing too?"

"Part of the school shooting? But why?" I don't even pretend to understand what's really happening.

"Who knows? Sam Mitchell said he thought it was some kind of false flag as part of gun control. I mean, we've seen it through the

176

years. Whenever there's a mass shooting, there's a call for stricter gun laws, right?"

"I don't see Bohm being a part of any type of disarmament." Chad looks to Rey. "Do you?"

"Nope. Not Bohm. He's more the type to want to force people to bear arms as to take them away. But who knows what those above him in his scheme wanted? Unarmed people are easier to control. So could be?"

"Nah. There's another reason. If Bohm was part of the shooting, it was for something else. My guess, he was brought in as part of the cleanup crew. Quinton too. Yeah, I can see that happening. It'd certainly explain Bohm ending up in Prospect when the stuff hit the fan."

Kimba looks at her shoe as she fiddles with the laces. "Let's ask him."

Chapter 27

Kimba
Monday, December 7

"I'll be back soon." I pull Naomi into a tight hug. "Mind Bev and go to bed when she says."

"Why do you have to leave when it'll be dark soon?" My daughter's lip sticks out in a pout.

"Because Daddy just finished work, and we have to meet."

"Is it a date? Like you used to go on?"

"Uh, well, no. Not a date. We're going to meet with Chad and . . . and someone else." I give her a smile and another kiss.

I adjust my daypack, a heavy canvas messenger bag, so it sits tightly against my hip. I'd become lazy with carrying my pack in the days leading up to the shooting in the dining hall, choosing to only wear my pistols. Since then, when I found myself without the needed emergency supplies, I've made a point of keeping what I need on me. Rey and Chad, who wear packs every time they leave, were even able to get me a few extra supplies.

I give Bev a final nod and tell her I'll be back as soon as I can.

My friend implores me to be careful, to be smart about everything. Then I'm out of the room and exiting the building, heading for our designated rendezvous spot.

It's taken us several days to sort out our plans of getting Bohm alone. The day in the storage room, we spent way too long talking with Chad and Bev. Our conversation ended within minutes of my time to report for meal service. The Pitneys were still disappointed we weren't joining up with the resistance, but they understood our concerns. Especially our need for more information about Bohm and his motives.

It's all just a little too slick . . . Eric Bohm being here, the situation with Sam and June Mitchell in Wyoming. Then add in Doris and me meeting up again, out of the blue, and Bev is right. It is like a soap opera! Or maybe Chad's correct and it's a poorly written novel. Doesn't matter.

I know Eric Bohm. I know how he thinks, and if he thinks an insurrection is a good idea, it's not. Plus, I felt it. When Rey prayed, I knew what we were to do. Or, maybe, I knew what we were not supposed to do. We are not to be a part of this. Definitely not a part of Bohm's plans, and I truly wonder if we should be involved in Colonel Ellis's reconstruction efforts.

I wish I had a way to get ahold of Nicole, to get her out of the Volunteer Unit. Right now, everything is all muddy in my head, and I don't know where the side of right is.

We were so passionate to be involved in rebuilding our country, but what were we rebuilding? Bohm is right about the country being a mess before. The division was evident and getting worse. People were turning against each other. By design? Maybe.

More than anything, I'm beginning to believe it may be Biblical. Maybe EJ Martin, the foreman on Lance Brower's ranch, had it right. Martin said he thought we were in the end times. This was part of the Great Tribulation.

I asked Bev about it, about the last days. She told me to read Revelation. I did and it scared me silly. The symbolism is confusing but also seems to line up with many things we've been experiencing. Not just in the last eighteen months, but before.

We were quickly moving toward a one-world government. To one currency as a cashless society. To everything laid out in Revelation. We just went along with it. We'd hear on the endless news cycle or read on the endless internet or social media about some new travesty, some new deal, and just say, "Well, isn't that interesting," then go on with our day.

Rey and I were so wrapped up in life, we didn't stop to pay attention to what was really happening. We knew about the evil in the world. We believed there were false flags. But we didn't know enough about the good in the world—about God—to be able to discern the what, where, why, and how of evil. The demise of the world we knew.

Now here we are, living in what we readily call the apocalypse. It falls off our tongues with ease. We've accepted our fate, our circumstances. It took a major world change—mass destruction, bombs going off, and the lights going out—for us to see what was truly happening.

Even in the process, in the days leading up to the bombs, many people were in denial. One catastrophe after another was easily explained. The government was blindly followed.

Some, like Rey and I, are coming to know the Lord during this time. Bev too. Even though she knew Him before, I can see her coming back into the fold, slowly and by tiptoe.

In the last few days, since our meeting in the storage room, even Chad seems to have a new interest. He may have scoffed at us for praying for guidance, but there's more. He was angry we weren't going along but now seems to understand our conviction to follow God. To not live by a lie and follow along blindly, hoping we are doing the right thing.

Our faith can't be in a mere man—whether that man is Eric Bohm or Colonel Ellis—it must be in God and His Son.

The Bible tells us Jesus Christ will return. At any moment, He may descend from Heaven and gather up His people. Reading Revelation for myself gave me a sense of urgency. I'd heard it preached many times before when we lived in Bakerville. Probably even on the occasions we attended church in the past, there were references to the end times. EJ Martin definitely mentioned it.

Reading the entire book for myself gave me a fuller understanding. The imagery of it was frightening and enlightening. Wars and rumors of wars, famines, and earthquakes have all been happening for years.

Well, I assume earthquakes are still happening. It's not like we know much about anything other than what's going on in Billings, Montana. There are plenty of continued rumors of war. The president never says anything except flowery words about how great our country is building back. But the scuttlebutt is the entire world is in wars or skirmishes of some sort.

Bev was right too. What Bohm is proposing will essentially result in a civil war in Billings. Some will be with him—thousands, if the reports can be believed—but others will be against him. It's likely friends and family could be on opposite sides.

Reading Revelation made me realize how short our time may be. Chad, Bev, and their children need to know the truth. I think Bev feels it too.

I heard her talking with Emma and Kylie about how Auntie Kimba may want to tell them about the Bible. She said to listen and not just with their ears but with their hearts too. Why she isn't telling them about the gospel herself, I'm not sure. But I'm going to find out—as soon as this issue with Bohm is resolved.

We're meeting at a ramshackle house a few blocks from the Y. I'm sure it was lovely before everything fell apart, but now the windows are busted out and it looks like a fire was lit in the front yard, charring the siding. The walkway is lined with overgrown shrubs on one side, the side not affected by fire, and burned stubs on the fire side.

As I approach, a guy walking nearby comes into view. A sentry? Possibly. When he turns and walks in his footprints, my suspicion is confirmed.

He gives me a curt nod.

My eyes drift from him to the perimeter of the building. A flash of movement in the second-story window shows another watcher. My heart's pounding in my ears. Is this a set up? I'm ready to turn and leave when Rey steps out the front door and motions me to continue toward him.

When I reach him, he takes my hand. "Quite the welcoming party, huh?"

"Lovely. Were they here when you arrived?"

"Showed up with Bohm." There's a hitch in his voice.

"What's wrong?"

Rey gives a slight shake of his head and glances to the edge of the house. He leans in to kiss my cheek, then whispers, "There's been a change of plans."

Bohm steps out of the house and onto the porch. "There you are." He gives me a brilliant smile. At least with his mouth. His eyes are hidden by the dark glasses he favors. He's wearing a long, heavy jacket over his usual suit and tie, along with a rugged-looking pair of insulated boots, a pair I've never seen him wear. How is it he doesn't seem to have the same footwear allotment we do?

"I'll admit, I was mildly surprised when Chad said you wanted to meet. I thought . . . well, I'm glad to see our previous issues aren't a problem. Water under the bridge."

Fastening on a smile, I give a curt nod. "Something like that." I look to Rey, who gives me a vague smile before we follow Bohm into a room set up with a couple of camp chairs. There's a small space heater running on propane. Where he found propane this far into the apocalypse is a mystery. Other than the chairs and the heater, the room is bare and wide open.

"You use this as a regular meeting place?"

"Sometimes. Have a seat."

The men all wait until I'm seated before taking their own chairs. I lean back and try to look casual, not easy in a mesh and polyester folding chair. Well, I should rephrase. *Casual* is easy. Getting out may be difficult. Trying to look casual but ready to spring up at a moment's notice is the challenge.

"As I said, I'm glad you're here." Bohm dips his chin and does the smile again. "We've got a long way to go to repair our country, to bring it back to what it should be. All of this seems . . . extreme. But it is necessary. You know as well as anyone, maybe even better than most people, how things sometimes need to get worse before they can get better."

"I'd definitely agree the death of millions is excessive."

"Yes, yes. I know it does seem so. But in order to bring things back to what they should be, we had to lose a little . . . shall we say dead weight?"

I feel a little sick to my stomach at his nonchalant phrase. My first instinct is to shut him up. Permanently. Instead, I paste on a tight little smile and give a nod. "Chad said you were in Wyoming when everything started. What were you doing there?"

"Working." He waves a dismissive hand. "Didn't plan on being there, thought I'd be . . . doesn't matter. The timeline changed. It is what it is."

"The timeline changed? Why is that?"

"Can't say. I contacted my associate after the planes went down. I knew there was supposed to be something big to start things off, but I wasn't sure exactly what it'd be. And I thought we still had a few months. Originally, the plan was for a repeat of September 11. You know, symbolic. If I'd have known it was happening sooner, you can bet I wouldn't have been in Podunk Wyoming."

"Prospect, right? Chad said Prospect. Did you know we were near there last winter?"

Chapter 28

Kimba
Monday, December 7

A flit of surprise crosses Bohm's face at Rey's declaration of our winter residence. He recovers in an instant. "Had no idea. You were in Prospect? I never saw you."

"Not the town, but in Prospector County. We heard about some of the things happening in Prospect."

"Oh, yeah, I bet. It was a lively town for sure. Dick Majors—did you hear about him?"

I clear my throat. "Richard Majors, yes."

Bohm throws back his head and laughs. "What a piece of work. He thought he was the king of the county. He and his son. Both had a few screws loose. They brought in this other guy, too, said he was some sort of deputy sheriff. Could've fooled me! The guy was a goof. I took him under my wing, thinking I could teach him a thing or two. Turned out, the guy taught me a couple of things. He was sadistic in a way I'd only heard about."

I raise my eyebrows.

Bohm lifts a hand. "I know, I know. I have some skills in that arena too. But for me, it was work. A job. This guy took pleasure in it. The things he did . . ." Bohm gives an exaggerated shudder. "Doesn't matter. He's dead now. Majors and his son too."

Rey leans forward in his chair. "What happened?"

"To the deputy? A woman he was looking for—he said she was his wife—I guess she didn't feel the same about him. She emptied her Glock into him."

"What about Majors and his son?"

"The town turned on him. They had some help from neighboring communities. That's when I realized it was time to find a new place. The deputy went with me until he met his unfortunate end along the way. I knew with the rumors of the military setting up in Billings this would be the place to be. Thought I'd find a few more folks here.

"When I saw you three get off the bus, I wasn't surprised. Figured you were, you know, aware of what was happening. Chad says it was just a coincidence you showed up here. I've never really believed in coincidences." His eyes travel from Rey to Chad, then finally rest on me. "Kimba, were you part of the operation?"

I shake my head. "We didn't know. Rey and I wondered who was responsible. We thought it might be some shadow government."

Bohm scoffs. "Yeah, something like that."

"What job were you on in Prospect?"

"Nothing that matters much. Just tying up a loose end."

"The school shooting in Eastern Wyoming?"

His laugh is humorless. "You always were good at putting things together. Yep. Another guy was supposed to wrap it up. He got about three-quarters done, but the last piece of the puzzle evaporated. They brought me in following a tip the subject was seen in Prospect."

"The other guy was Brad Quinton?" Chad asks.

"Quinton?" Bohm narrows his eyes. "What do you know about him? Why are you asking about ancient history?"

Chad lifts his hands in a surrender motion.

"We ran into Quinton, Rey and me," I say.

"Did you, now? Piece of work that guy. You don't happen to know if he finished the job, do you?"

"What was the job?"

Bohm waves a hand. "Doesn't matter. Let's move on."

I deliver a patient smile. "We're just tying up our own loose ends. Like you, coincidences concern me. To discover you here, to find out you were nearby where we were . . . you know me, I like answers."

Bohm leans back in his chair and seems to relax, if only slightly. "Like I said, ancient history. I was finishing up a job, that's all."

"You know one of the conspiracy theories about the school shooting was it was a gun grab."

"It wasn't a gun grab. It was a hit."

Rey makes a humming noise. "A hit, huh? I guess that's one way to disguise it. Very trendy."

"One of the teachers. A witness protection type of deal."

"Guess the mob was pretty serious."

Bohm's smile is reptilian. "State secrets require extra measures. You can only stage a suicide so many times before people start to talk."

Chad gives a slow shake of his head. "My favorite is the double shotgun blast to the back of the head suicides. Very convincing."

"My point exactly."

"Yes." I choke out the word. "Always so much better to shoot up a school full of children."

He moves his head and shoulders in a lackadaisical way. "So, there you go. We square? All your curiosities covered? We can get down to business?"

Rey takes the lead. "Chad says you have the numbers to take over the town?"

"There're a lot of unhappy people here. Rightly so." He looks at me. "You can't be pleased with the way you've been relegated to dishwasher. Not a woman of your special abilities."

"I understand the reasoning."

"Wouldn't Chad's little wife take care of your kid if things went bad?"

"She would." Chad nods. "We would. Just like Rey and Kimba would take care of our girls."

"Exactly. It's a stupid rule." Bohm crosses his legs, ankle over his knee. With the way the camp chair tilts back, he looks like he may tip over. "Yep. Chauvinism at its finest."

A door slams somewhere nearby, followed by a shout and running feet. Bohm awkwardly jumps up, knocking over the flimsy chair in the process. I'm also on my feet, as are Rey and Chad a beat later.

My hand's on the butt of my Glock. "What's happening?"

A red-faced man stumbles in the door. "Troops approaching."

Bohm seems to relax. "Major Dudrock and his group? They're expected."

"Not Dudrock. These aren't friendlies."

Bohm spins in my direction. "You! You did this."

I lift my left hand and shake my head. My right stays on my gun. "I didn't *do* anything."

Everything happens at once. My eyes are on Bohm as I catch movement out of the corner of my eye. The red-faced guy pulls his gun. A shot sounds off. Bohm's gun is out, and I'm moving. Neither the camp chairs nor the small heater will provide any cover.

"Go! Go!" Rey orders. There are several more gun blasts as I slip out the door and into the hallway.

"Stop! Hands in the air!" The shouter doesn't even wait for me to oblige his order. "Get her!" he yells, right before I'm hit from behind.

I hit the faded tile with a thud, turning my head at the last moment to protect my nose. It's still a hard hit and knocks the wind out of me. The guys don't care. Someone grabs me from behind and yanks my arms as I'm roughly pulled to my feet.

"Hey! That hurts."

"Should've thought about that before you joined the insurgents."

"Insurgents? I'm not— "

"Shut your trap!"

The slap comes hard and fast, ringing my ear and snapping my head to the side. The taste of blood is immediate. More of these guys' ilk are in the building.

Rey yells something, then Chad does. There's a crash—maybe the heater toppling over.

"Get them all out of here. Take them to the colonel."

"Colonel Ellis?" My voice comes out in a croak.

"I said to shut your pie hole!" He puts his face next to mine, the remnants of his lunch spraying across my face. I feel like puking. Lifting my shoulder to my cheek, I wipe off what I hope is the worst of it. The light touch to my face stings from where I was smacked.

With my hands cuffed in front—with actual cold, metal handcuffs—I'm frog-marched down the hall and out the front door. The guard makes appreciative comments about my gun as he shoves it in his belt at the small of his back.

Outside, the air is crisp and snow is lightly falling. I take a few deep breaths, trying to remember the relaxation methods Bev taught me. Much like the box breathing I'd relied on for so many years when on a mission or under pressure, her way of breathing is a slightly different pattern and much more oxygenating. I need that right now. I need to clear my head and figure a way out of this.

Chad's behind me, being overly vocal about his thoughts on being cuffed and man handled. I hear a grunt farther back, a grunt I recognize as my husband's.

"This is your fault," Bohm yells.

I glance over my shoulder in time to see Bohm launch himself at Chad. The guy holding me lets out a hoot of laughter, while the one who is supposed to have control of Bohm is grasping at air, trying to

186

get ahold of any part of him he can. The crack of a rifle eliminates the laugh of the guy holding my arms, along with a chunk of his skull.

"Kimba!" Rey's yell is obscured by another rifle shot. I make a dive for the withered bushes lining the sidewalk. The dead guy who was guarding me is close enough I can retrieve my pistol from his belt. I yank my hand back quickly when another shot puffs up the snow a foot away.

"Go! Go!" Rey yells from the edge of the porch. His shouting earns a shot directed at him.

I waste little time sprinting to the side of the house. The shooter—or I should say *shooters*, since it is obvious there is more than one trying to pin us down—riddles the corner of the house as I duck behind. I take a knee and scan, my gun held awkwardly in my cuffed hands.

Rey is still huddled by the porch, his hands behind his back. I don't see Chad anywhere. Bohm neither. Someone's shooting from inside the house. Several someone's, in fact. Army? I saw quite a few looking through the rooms of the house when I was being hustled out.

Almost as quickly as it started, it ends.

"Rey," I hiss. He gives me a nod and scurries to my side without incident. We lean against the house, awkward in our handcuffs. "Chad?"

His breath tickles my ear when he answers. "Went around the other side. Bohm was still pounding on him as the shooting was happening."

"No kidding. Makes sense considering he knew he wasn't a target. The fight . . . he staged it as a distraction."

"That's my guess."

"And the Army . . . they'll blame us for this."

"Well . . ."

"You okay, bro?" Chad calls from the back corner of the house.

"Yeah, were good."

When Chad steps toward us, the first thing I notice is he's swinging his arms. "How'd you get unhooked?"

He lifts his hands. "Magic. And a little help from a friend."

A man in uniform steps around. "I have a key." He looks at Rey and lifts his chin. "Looks like you got trimmed." He raises his voice. "We could use a medic over here."

Rey turns slightly and looks over his shoulder. "Thought it stung a bit."

187

"Turn," I order as I dig in my bag for first aid supplies.

He spins enough for me to see blood trailing down his jacket; a puff of polyester filling is stuck where it doesn't belong. The entire side of his backpack is blown out. Rey sways slightly. Chad is instantly by his side. "I got you, bro. We'll get the cuffs off and get you fixed right up."

Chapter 29

Beverly
Tuesday, December 8

"How is he?"

Kimba plops on the loveseat, emitting a noise of disgust. "It's ugly. Left a trail all across his back. How it didn't do more damage . . ." She repeats the noise. "I'd like to kill him myself for what he did." She meets my gaze with a hard look. "Your husband too. What were they thinking?"

I set my shoulders. "It's not like they had much of a choice."

The noise again. "There's always a choice."

The girls are still asleep, each tucked away in their own room. Sal already left for his grinder job. Chad never came home last night. When Kimba brought Rey back, she said they'd been separated. Chad was taken for debriefing while Rey for medical treatment. When no one said they needed to be debriefed, they came home.

The girls, Sal, and I had picked up our food and meals for the three of them. When it was obvious Chad wasn't coming home, I made Sal and Emma share Chad's plate. The younger girls had already gone to bed by then. Emma argued, saying her dad would need the food.

While I agreed, it was better to let him go hungry a night—if he did get home—than to waste anything. Although we don't have the food concerns we did in Bozeman last winter, there's still a limit.

Maybe more of a limit than I want to admit.

Just in the six weeks we've been here, I've noticed a change in the allotment of food we're given. The potatoes and turnips are still in abundance, but the meat has decreased. There's little variety in other vegetables.

The ergot in Bozeman was a hot topic here when we arrived, with all their cereal grains being examined for the fungus. Officially, all grain was clear. Unofficially, I suspect they did find some contaminated, then took care of it and chose to keep the information quiet in hopes of preventing mass hysteria from the possibility of ergotism.

Captain Mercer had said they thought some of the people who were believed to be infected in Bozeman were really not. Instead, they imagined the symptoms. She'd said this form of groupthink is very real and can quickly spiral into a panic under the right conditions.

Assuring people in Billings that their food supply was safe was probably a smart thing to do. There're enough issues here that cause people to be on edge. Adding in something like the threat of ergot could send the city into a downward spiral.

I understand Kimba being angry. Especially considering the way she was blindsided. Rey and Chad fully expected the meeting with Bohm to go as we'd planned the day in the storage closet. They would confront him and get answers to their questions. I was against it. Who really cares why Bohm was in Prospector County or how he'd spent his time before arriving in Billings? All that mattered was the here and now.

Kimba and Rey were so passionate about not joining in with Bohm and his plans to take over the reconstruction efforts. They insisted it would go bad. During the conversation, they reminded Chad of other encounters with Bohm when he was on Jankins's team, plus shared stories of what they knew of Bohm or incidents they believed could be attributed to Bohm.

It was the most I'd ever heard about their time working together, and definitely more than Kimba had ever shared about her government work. I could've done without learning most of it. I knew what they did, of course. But the details, the ruthlessness, the way they could kill and not be changed forever . . . I'll never understand it.

Changed forever . . . they were definitely changed. The way Kimba is, for sure it can be directly tied to her work. Her aloofness with her own children was likely a coping mechanism born out of the fact she was a hired gun for so long.

She's different now. At first, I thought the changes were because of the world falling apart and then losing her son. Now I know it's more. She isn't perfect. Far from it. Still, she's different. I like her a lot more too.

There's a new kindness about her. Even as she sits here in this tiny living space, seething over the situation, the change is obvious. It's God. It's Jesus shining through her. Some people might believe this change has weakened her, changed her from the killer she was to some kind of feeble woman. That's not it at all. The spirit God gave her is strong. Loving and kind, yet capable and determined.

For all the time I've known her, I've merely tolerated her. Yes, we were friends, but only to a point. I've always judged her and her behavior.

I'd cluck my tongue over the way she treated her children and husband poorly. I'd seethe over the way she took advantage of the successful business they had, a business my husband was a huge part of, but she didn't give him the credit he was due. I'd dread when they'd come to our place for a visit, or we had to go to theirs. And the weekly streaming calls . . . ugh.

Chad knew Kimba and the way she was drove me crazy, but he didn't know just how crazy. Spending time with Kimba did at least make me feel like I could easily get the title of Mom of the Year. At the same time, I'd feel terrible about myself. I never looked right or said the right things around her. She was always so . . . so perfect. I was always so dowdy. Add in being overweight and too short.

Even with all her faults, I can now see a big part of my difficulties with Kimba was jealousy. Although I would still choose to be more involved in my children's lives than she was, everything else looked pretty good to me. She was so confident and together. Beautiful and stylish. She was everything I wanted to be but knew I never would.

None of that matters now. Not only has her heart changed, but so has her outward appearance. She's still beautiful, maybe even more now than she was when her makeup and hair were always perfect. With her fashionable clothes gone and my forced weight loss, we're certainly on more even footing as far as appearance.

Once again, Kimba has something I want.

As a child, I'd wholeheartedly given my life to God when I naively asked Jesus into my heart. The simple way my mother had explained the gospel to me made sense. I understood I was a sinner—my father had made that abundantly clear for as long as I could remember. My mom explained it wasn't my fault, that it was inherent in me just like it was in her. Just like it was in my father.

"For all have sinned and fall short of the Glory of God," she'd said. But that wouldn't matter once Jesus was in my heart. Then I'd want to do good, and the blood Jesus shed on the cross for me would hide the innate sin from God's eyes. Once His blood covered me and my sin, God would welcome me into Heaven as my Father.

During my teen years, as my earthly father became increasingly unstable and my mother tried to hold things together, to cover for him so the congregation wouldn't find out just how truly sick he was, I started to question God. I mean, really, who wouldn't? If God was so powerful, couldn't He give me a healthy father?

I couldn't wait to leave home and go to college, to finally have a life of my own without the constant criticism. Without the physical abuse. Without being told how terrible I was. Fat, ugly, and how no man would ever marry me.

When my father lost his church, he almost seemed relieved. I spoke with Mother on the phone that day, and she said she'd never seen him smile as much as he had since the elders told him.

He even came in the room and asked to be put on the phone. "Beverly, girl, we're going to start fresh. This is exactly what we've needed for years. A new congregation. A new town. Maybe we'll even move closer to you."

The next day, someone told me there was a call on the hall phone—that was years before cell phones were mainstream and we still had phones with cords. The dorm didn't even have phones in our rooms, just a payphone at the end of the hall for all of us to share. I expected it to be my mother again since no one else ever called.

It was the police. I wasn't really surprised. Not much, anyway. His killing her and then himself made perfect sense. He'd always been a total control freak. That was how I saw God too. Controlling and demanding. If my father was a preacher, supposedly sharing God's Word and His way, then my father must be just like Him, right?

Living my life without God in it was easy. I rarely thought about what I might be missing. Church fellowship had been nice. I especially loved Revival Week when an out-of-town preacher would come in. Each night before service, the congregation had a potluck—or as my father insisted it be called, a pot blessing—and we'd all eat together.

As a child, I loved Vacation Bible School too. And then when I was older, I was a helper. Being the preacher's daughter did get me treated differently than the others. I didn't mind and understood it was just the way things were. Those happy memories were fine, but not enough to make me search out a church or God ever again.

Not until now. Since Kimba and her family arrived, God takes up a lot of my thoughts. I'll often find myself thinking of verses they may want to learn. When Kimba asked if I'd help them with finding and memorizing verses, my first instinct was to say no. Definitely not. I got her the concordance, thinking the book would be enough help.

When they asked about part of a verse, one they thought they knew and couldn't find, I helped them sort it out. While they may have had a general idea of the verse, they had it so mangled that the concordance was little help. Then it almost became a game of how wrong they could get scripture and I could still figure out what they were looking for. Then it became more. And now . . .

"Kimba?" Her head snaps toward me in question. "I was . . ." I tilt my head as I search for the words. "Will you pray with me?" The question comes out in a rush. I feel my cheeks heating. Why am I embarrassed to ask this?

She blinks a couple times. "Of course I will. Are you worried about Chad? I think— "

I lift a hand and shake my head. "I know he's fine. Probably just caught up in whatever they needed to do."

Kimba motions to the empty spot next to her on the loveseat. Once I'm in position, she takes my hand. "What are we praying about?"

"I . . . well, I guess I need the Sinner's Prayer."

Kimba's brows shoot up.

"I mean, I know I'm a sinner. Years ago, when I was a child, I knew I was forgiven, but now . . . I want to know that again. To have God as a part of my life. To be . . . to be able to call you my sister in Christ."

"Oh, Bev, I'd like nothing more." She pulls me into a hug, squeezing me much too tightly. "I think . . . isn't it the same?"

"I don't know. Scriptures tell me God—Jesus—will never leave me or forsake me. I believe that. He wasn't the one who did the forsaking, it was me. I walked away from Jesus."

"Like the son did his father?"

I tilt my head at her. "What son?"

"You know, the prodigal son."

It suddenly becomes clear. Jesus told the story of the son in his father's household. He left home, went out on his own. Then he realized he wasn't living the life he should. He went home. He repented and was welcomed. "Do you think it's the same?"

Kimba's shrug is exaggerated. "I'm still a newbie. But if God can welcome someone like me into his family . . . you know, a spy and a killer." She lifts her hands. "I'd think He could welcome you back. Let's pray."

We hold both hands and bow our heads. My words are halting and simple, filled with tears as I do my best to apologize to God. I'm several words in when I realize God already knows my heart. My words may not be perfect, but He knows me. He's always known me. Just like He promised, I wasn't forsaken.

When I'm done, I feel as clean as when I was a child and my mother lovingly led me to Jesus. Kimba pulls me into a tight hug. We're interrupted by a knock on the door.

Chapter 30

Kimba
Friday, December 11

A potato peel drops to the table. The rhythmic chopping of Bev's knife on the wooden cutting board beats out a cadence. Peeling potatoes, preparing and serving meals, doing dishes . . . it's good to be back to our normal routine. At least for now.

The last few days have been crazy. The morning with Bev on the loveseat when she rededicated her life to Christ was amazing. I was so exhausted after being out late with Rey while he was treated. His injury took a toll on me.

It was different, though. While I'd felt so lost when Nate died, and totally distraught when Rey was injured in Bozeman, this time I was concerned but knew I wasn't alone. I trusted that, no matter the outcome, things would be fine. I'd be fine. Naomi would be fine.

Trust has often been an issue for me, which makes sense with my history and life choices. I mean, I used to work around scoundrels who were known to lie. Cheered for it even. My own life had been a lie in many ways . . . in *most* ways.

Putting on a show to manipulate and get what I needed, or simply wanted. A life of lies. Rey too. We weren't even always honest with each other. Not by a long shot. We got married because I was pregnant with Nicole. He asked, and I agreed. We stayed together all these years because of the children.

We rarely argued. I think that says a lot about our relationship. We had so little passion between us, there was no need to argue. We just did what we needed to do. He was often gone with our business, working on some assignment with Chad. I mainly did office work, often longing to be in the field but tied down by the kids. That's how it felt. Tied down.

It wasn't that I didn't like being a mom; it was fine. I just thought my life should've been more. My cheeks warm as I remember how selfish I used to be. At best, I was a mediocre parent.

Last winter, while living at the Bakerville ski lodge, we went to a Christmas program put on by the younger children. Afterward, Nicole said that as she watched me and Rey clap and cheer for Nate—who'd insisted he was really too old to be in the program but smiled widely during it, and Naomi looking so sweet and angelic as she wore the wings of a Christmas Angel—it reminded her of the time I was supposed to go to a special event with her first-grade class and I never showed up. She said she'd waited and waited while the other parents arrived.

I apologized and told her how sorry I was I missed it. But the truth is, I don't even remember. I have zero recollection of any program or event I was supposed to attend and didn't. *What a great mom I was.*

It's not like I'm perfect now. But things have changed. Somehow, after the world fell apart and the lights went out, I became the mom I never knew I could be. I've discovered just what a joy my children are. My breath catches. *Nate.* He was truly special. Although he was almost thirteen when he died, in some ways I feel like I only had less than a year with him.

Realizing the world didn't revolve around me and beginning to notice my husband and children did take some time. We say the Kim act I put on for Sabrina and Sylvia Ericksen early in the collapse was a show, and again recently for Lance Brower when he tried to take over the Double D, but there's more truth to Kim than I'd like to admit.

Kimba is just as selfish as Kim, just as annoying. She simply hides it better. At least the Kimba from before. I didn't like her then, and I don't like the memory of her now. God is doing work in me. Christ is making me new.

Bev and I have spent a lot of time talking about things since the morning after Rey was grazed in the shootout, about how we're both excited to let God mold us. I got a good laugh when she confessed she didn't like the old Kimba very much either. It feels good to be honest with each other.

Beverly's recommitment to Christ was cut short when Chad arrived home. With her eyes glistening, she'd ran into his arms and dropped kisses on his face.

"Whoa, babe. I'm sorry— "

"Shh. I'm just glad you're here."

After we let him know Rey would be fine, Chad started to tell us about his night. Rey called out from our room and asked Chad to hold off a minute.

With the crease from the bullet going the full length across his back, from shoulder to shoulder, Rey was moving slow. The medic said it was a miracle the bullet had entered between his small backpack and his body, leaving barely a scratch at the beginning but mushrooming as it went.

The exit not only blew out the coat and backpack but left him needing three stitches. If it had gone less than half an inch one way, only his pack would've been damaged. Of course, half an inch the other way . . .

Once we'd settled Rey onto the loveseat, Chad said it was over.

Colonel Ellis's people were able to get enough info from the men they captured to find the other ringleaders. Bohm was in the wind, having managed to escape. Ellis was less than happy about the loss of his men, the one who was with me and the one with Eric Bohm. The two who were with Rey and Chad were also injured, but only minorly.

Rey wanted to warn me about the change of plans, but Bohm had interrupted us. Chad and Rey had zero choice in the double cross. They'd been on their duty earlier in the day and were called to headquarters. They were surprised to find Colonel Ellis there. While they hadn't met him in person before, they'd seen him from afar a few days earlier when the colonel returned from medical leave.

The colonel said he knew all about the insurrection and about Major Dudrock and several of his men being involved. He'd been told someone saw Chad talking with Bohm. Seems even Colonel Ellis knew Doc Bohm prior to the collapse.

Bohm had put up a bit of a stink when the colonel didn't add him to his regular detail. They'd worked together some time in the past, and Bohm thought that would get him a position. Ellis knew enough, more than enough, not to trust Bohm and had been keeping an eye on him ever since.

The way the colonel approached Chad and Rey left little choice in how things would go. Basically, he said, "If you're part of Bohm's plans, tell me now. I'll make the ending quick for you." He'd said this with his hand on the butt of his pistol and two of his security detail pointing M4 carbines at them.

197

Chad and Rey came clean and said they'd talked to Bohm but were not going to be part of it. When Chad asked why Ellis was approaching him and Rey, Ellis said he had a letter from a friend, delivered by messenger from Bozeman, asking if Ellis had met our group.

Captain Mercer's memo was regarding something else, but our information was added as a footnote in which she said we could be trusted and may help the cause. What exactly *the cause* is . . . I'm still unsure.

I guess Mercer mentioned me, too, because when Ellis showed up here yesterday to check on how Rey was healing, he offered Rey, Chad, and me new positions on his special security detail.

As soon as I'm finished with kitchen duty, hopefully one of my last, the three of us are going to headquarters at the Moss Mansion to learn more.

Major Dudrock and his gang were all rounded up. There was a public execution for treason the day before yesterday. Others who were part of it, but not the masterminds, have been put on work crews reminiscent of the old chain gangs.

Eric Bohm wasn't found. Knowing him, he's heading to Rapid City, Cleveland, or one of the other operating centers to try this all again. Ellis says it won't work; the radio relay system the bases use has been utilized to cryptically spread the word about the attempted insurrection.

After Ellis mentioned the radio, I took a chance and asked if there's any way he can find out where Nicole is. "I've been waiting for a letter, but with the weather . . ." I shook my head.

"I'll see what I can do," Colonel Ellis promised. "I should tell you, there has been mail. Seems Dudrock was holding it as part of his plan, for whatever reason. We're working on sorting it and will have it all delivered in the next few days. It'll be an early Christmas present for those who get something. Nothing much better than hearing from friends and family."

After all the kitchen duties are wrapped up, I practically skip to our apartment.

"Slow down." Bev laughs. "They won't leave without you."

"You sure? Rey was pacing like a caged bear last night. He's ready to get back to work."

"I'll miss having you to chat with while we work."

I stop moving and reach for Bev's hand. "I don't have to do this. If it's— "

She shakes her head. "You'll do it. From what the colonel said, it's going to be a special position. His personal detail?"

My shoulders go to my ears. "That's what it sounded like. I guess we'll know more later."

"And maybe he'll already have news about Nicole. Wouldn't that be wonderful?"

We're walking again, at a slightly more sedate pace. "It would be. I don't know, though. It might take a while to find her. From the little I've heard, it doesn't sound like the Volunteer Unit has a great recordkeeping system."

Inside our room, I hurry to put on my outerwear. The men are both ready, with Chad at the chair tying his boots. His greeting to his wife is lukewarm. He won't admit to it, but I think he's angry at her.

The morning after the shooting, when Rey came out of his room, he reached a hand to Bev. "I heard. I'd hug you, but welcome back to the family . . . uh, sister."

Chad visibly stiffened, looking from Rey to me and then to Bev. His eyes narrowed. "The family, huh?"

She gave him a shy smile and tilted her head. "I told you how I've been— "

He raised a hand. "I know. It's fine. Go ahead and do your God thing. I figured it'd happen eventually. The girls?"

"Kylie accepted Jesus last night. We prayed together. Emma . . . well, she's afraid you'll be upset with her."

Chad's brows knit together. "Of course not. It may not be my cup of tea, but I wouldn't stop her or you from it. Just don't expect . . ." He shook his head. "I'm not there. At least not yet. Maybe I— "

Bev put a hand on his arm. "I'm already praying."

I'm sure she saw his eye roll. Chad and Bev had been doing so good since everything about Gary Searle came out into the open. It's sad this may come between them. Like Bev, I'm praying too.

"Did you see Sal?" Rey asks, while I put on my snow boots.

"Not since lunch. What's he working on this afternoon?"

"Not sure. He popped in here all excited, saying he'd been called to headquarters. He went to his room and came out soon after. On his way out the door, he said he'd let us know as soon as he could. I think

199

he's hoping he got a new position, too, and maybe won't be a grinder much longer."

"That'd be good for him. But I hope . . ." I shake my head. "I don't want him in a dangerous job. He's— "

"We love him, and we'll pray for him. He's part of our family," Bev finishes.

The air is crisp and clear, with the sun shining brightly. One of the best things about winter in the Rockies is the sunshine. There aren't as many sunny days as we had in Denver, at least it doesn't seem like it, but it's still lovely. A gust of wind comes up and gives me a chill. I tighten the string around my hooded sweater, then pull the hood of my too-light winter jacket into place.

Will our new positions allocate warmer winter wear? Will we move from the Y to other housing? Like Beverly, I'm tired of communal living. Not to mention, the building wasn't designed for the off-grid life we're now forced into.

The addition of the wood cookstove, and a few other strategically placed woodburning stoves, barely keeps the place above freezing. Our room, a windowless former racquetball court, isn't terrible, but it's not overly comfortable either. We all wear several layers of clothing and shoes, even inside.

If we do need to continue living there, I'm praying the new positions will at least allow us more blankets and other cold-weather essentials as part of our allotted rations.

We're about halfway between the Y and Moss Mansion when Chad bumps into a guy coming around the corner from the other direction. Rey and I, holding hands as we walk, barely stop in time to keep from crashing into Chad's back.

"Sorry about that, friend." Chad nods and steps to the side.

"It's no problem."

My heart goes to my throat as my eyes shoot to the man.

"You." Chad reaches for his sidearm, but he lets out a yelp and is going down before Rey and I can even react.

I'm grabbed from behind, my arms pulled tight against myself into a bear hug. Out of the corner of my eye, I see Rey sink to the frozen sidewalk. Chad is also on the ground, and Bohm's standing over him with a bloody knife in his hand.

"I thought about letting you live." Eric Bohm points the knife in my direction. "I know you weren't involved in the double cross. Just these two." The tip of the knife is directed at my husband, while Bohm puts a heavy boot on Chad.

Chad lets out a low moan.

"Thought I'd give you a couple of days to sort things out. Then I heard about the offer Ellis made you, and here you are, happy as a clam to be colluding with the enemy. *Enemy, Kimba.* Don't you get it? People like Ellis are the reason our country fell apart. The reason why we had to change things."

I lift my chin. "You can still let us go, Bohm." I turn my head slightly so I can see Rey. My stomach clenches at the growing pool of blood surrounding him.

The guy who has him catches my glance. He licks the blade of his bloody knife. "Little late for that. For this one, anyway."

Bohm clicks his tongue several times. "Too bad. I'd like to tell you your daughter will be fine, that Chad's mousy woman will take good care of her." He steps harder on Chad, eliciting a groan.

"But that would be a lie. You see, Kimba, I'm going to kill them too. You know, the sins of the father and all that. Everyone in your household will pay for the men's deceit. There's no place in this new country for turncoats. What we're building is only for the strong. Once these debts are paid, we'll take care of Ellis. Then we'll be ready for the next stage."

"The next stage?" My voice is thick as my mind tries to figure a way out of this. My pistol is still on my hip. The guy holding me didn't bother to relieve me of it. If I can get my arms free, maybe we'd have a chance. I hazard a look at Rey and feel sick at what I see.

"Things may not have gone exactly as planned. The timing may have been off, and losing the port cities . . . well, that's an issue. But the overall plan will still move forward. Reinforcements will arrive soon. You must know we have help from— " Bohm's body jerks a microsecond before the percussion of a light semi-auto rifle bounces off the buildings.

I stomp my foot hard on the instep of the guy holding me while I throw my arms straight up. His grip loosens. I step to the left and slam my elbow into his sternum as several more rifle volleys sound. I pull my Glock and squeeze the trigger three times.

With my captor on the ground, I spin toward the guy who used the knife on Rey. He's already down, thanks to the rifle shooter. I focus my attention on Bohm. The knife he had is several feet away.

He also won't be getting up. The mystery gunman's shot went in Bohm's left arm, then traveled through his torso and took bits of heart and lung with it, and blew out the right arm, shattering the bone as it went.

I drop to a knee and look across the road, searching out the shooter.

"Are they . . . is it done?" a shaky voice calls.

"Sal?"

He scootches from behind a car, one that's been sitting since the EMP at least, staying low. "Are they . . . did I kill them?"

"We're clear. We need a medic!" I quickly holster my weapon and scurry to my husband. His eyes are already glassy, staring at the blue sky which he'll never see again. I rest my hand against his cheek.

Chad moans, but I don't want to leave Rey. Even in his death, I want to stay with him. I glance to Chad before looking back at my husband. I drop a kiss on his lips along with several hot tears. "I'll be right back, my love."

At Chad's side, I tell him not to move, that help is on the way. "Rey?" His question comes out as several syllables.

I shake my head. "He . . . he's gone."

"Too late . . . for me too. They'll be safe. Our children. Bohm's dead?"

"Bohm's dead. Yes, they'll be safe."

"Tell Bev— " He coughs up frothy blood. "Tell her . . . yes . . . sorry." His mouth opens and his face relaxes. He looks calm. Almost happy.

I'm sitting on my bottom in the snow between Rey and Chad. I hold my husband's hand and rest my other palm on my friend's shoulder until the soldiers arrive, with Sal in the lead.

"I tried to hurry."

"You did fine, Sal. It was . . . there wasn't anything else to do. They were . . ." I stare up at his tearstained face. "Where'd you get the rifle?"

"They gave it to me." He lifts an arm in the direction of the soldiers as they check the bodies. "I'm no longer a grinder. I'm part of the sentry squad now. It looks a lot like a rifle my dad had, so . . ." His left shoulder goes up to his ear. "I'm sorry I was too late."

202

Chapter 31

Beverly
Thursday, December 24

"How's it look?" I step back and admire the adjustment I made. The red tinsel garland is much too festive.

Days ago, Kylie asked if we'd have Christmas decorations in our new house. With Chad and Rey dead just over a week then, I couldn't bare it. I couldn't bare much. There was no funeral. Not much of a memorial even.

Colonel Ellis offered the use of a room at Moss Mansion for the memorial. Our family, a few of the Civilian Defenders, a handful of regular military folks, and the colonel attended. In the spring, when the weather clears and digging is easier, there will be a mass burial of everyone who died over the winter.

The Moss Mansion was tastefully decorated for Christmas, even at the December 13 memorial. The mansion had been open for tours before the world changed, and several staff members were still around Billings.

There wasn't a lot of support to turn the place into the Army's headquarters—not that they were really given a choice. Ellis said the operations manager and a few people from the Moss Mansion Board of Directors showed up a few days after Thanksgiving and started decorating, pulling out ornaments stored from before the world fell apart and turning the twenty-eight-room place into an old-fashioned Christmas extravaganza.

While much of the extra furniture and decor had been removed when Ellis took over the place, what remained was a perfect complement to the old-fashioned adornments.

The day after the memorial, Kimba and I began packing up our little apartment at the YMCA. Her job offer to be a part of Ellis's security detail stood. Housing nearby the mansion is included as a perk for the small, elite squad. Ellis had already secured a duplex for our two families and allowed the housing arrangement to continue.

He seems to understand we're family, Sal too. With his new position as sentry, he could stay in the Y and live in one of the male dorm rooms. Ellis waved a magic wand and got him on a different sentry unit, working directly out of the mansion. He's staying in Kimba's half of the duplex since it's a larger three-bedroom.

"I think you need another string." Kylie bobs her head up and down, handing me a green shiny garland. "Don't you think, Emma?"

Emma lifts her eyes from where she was fiddling with the edge of her shirt. She scrunches her face. "I guess." Losing Chad isn't easy for any of us, but especially my oldest daughter. She was always his little girl. It's the true cliché of the oldest daughter being the apple of his eye. Even with him gone so much for work, it didn't change the bond they had.

I think a lot about Chad's final minutes, when he knew he was dying and heard Bohm say we were all going to be killed. The fear, the anger he must have felt. And then to know that it wouldn't happen. We'd be safe, thanks to Sal. Thanks to Kimba.

Kimba told me Chad said he was sorry. Sorry for dying? Are there other things? I could drive myself crazy thinking about it. I'm also driving myself crazy wondering . . . wondering if I'll even see him again? In those final moments, did he give what was left of his life to Christ? Is he like the thief on the cross? Did Chad respond to the gospel and was taken to paradise?

When Kylie asked again yesterday if we could decorate for Christmas, I'd started to say no when I saw the look on Emma's face. Hope, maybe. When I said I'd see what we could do, she then asked if I thought we should have a breathing session and invite Kimba and Naomi too. Maybe even Sal.

It was the last thing I wanted.

Breathing, relaxing, mourning. Ugh. We did it anyway.

Combining breathing with scripture, it did help. Don't get me wrong, my heart is still shattered. All I really want to do is curl up in a ball and spend my day that way. Emma seems to know, though, that as much as we're hurting, we have to keep going. We have to find a way to heal.

Life in the duplex is considerably different than life at the Y. Not only do we have privacy, but living on our own means we have the responsibility of all our meals and household chores.

Kimba will start her new job the day after Christmas. Ellis said he wanted to give her time to get settled and make sure her head was right before she went to work. She's doing well with Rey's death. Better than me in some ways. Worse in others.

Having lost her son six months ago and now her husband, along with her oldest daughter being away, has taken a toll. She's reading her Bible regularly, and we talk a lot about the verses she finds, using the concordance as a guide. While I may have many memorized, my grieving brain isn't doing well at pulling them up. She seems to know that and has taken her study upon herself.

Like Kylie and me, Emma has also given her life to God. She's teamed up with Kimba on studying the Bible.

Kylie hands me the second string of garland. "When will Kimba and Naomi be back?"

"Soon. They were just going shopping and checking for mail."

"Do you like having to cook food just for us?"

"It's certainly quicker." I glance to the woodstove at the edge of the room. It's not a cookstove like the one in the Y, but the top gets hot enough for boiling, which lets us make stews and soups. Living here, we receive weekly ration cards.

A chicken was part of Kimba's rations for the week, and I've been wondering how we can cook it. It might roast nicely inside the firebox, but we'd have to let the coals die down and the house would get too chilly. Most likely, we'll stew it on the top.

To help earn my keep of living here, I've been added to the mansion's cleaning crew. My ration cards didn't include a chicken but were still very generous considering, like Kimba, I've yet to start working.

There's no school set up for those living in the housing around Moss Mansion, so Emma will watch the younger girls and help them with schooling during the times Kimba and I are on shift. When I'm home, we'll go over what they've learned. It's a lot of responsibility for Emma—responsibility I wish wasn't required.

When we were offered this house, I told her we could stay at the Y where she'd have friends and schooling, where she wouldn't need to help with meal prep and keeping the fire going. She rolled her eyes in her usual manner. "I've read *Little House on the Prairie*. I understand how things used to be . . . how they are again. It's fine."

Emma brings me back to the present with a rare smile. "I like it. The colors are nice together. Are we going to decorate Kimba's side too?"

"They may have done it already. Kimba already had decorations before I asked her if she could find us some. I think they were going to put them up last night."

Kylie claps her hands. "Can we go see them?"

"Maybe when they get back."

We fiddle with more decorations. There's no tree, but there are plenty of ornaments and other things we put around. When we're finished, it's definitely not the understated sophistication of the Moss Mansion, more like the department store in the movie Elf. Over the top and slightly gaudy. It's also cheerful.

I know someday my heart will not feel completely shattered. Someday, my smiles won't be forced, and my voice will truly be cheery. For today, for this Christmas, over the top and gaudy seems like a good fit.

A noise on the shared porch has Kylie running to the window. "They're back! Should I get my boots on so we can see if they decorated? Oh, they're coming to our place." She runs to the door and swings it open. "Did you decorate your house?"

Kimba lets out a light laugh. "We did." Her eyes scan our front room. "I see you've been busy too." She stomps her boots on the carpet by the door and instructs Naomi to do the same, while also urging her inside and out of the cold.

"I've got the food. And you're never going to believe this, they finally put the mail out! I thought Ellis might keep holding it. They read it all, I guess, to check for more insurgents. That's why it took so long."

I make a face. "Did you get a letter from Nicole?"

"Not yet. But at least Ellis was able to find out where she is for me. And I know she's okay."

I bob my head. Ellis told us after the memorial service that Nicole's stationed out of Sandpoint, Idaho. She finished her training with the Volunteer Unit. He said he'd put in a good word with the regular Army base commander and see if he could use her.

Ellis said, if he hadn't been out on injury, Captain Mercer's note would've guaranteed Nicole a spot in his unit in Billings. Major

Dudrock hated Mercer, so it makes sense her recommendation didn't help Nicole at all.

Ellis also said he'd get word to Nicole about the death of her dad, but Kimba asked him to wait. She wants to be the one to tell her. "You have letters from your friends? Replies to the ones Nicole sent off?"

"We do! I know you don't know any of them— "

"I feel like I do, as much as we've talked about your Montana journey and the life you had in Wyoming. In some ways . . ." I bite my lip and stop my words.

"In some ways what?" Kimba sits on the bench by the door and unlaces her boots. "Take off your boots, Naomi. We'll stay and visit. Emma, will you put the teakettle on? They gave me hot cocoa, apple cider packages, and tea in our rations. We'll have a treat." Kimba glances back to me. "In some ways . . . ?"

I shake my head. "It's silly, really. The way you talk about the people in Bakerville and the ones you traveled with, it's almost like you've known them forever."

She leans back on the bench. "It feels like that. In fact, I was thinking, maybe . . . if you're willing, we could go back to Bakerville in the spring."

Chapter 32

Kimba
Thursday, December 24

Bev turns to fiddle with the decorations she just put up. The decorating is a distraction, just like it was for me. That and for the girls. Even though we're all still grieving, we're trying. Somedays, I feel myself edging toward the pit I was in during those early days after Nate died.

That time was different. I knew Rey and Nicole were also grieving, but they were able to keep it together enough to be there for Naomi. In some ways, that allowed me to give myself permission to languish in my misery. Now I don't have that luxury. With Rey dead and Nicole gone, I'm all Naomi has.

Satisfied with her adjustments, Bev turns around from the garland. "What do your friends have to say?"

"I didn't read them yet. Thought I'd wait and maybe . . . I was thinking we could read them together. Do you mind?"

Bev's brown eyes fill with tears as she gives me a partial smile. "Sure. That's fine. Did you hear from everyone you traveled with?"

I shake my head. "Not the Dosen boys or any of the others at the Double D. But everyone else, yes. Tamra Nicholson, Sadie Monroe, Rochelle Bennet, and even Doris Snyder in Bakerville. I'll admit, Bev, part of it's . . . well, if there's bad news, I don't want to be alone."

"Should we wait for the water to boil?"

Bev adds more wood to the fire, as Emma pours water from a nearby gallon jug into the kettle. As we wait, I hand Bev the four letters. "Will you read them? I thought . . ." I look to the girls. "Maybe skim each one first? Then you don't have to read word for word if it's not necessary. Just hit the highlights? Does that sound good?" I motion to the girls and tilt my head.

"You're sure?"

"I think so, yes. We could probably do one while waiting on the water."

"Who do you want to start with?"

I bite my lip. Tamra was the person I knew the least. Truthfully, I didn't really know her at all before we left the ski lodge last March. What I did know of her, I didn't much like. She was a bit on the snooty side, often making faces of disgust and seemed to think she was better than everyone else. As I did get to know her, I realized it wasn't conceit as much as insecurity.

"Tamra?"

I give Bev a nod, and she finds the correct letter. We'll save the envelope to use as a note sheet, then it'll become a fire starter. Her eyes travel down the paper. She smiles and then passes it to me. "Go ahead. Read it aloud. It's . . . good."

Tamra's letter is very newsy and light. Tamra and her girls, Beth and Debbie, are settled well in Joliet, a small town only an hour outside of Billings. Or what used to be an hour in the old days of easy travel. They're still living with Tamra's parents and bracing for another cold winter.

She said Rochelle and PJ Cameron stopped for a visit back in June when they picked up the wagon PJ had left for safekeeping. Rochelle not only found her son, who was away at summer camp when the attacks started, but had a whole passel of other children with her, several of them babies. Three of the babies were adopted by families in Joliet. She finished with wishing us well and asking we keep in touch.

"Does Rochelle talk about the other children?" Naomi asks with wide eyes.

"Let's see." I nod to Bev.

She shuffles the remaining envelopes to find the one from Rochelle. After removing the paper, her eyes quickly travel down the page. Her brows knit and a frown crosses her face. My heart is pounding in my throat until her features soften. She smiles. "It's a happy ending." She passes me the letter.

It starts off great, with Rochelle detailing how she found her son. He was so grown up and very healthy. She was asked to take some younger children at the camp with her to an orphanage or find them homes. Traveling by horseback took some time, but they finally made it to Tamra's house. Then they ran into trouble in the small town of Belfry, only ten miles from the state line.

"I was gathering water from the river when someone said my name. I couldn't even look up; I was paralyzed with fear. It was Fred Lassiter. My husband by force, who'd purchased me and my girls like cattle and held us hostage. What happened next was a bit of a blur as the bullets started flying. In the end, Fred was dead, and my sweet son was injured.

"It was touch and go for several days. The damage to his arm was so severe, he had to have it removed. He grieved the loss of his arm for some time, as would be expected. But as I write this, he's learned to adapt and is the amazing young man he always was."

I pause my reading and lean back on the couch, my brain working to sort out this information. "Do you remember how I told you about Bohm saying he spent last winter in Prospect?"

Bev bobs her head. "And he left there after the town rebelled, right?"

"Right. He said he left with another guy. Said he'd been a deputy of some sort but was really a sadist."

"Sure. And the guy he was traveling with was killed— " Her eyes light up. "You don't think he's the one your friend is talking about, do you?"

"It fits. The way Bohm said it about how the guy ran into his wife and she emptied her Glock into him . . . Bohm specifically said Glock, and Rochelle carried a 10-millimeter Glock. Rochelle's husband was a terrible person too. From what I know about him, it fits some of the things Bohm said."

"Could be." Bev nods.

I return to the letter, reading about the children who are now part of their family. They'd been taken in at the summer camp, but there were too many kids and not enough adults. They're now part of her family, giving her a total of nine children. And two of the girls, barely teens, just had babies, adding to the brood. At the end of the letter, Rochelle said future letters could be addressed to Rochelle Cameron since she and PJ married in late July.

"I knew they'd get married." Naomi has a dreamy look. "They loved each other a whole bunch."

We spend several minutes talking about Rochelle and PJ and what their life must be like with so many children around, then the teakettle whistles. Bev and I have mint tea, while the girls all have apple cider.

Once we're settled in again, Bev scans the letter from Sadie Monroe. She shakes her head. "It's sad but is okay for the children to hear. Nothing too . . ." She shakes her head again.

"Would you?" I motion to the letter still in Bev's hand.

She clears her throat before reading aloud. Leanne and Donnie were married only for a few hours before Donnie was killed in a fire. Leanne had side effects from smoke inhalation and her recovery was slow.

There were troubles with the community that resulted in a shootout when one of the guys, who Sadie said was probably crazy, shot the community leader. He was severely injured but is doing okay and should be fine.

Things are better now, and Sadie's aunt Karla is a big reason for it. Where the community had previously closed themselves off from the town, earning all sorts of rumors about being a cult and a bunch of weirdos, they've now merged with the town of Lewistown. Karla is the liaison between the towns and even holds the title of Deputy Mayor.

"Terrible about your friend losing her husband so quickly after the wedding." Bev's sigh speaks volumes.

"My heart hurts for her. Leanne had a terrible time with everything since the attacks. She found her family murdered. That's how she ended up at the ski lodge. She just didn't feel she had anywhere else to go. Then, when we made our plans to find Rochelle's son and take the Dosens home, she asked if she could join us and go to her aunt's place.

"Donnie only went because he had a thing for Leanne. He said he wanted to get her home safely. She didn't like him much in those early days, but it soon became obvious they made a good pair. They complemented each other."

Bev and I spend several minutes sipping our tea and staring at the fire. The girls seem to understand we need time to absorb this latest news and grieve not only for Leanne but for ourselves.

I tip up my cup, emptying it in a final large gulp.

Bev follows suit, then noisily sets her mug on the side table. "Just one letter left. It's from your friend Doris."

There's a twinkle in her eye when she says her name. Doris Snyder a.k.a. Meagan Wright was a well-known figure throughout the time I've known Bev. More than once she'd heard the story of how Meagan wronged me. Then, after we finally made it to Bozeman, she heard me sing her praises as I came to know Doris and discard the anger over Meagan.

"I hope Grandma Doris is okay." Naomi's cup is halfway to her lips.

I nod my agreement and then turn toward Bev. "How about I read this one without you skimming it first?"

She hands me the letter with a nod. My hands are shaking as I unfold the single page. The script is tiny and precise, with writing on the front and the back, using every bit of space available.

"My dearest family,

"It was with a grateful heart I received your letters. I've written this in my head many times while I've waited for your follow-up with an address. I'm so, so sorry for the loss of our sweet Nate. I know the pain you are feeling. My prayers are with you continually as you grieve.

"Please pray for me too. Lindsey was killed in April when we were attacked by people from Prospect. My only solace is she died instantly. We lost several others that day, including one of the children, Chaplain Rick, and Toby James. I know you knew the chaplain well, having attended many of his services. Toby James was the nice boy who helped me up to the ski lodge each day."

Tears stream down my face. Naomi crawls up next to me and leans into me.

"I know vengeance is supposed to belong to God, but I'll admit I felt a sense of relief and gratitude when we merged with the rebellion forming in Prospect and stopped Richard Majors's killing spree. The town—our entire county—is now free of his murderous reign.

"Oh, the things we discovered after freeing the town! The things he was doing were barbaric. Fred Lassiter, that snake, had ended up in Prospect and was part of Majors's upper echelon. Somehow, Lassiter managed to escape with a guy everyone called Doc."

I stop reading and meet Bev's eyes. She gives a combination nod and shake of her head before urging me to continue.

"The two of them captured and tortured a couple of our townspeople before escaping. At the time, we didn't know why, but now it makes sense. Lassiter was looking for Rochelle! I saw her the other day and know she received a letter from you also. She said she

was sending a reply. I don't know if you've received it yet, but all I'll say is, Fred Lassiter got what he deserved.

"When I first heard the stories of the guy they called Doc, it was like deja vu. He did terrible things here, things that sounded so familiar. Too familiar. Things we'd been trained to do. They even made wanted posters of him, with a sketch and his full name. You won't believe this, Kimba, but it was Eric Bohm. Eric "Doc" Bohm was here in Prospector County!"

The words blur on the page. I wipe my eye with the back of my hand. Bohm was brought to justice, but too late to save my husband. To save Bev's husband.

"Is he the one?" Emma asks. "The same one who killed my dad and Rey?"

"He's the one." Bev's voice cracks at the end. Our eyes meet, and she urges me to continue. I skim the paragraphs about Bohm and the way we knew him and more on the terrible things he did in Prospect. The children don't need to hear this.

"Even with the trouble in Prospect squelched, things aren't perfect here. And as spread out as our community is, like last winter, we've again moved to the ski lodge. We had a wonderful harvest and are happy we'll have much more than just sugar beets as our main food this year.

"Evan and a group of others went back to the river for waterfowl hunting. I'll be sending this letter with him so he can pass it off to the military unit set up along the highway in the old restaurant. They're considered part of the peacekeeping force in the area.

"Many in our small community have joined the Volunteer Unit, or those who were in the military before and qualified are back in a regular unit. Others have moved on, with the roads reopening and the peacekeepers in place. Still, others have died.

"My dear friend Mollie Caldwell passed away early in the summer. She'd been sick for some time but kept fighting until the end, even being a part of the battle with Majors. Her second grandchild was born shortly after her death.

"Then, with barely time to grieve the loss of her mom or celebrate the birth of her niece, Mollie's youngest daughter and her husband joined up and were whisked away. A letter arrived a few weeks ago saying they're in South Dakota."

"Who's she talking about?" Naomi asks. "Is Mollie the one who had meetings at her house?"

"Yes, the lodge where we met in the den. That was Mollie. Remember her daughter had the baby boy?"

"I remember. She was nice to us. That's sad she died, but nice about a baby being born."

"It is nice." I turn slightly toward Bev. "Didn't we hear the governor of South Dakota wasn't accepting help from the military? Just using National Guard?"

"That's one of the rumors."

"Hmm. Wonder what's going on with Mollie's daughter going there then?"

"Write her back and ask?"

Naomi scoots closer to me on the sofa. "I want to write Grandma Doris and make sure she's okay after Lindsey died."

I put an arm around her. "I'm sure she's sad just like we are. But, yes, we'll definitely write to her."

"That's good. I think . . ." My daughter bites her lip. "Do you think we can go back to Bakerville? I know you want to go home to Denver, but . . ."

I meet Bev's gaze. She gives a slight nod.

"Yes, Naomi. I do think we can go back to Bakerville. I think that's exactly where we belong."

★★★★★

Thank you for spending your time with Kimba, Beverly, Victoria, Sadie, Rochelle, Tamra, and the rest of the group on their Montana journey! If you have five minutes, you'd make this author very happy if you could write a short Amazon review.

I appreciate you!

Saying goodbye forever to so many in this series wasn't easy. Asher Dosen, Donnie McCullough, and Nate and Rey Hoffmann were part of the original *Havoc in Wyoming* stories, and all of them were close to my heart. Even though Chad Pitney was only in the final book, he and Beverly have been in my mind since Kimba and Rey first announced they were going to their friend's place in Bozeman.

You may remember Kimba focusing on box breathing during *Ruthless Havoc: Montana Mayhem Book 5* as she tried to focus and heal from the death of her son. Beverly introducing Kimba to breathwork seemed a perfect fit.

I, too, was recently introduced to breathwork by my dear friend Tammy Trayer of Breathe to Healing and Trayer Wilderness. Where Kimba was initially skeptical, not knowing exactly what kind of froufrou stuff Bev might be introducing her to, I didn't have that concern. Tammy is a woman of God. I knew whatever she was doing would be Christ-centered and she'd never lead me astray. Be sure to keep reading for a note and special offer from Tammy Trayer to learn more about breathwork for yourself.

I suspect we'll catch up with Kimba, Beverly, and their children in the future— possibly back in Bakerville. In the meantime, we'll be moving slightly east in our adventures.

Bitter Mayhem: Dakota Destruction Book 1

After a series of coordinated attacks devastate the United States, Katie and Leo sacrifice everything to help their country.

Katie was one semester away from a degree in graphic design, living a carefree life with her boyfriend Leo.

Then the apocalypse happened.

College is but a memory, and danger is around every corner.

Katie and Leo decide to join the Volunteer Unit, to make a difference as the country begins to rebuild. But after they find themselves in South Dakota, a tragic disaster makes the Volunteers unwelcome.

Is it time to go home and start fresh, or can something good come out of this terrible situation?

Preorder your copy of *Bitter Mayhem* today!

A Special Note from Tammy Trayer

So often, we view prepping and preparedness as solely stocking up on things. Millie Copper has blown that out of the water as she has shared the skills and tasks necessary to survive in a fallen world. Breathwork is one of those skill sets that are not only a healing skill but indeed can be a life-saving skill that everyone should know. We are gifted with the blessing of breath and greatly take it for granted until we don't have enough of it, and most people are unaware of the untapped renewing and healing benefits of using our breath properly.

I feel that it is vital for every man, woman, and child to know how to tap into our amazing abilities within our bodies, the gift of our own God-given breath. Not only can you calm the body very quickly, you can also increase your clarity, energy levels, creativity, help manage PTSD, depression, chronic pain, chronic illness, auto immune issues, and even detoxing just to name a few.

I educate, teach, and offer private and group Breathwork sessions at BreatheToHealing.com. As a Millie Copper fan and reader, I would like to bless you with a free session so you can see for yourself the fantastic benefits of Breathwork. Use this link to get your free Breathwork session: https://breathetohealing.com/milliecoppergift.

God Bless,
Tammy Trayer † 🖤
BreatheToHealing.com
Instagram: BreatheToHealing.com/instagram
YouTube: BreatheToHealing.com/youtube

Also by Millie Copper

Montana Mayhem Series

Unending Havoc: Montana Mayhem Book 1

Ruthless Havoc: Montana Mayhem Book 2

Merciless Havoc: Montana Mayhem Book 3

Cruel Havoc: Montana Mayhem Book 4

Relentless Havoc: Montana Mayhem Book 5

Havoc in Wyoming Series

Wyoming Refuge: A Havoc in Wyoming Prequel

Havoc in Wyoming: Part 1, Caldwell's Homestead

Havoc in Wyoming: Part 2, Katie's Journey

Havoc in Wyoming: Part 3, Mollie's Quest

Havoc Begins: A Havoc in Wyoming Story (Part 3.5)

Havoc in Wyoming: Part 4, Shields and Ramparts

Havoc in Wyoming: Part 5, Fowler's Snare

Havoc Rises: A Havoc in Wyoming Story (Part 5.5)

Havoc in Wyoming: Part 6, Pestilence in the Darkness

Christmas on the Mountain: A Havoc in Wyoming Novella

Havoc Peaks: A Havoc in Wyoming Story (Part 6.5)

Havoc in Wyoming: Part 7, My Refuge and Fortress

Nonfiction Books

Sourdough for Your Food Storage: Add Nutrition and Variety to Your Baked Goods

Sprouts for Your Food Storage: Add Nutrition and Variety to Your Diet

Stock the Real Food Pantry: A Handbook for Making the Most of Your Pantry

Design a Dish: Save Your Food Dollars

Real Food Hits the Road: Budget Friendly Tips, Ideas, and Recipes for Enjoying Real Food Away from Home

Stretchy Beans: Nutritious, Economical Meals the Easy Way

Find these titles on Amazon:
www.amazon.com/author/milliecopper

Acknowledgments

Thanks to:

Ameryn Tucker, my editor, beta reader, and daughter wrapped in one. I had a story I wanted to tell, and Ameryn encouraged me and helped me bring it to life.

Dee from Dauntless Cover Design.

My husband, who gave me the time and space I needed to complete this dream and was very patient as I'd tell him the same plot ideas over and over and over.

Three more daughters and a young son, who willingly listen to me drone on and on about story lines and ideas while encouraging me to "keep going."

My amazing Beta Readers! Thanks to Barbara, Becky, Brian, Glen, Ilona, Judy, Katrina, Tammy and Tracy for your help in creating the final story. Your insights and abilities to see the things I miss are very much appreciated! And a special thank you to Tim, specialist in all things that go boom, for always answering my questions and pointing out things I wouldn't even think about.

And to you, my readers, for spending your time with our band of weary travelers. If you have five minutes, you'd make this writer very happy if you could leave a review. I appreciate you!

About the Author

Millie Copper, writer of Cozy Apocalyptic Fiction, was born in Nebraska but never lived there. Her parents fully embraced wanderlust and moved regularly, giving her an advantage of being from nowhere and everywhere.

As an adult, Millie is fully rooted in a solar-powered home in the wilds of Wyoming with her husband and young son, milking ornery goats and tending chickens on their small homestead. In their free time, they escape to the mountains for a hike or laze along the bank of the river to catch their dinner. Four adult daughters, three sons-in-law, and three grandchildren round out the family.

Since 2009, Millie has authored articles on traditional foods, alternative health, homesteading, and preparedness–many times all within the same piece. Millie has penned five nonfiction, traditional food focused books, sharing how, with a little creativity, anyone can transition to a real foods diet without overwhelming their food budget.

The twelve-installment *Havoc in Wyoming* Christian Post-Apocalyptic fiction series uses her homesteading, off-the-grid, and preparedness lifestyle as a guide. The adventure continues with the newly released *Montana Mayhem* series.

Find Millie at www.MillieCopper.com
Facebook: www.facebook.com/MillieCopperAuthor/
Amazon: www.amazon.com/author/milliecopper
BookBub: https://www.bookbub.com/authors/millie-copper

Made in the USA
Monee, IL
21 October 2022

16332036R00135